KATANA NIDAN:

THE UNWRITTEN KOAN

By Ken Warner

For all of the teachers
I had in my youth.
Your impact on my life
has proven immeasurable.

Two monks were arguing about
the temple flag waving in the wind.

One said, "The flag moves."
The other said, "The wind moves."
They argued back and forth but could not agree.

Hui Neng, the sixth patriarch, said:
"Gentlemen! It is not the flag that moves.
It is not the wind that moves.
It is your mind that moves."

The two monks were struck with awe.

Zen Koan

Contents

KATANA NIDAN

Prologue: Betrayal

Hawaii, thirteen years ago

"Adrian, are you ready?" Kristine called from the living room as she pulled on her high heels. Kristine Kahanu was tall and slender. Her long, jet-black hair flowed like silk down her back; her dark eyes hinted at her Japanese heritage.

"Almost," said Adrian, facing the mirror in the bedroom. Adrian was a few inches shorter than Kristine. Native Hawaiian in ancestry, he was tan and muscular. His dark eyes sparkled as he worked on the knot in his necktie. "Is Alissa here yet?"

"No," said Kristine, walking into the room. She stood behind Adrian and put her arms around his waist, her chin on his shoulder. "But she should be any minute."

"It was nice of her to babysit tonight."

"She doesn't mind," Kristine replied. She walked over to the crib in the corner of the room. "Anyway, she said that she and Ron have been talking about starting a family. I think she considers this practice for when she has a baby of her own."

"Well, she's in for a rude awakening," Adrian said with a chuckle. "No baby in the history of the world has ever been as happy as Katana."

"I know," said Kristine, smiling down at her daughter, sound asleep in the crib. "No one believes me when I tell them that she doesn't keep us up all night."

Just then, the doorbell rang.

"Speak of the devil," said Adrian.

Kristine went to open the front door. "Hi, Alissa."

"Hi," said Alissa, bustling into the living room. "Sorry I'm late. My mom called as I was walking out the door."

"Oh, no problem," said Kristine. "Adrian's not ready yet anyway!"

"Says who?" Adrian replied as he walked out of the bedroom, his tie now fully tied. "I'm ready if you are."

"Thanks again, Alissa," said Kristine with a smile.

"Katana's asleep. I doubt she'll give you any trouble," said Adrian, sitting down on the sofa to put on his shoes.

"She never does," Alissa replied, walking into the bedroom. Adrian looked over at Kristine and winked.

The phone rang as Adrian searched for his keys. He picked it up and said, "Hello," but he couldn't hear anything but static. "Hello?" he said again.

"Adrian," said a voice, barely audible over the static.

"Yes, this is Adrian."

"Adrian, this is Jesse. Jesse Thompson."

"Jesse..." said Adrian quietly. Kristine looked at him apprehensively.

"Adrian, I need to talk to you. Meet me at Yoshida's dojo in twenty minutes."

"Yoshida... What..." Adrian's words were catching in his throat.

"Jesse, Yoshida is in China. What's going on?"

"No. He's back. He's coming, too. Twenty minutes." Adrian heard a click.

"Jesse?" he said. "Hello?"

"What does he want?" asked Kristine.

Adrian looked at her with an expression of deep concern. "He wants me to meet him at the dojo in twenty minutes."

"What?! He's here—in Hawaii?"

"So it would seem," he said. "He says Yoshida is with him."

"I thought Yoshida was in China until next week."

"Yes, that's what he told me. I'm going to call the dojo." Adrian dialed the number. He heard the answering machine pick up. "There's no one there."

"Try Yoshida at home," Kristine suggested, sitting next to him on the sofa.

Adrian dialed again, and waited as the phone rang. "No answer."

"Adrian, I don't like this," said Kristine. "He has a huge fight with Yoshida, and disappears for over three years. Then he shows up out of the blue and..."

"And wants me to meet him, and says Yoshida is coming, too. I know. I need to go see what he wants."

"I don't think this is a good idea," she said.

"Kristine, if Jesse Thompson is back, something is going on. I need to find out what."

"Then I'm going with you." Adrian looked at her for a moment. "Fine."

"So much for our three-day-late New Year's dinner," she muttered. She rose off the couch to talk to Alissa.

Adrian and Kristine got in their car. Twenty minutes later, they were driving along an isolated road at the top of a cliff overlooking the ocean. Yoshida's dojo sat at the end of the road, in a clearing in the woods. It was a single-story, wooden structure.

Adrian parked the car right in front of the building. "Get in the driver's seat, and be ready to go in case anything happens," he said to Kristine. They both got out of the car. Kristine ran around to sit behind the wheel.

Adrian followed the sidewalk to the entrance. It was locked. He pulled a key out of his pocket, unlocked the door and went inside.

The dojo was dark and empty. Adrian checked the office and the changing rooms, but nobody was there. He went outside and walked around behind the building. Nothing. He was returning to the car when a voice called out behind him, "*Master* Kahanu." Adrian stopped dead in his tracks. "Sam and I just made master a few months ago, Jesse," he said, turning around. "How do you know about that?"

"Word gets around," said Jesse Thompson. He walked slowly toward Adrian, leaving the door to the dojo open behind him.

Jesse was wearing jeans and a T-shirt—much better for fighting than a suit and tie, thought Adrian. He took off his jacket and handed it to Kristine through the window. "Stay put, and keep the car running," he said.

Adrian walked toward Jesse. He stopped ten feet away. "Where's Yoshida?" he asked.

"He should be here any minute now," Jesse replied with a smirk.

"What do you want, Jesse?"

"There's someone here who wants to meet you," he said, and stepped aside, giving Adrian a clear view of the entrance. At that moment, a tall figure stepped over the threshold. The man wore full samurai battle armor, gleaming white in the shadows. A skeletal face was visible through the opening in the facemask, and two pale green eyes glowed faintly in deep eye sockets.

"Jaaku..." hissed Adrian. He turned to run back to the car.

But Jesse was ready. He dove forward and threw one arm around Adrian's neck, pulling him back. Adrian thrust an elbow into Jesse's ribs, grabbed his arm and flipped him over onto the sidewalk. He pinned Jesse down with one knee, keeping a hold on his arm with one hand, ready to break the elbow if Jesse tried to move.

"Excellent," said Jaaku, his voice little more than a whisper. He walked toward Adrian. "Jesse told me you were very... talented. You will make a fine addition to my Arashi."

"I'll never join you, Jaaku," said Adrian with a disgusted look. He held out his free hand to throw a glowing red ball of energy at Jaaku.

Jaaku caught the fireball between his hands. "No, perhaps not," he hissed. He added his own energy to the fireball—growing it to enormous size—and threw it back at Adrian. The fireball looked like a comet streaking through the night sky, a long tail streaming off of it. It hit Adrian in the chest and knocked him through the air.

Kristine screamed. There was a brilliant flash of light behind Jaaku, right in front of the dojo.

"Jaaku!" shouted the man who had materialized in the flash of light.

"Yoshida!" yelled Adrian. There was relief in his voice.

Jaaku turned to face Yoshida. "I thought you might be joining our little party."

At that moment, Jesse took advantage of the distraction and lunged at Adrian—but Adrian was ready for him. At the same time, Jaaku dove at Yoshida, sending them both into the dojo.

But as Yoshida fell back, he disappeared. Jaaku rolled forward and regained his feet. Yoshida materialized again in the center of the dojo.

"So you finally found the one," said Jaaku.

"You are mistaken. You cannot attain immortality this way, Jaaku."

"We shall see," hissed Jaaku, advancing on Yoshida again. Jaaku threw a series of lightning-fast kicks at Yoshida's head, driving him back, toward the wall. Yoshida dodged each of these with ease. When he reached the wall, he jumped up in the air. He kicked off the wall with both feet, flying over Jaaku's head. He flipped over and landed facing Jaaku.

Jaaku rushed toward him. This time Yoshida attacked, throwing a vicious barrage of punches and kicks. Jaaku blocked all of these, and then jumped straight up in the air. He seemed to float there for a moment, just out of Yoshida's reach. Yoshida took a step forward, jumped in the air, and slammed a side kick into Jaaku's chest plate.

Jaaku smashed into the wall and fell to the floor in a heap.

Yoshida ran toward him. Jaaku sprang to his feet. The two struggled back and forth, throwing a flurry of kicks and punches, neither able to gain an advantage on the other.

Finally they both backed off and circled each other, looking for an opening. Jaaku lunged in, but Yoshida vanished. He reappeared right behind Jaaku, threw his arm around his neck and pulled him down to the ground in a chokehold.

At that moment Adrian ran in the door. There was blood trickling from his mouth. "Run!" yelled Yoshida, pulling tighter around Jaaku's throat. "Get out of here!"

Adrian nodded, and ran out the door.

Jaaku struggled against Yoshida's chokehold for a moment longer. Then he disappeared.

"No!" yelled Yoshida. He got up to run out of the dojo. He exited in time to see Adrian's car careening out of the parking lot, and Jaaku kneeling next to Jesse's unconscious form, sprawled out on the sidewalk.

Jaaku stood up, took one look at Yoshida, and turned to face the parking lot. He took a step forward and vanished again. He reappeared out on the road this time, directly in the path of Adrian's car. Jaaku held up one hand and shot an enormous fireball at the car.

"NO!" Yoshida screamed, and disappeared, materializing right next to Jaaku. He tackled Jaaku, sending them both crashing into the pavement. But it was too late. The front of Adrian's car was now in flames. Kristine swerved to avoid hitting Yoshida. The car went off the road, and flew over the cliff.

Jaaku disappeared out of Yoshida's grasp, reappearing next to Jesse. He knelt down, hoisted Jesse over his shoulder, and vanished in a brilliant flash of light.

Yoshida ran to the edge of the cliff and looked down in time to see Adrian's car hit the rocks far below. It exploded in flames.

He dropped to his knees, bowed his head and wept. The stars wheeled in the night sky, the waves crashed against the base of the cliff, and the wreckage of Adrian's car burned angrily on the rocks. And there Yoshida knelt, and wept until he could weep no more.

Chapter One: Billy

Vermont, present day

Katana was asleep, lying face down diagonally across her bed. Her long black hair was spread out in a messy tangle, her left arm dangling off the edge of the bed. She was wearing a pair of boxers and a white tank top. She was all muscle and bone. A month away from her fourteenth birthday, she'd grown several inches over the past year. She had the elongated look of someone who was getting taller so quickly that she hadn't had time to grow into her body yet.

A large fan was whirring in the window next to her bed—they'd been experiencing a heat wave for the past few days in Croton, Vermont. Katana was doing everything she could to keep cool, but with little success. She'd been sleeping over at her best friend Chris's house because the Boyds had central air. But Chris's parents were away for the week, so the kids were staying at Katana's house, suffering through the heat.

"Katana, I'm going to work. I'm doing a double shift today," said Katana's aunt, Leanna as she walked into the room.

Katana stirred. "Okay," she muttered.

"Are you and Chris going to Turtle Beach today?"

"Mm-hmm."

"All right, well don't forget to finish your chores before you go. I'll see you tonight." Leanna bent over and kissed Katana on the back of her head, then bustled out of the room.

Katana turned over on her back and stretched. She tried to see what time it was, but the sunlight streaming through the window was blinding her. She sat up and held out her hand to shade her jade green eyes from the glare. It was seven thirty. This was much too early to be awake in the summer. She fluffed her pillow and lay back down.

But it was no use—it was stiflingly hot. She was awake now. She got up and walked out to the living room. Leanna's apartment occupied the second floor of a two-family house a few minutes outside of the center of Croton. It wasn't very big—it had a living room, an eat-in kitchen, two bedrooms and one bathroom, although it was large enough for Katana and her aunt.

Chris was sound asleep on the foldout couch. Katana walked around the end of the bed and sat down at a small desk. She pushed the power button on the computer. Nothing happened.

"Piece of junk," she said with a sigh. She moved back across the room toward the kitchen.

"Wake up," she said. Chris didn't respond. Katana walked over and pulled the pillow out from under his head. Chris merely grunted and went right on sleeping. "Come on, wake up!" she said, hitting him in the head with his pillow. This did the trick.

"Hey!" said Chris. He grabbed his pillow and rolled over to go back to sleep.

"Let's go," said Katana. "It's like ninety degrees out again. I wanna go to the beach."

Chris muttered something that sounded like, "What time is it?"

"Seven thirty. Come on, get up."

He rolled over on his back, rubbing his eyes. Chris, too, had grown significantly over the past year. He appeared very bony. He was wearing shorts and a wrinkly T-shirt. He'd been letting his curly, dark brown hair grow out. Katana thought it looked like a small shrub growing on the top of his head.

"You really need a haircut," she said, walking into the kitchen. She got out cereal and milk and sat down at the table to eat.

Chris shuffled into the kitchen, got a bowl out of the cupboard and sat down across the table from Katana. "We gotta stop at my house on the way to the beach," he said. "I forgot my bathing suit."

"That's fine. We can see if Sara's on. My computer's still busted." Sara Brown was their friend who lived in Japan. Katana and Chris talked to her online whenever they had a chance.

"What time is it there? Is she gonna be up?" asked Chris.

"They're fourteen hours ahead, so it's like nine thirty at night. She'll probably be on."

After breakfast, Katana washed the dishes and Chris took out the trash. Katana changed into her bathing suit, and threw on a pair of shorts. They walked to Chris's house.

Chris's family lived in an old colonial built in the 1700s. It was a few minutes away from Katana's house, and sat on several acres of land that was covered with pine trees.

"Ugh," Chris said as he opened the front door. "I forgot to turn off the air conditioning."

"Remember to shut it off when we leave," said Katana. "I thought your mom was gonna kill you last time you left it on."

Chris dropped his backpack and ran upstairs to change into his bathing suit. Katana went into the living room and sat down at the computer. She signed on to her screen name and saw that Sara was indeed online.

KATANAKAHANU: Hey!

NINJAMASTERSARA: hey Kat

NINJAMASTERSARA: I have so much to tell you

KATANAKAHANU: what's up?

NINJAMASTERSARA: Nash came over for dinner tonight

KATANAKAHANU: Nash is in Japan?

NINJAMASTERSARA: yeah, and something's up

NINJAMASTERSARA: he was talking to my dad after dinner about some mission

NINJAMASTERSARA: they kicked me out of the room but I was listening thru the door

KATANAKAHANU: what's the mission?

NINJAMASTERSARA: I don't know, but Nash said it's gonna be dangerous

NINJAMASTERSARA: something about someone going to china I think

KATANAKAHANU: Who?

NINJAMASTERSARA: I don't know but it sounded like it

was someone from Hall of the Dragon

Chris came back downstairs. "Okay, let's go," he said. "We're not supposed to be here while my parents are gone."

KATANAKAHANU: I gotta go

KATANAKAHANU: Chris's parents will be back next week so we'll be on more again

NINJAMASTERSARA: ok, see ya

"Did you shut off the air?" Katana asked as they left the house.

"Oops..." said Chris, and ran back inside. He came out and locked the door, and they headed to Turtle Beach.

"Sara says Nash was over for dinner," said Katana. "She heard him talking to her dad about someone from the Hall going on some sort of mission." Jordan Nash was the tai chi master and headmaster of the Hall of the Dragon, a boarding school for students from seventh to twelfth grade who studied martial arts. The masters in residence taught kempo, tae kwon do, wushu, aikido and tai chi.

"What kind of mission?" asked Chris.

"She didn't know," said Katana. "They were talking in private, but she listened through the door."

"Yeah, that sounds like Sara," said Chris. "I wonder if it has anything to do with the scroll." A man named Master Chow founded the Hall of the Dragon in 1850. He had allegedly trained with the Immortal Master and mastered all five arts, a feat that no one had been able to accomplish since. When Chow left the Hall of the Dragon, he left behind the Scroll of the Five Masters. The scroll was supposed to hold the secret of immortality. Only the next

Master of the Five Arts would be able to understand it.

"I bet it does," said Katana. "I hope Jaaku hasn't been able to figure it out."

Sara had told her about Jaaku when Katana first arrived at the Hall, but they'd thought at the time that he was only a myth. It turned out that Jaaku was all too real. He had been a samurai warrior in the 1700s in Japan, but had ultimately left behind the ways of the samurai. He'd gone to China to learn the dark art of dim mak. Students of dim mak could manipulate an opponent's chi—the life energy in every living thing—to do things like cause paralysis or pain. Jaaku had even learned the art's highest power— the death touch. He could take someone's chi and absorb it into himself, leaving the other person dead.

Master Osaka had told Katana that Jaaku had originally believed he could become immortal by constantly stealing chi from other people. But after nearly three hundred years of doing this, Jaaku's time was running out: the more chi he stole, the less he could absorb.

Jaaku had found out about the Scroll of the Five Masters during Katana's first year at the Hall. He'd sent members of the Arashi—a secret society devoted to practicing and teaching the art of dim mak—to steal the scroll. They'd succeeded with the help of Master Sato, the aikido master at the Hall. Jaaku had taken Sato's prenatal chi and used that connection to control him and force him to let the Arashi into the school. Katana and her friends had caught Sato and three of the Arashi stealing the scroll and tried to stop them. But the Arashi had proven much too powerful.

Sato himself had ended up bringing the scroll to Jaaku. But Sato, Master Van Heldon—the tae kwon do master at the Hall—and Katana's friend, Robert, had all died before that night was over.

"Did you remember the suntan lotion this time?" Katana asked when they got to the beach and spread their towels out on the sand.

"I think so," said Chris, rummaging through his backpack. "Yeah, here it is."

"You better put on a lot this time." Chris's complexion was pale, and he burned easily. His back and shoulders were still a painful shade of red from the last time they'd gone.

He handed the bottle to Katana and she applied copious amounts to his back.

"Aren't you gonna put any on?"

"Nah. I wanna get as dark as I can before summer's over." Katana's complexion was much more suited to the summer sun than Chris's was; she'd already achieved a rich shade of brown.

"Leanna's gonna kill you. 'You're gonna get skin cancer,'" he said, imitating her voice.

They ran down the beach and jumped into the lake, but the water was so warm it did little to cool them off.

"Swimming in the ocean is way cooler than this," said Katana when they walked back to their towels. The Hall of the Dragon was located along the Pacific coast in California, between Redwood National Forest and the ocean. Katana had gone swimming at the beach across from the school a few times the previous year.

"Yeah it is," said Chris, lying down on his towel. "Did Sara say who's going on the mission?"

"No. She said it sounded like it was someone from the Hall, but she couldn't hear who."

"Maybe it's Osaka again," suggested Chris.

"I don't know," said Katana. "Let's ask Mike—maybe he knows something."

Katana and Chris lay out in the sun for a while then went back in the water again. Finally they decided it was too hot and headed back to Chris's house.

"Let's hang out here today," said Chris. "At least it's air-conditioned."

"I thought your parents didn't want us here while they're gone?"

"They don't, but they don't have to find out."

They spent the rest of the day watching Chinese kung fu movies—their favorite was one called *Fighters of Shaolin*—and playing video games. Late that afternoon they walked to Sensei Mike's school in the center of Croton. They went in early most days to help Sensei Mike with the kids class that took place right before their own.

"Hey guys," said Mike as they walked in. Mike was a full head taller than Katana. He had bouncy blond hair and a very muscular build. He wore a white karate uniform and a black belt that was torn and tattered with age.

"Hi Mike," said Katana.

"Isn't the air conditioning working?" asked Chris.

"It is, but not very well," replied Mike. "I think it's too hot for it to handle. Don't worry, we'll go easy tonight."

Katana and Chris went to get changed into their uniforms. A large, empty room occupied the middle of the school—this was the main practice area, or dojo. It was covered with tatami mats. A short table at the front of the room functioned as an altar. It contained a small bamboo plant, two incense holders and a jade carving of Buddha. Behind the altar hung a scroll with the Japanese character for "Do," or the Way. Large mirrors covered the rest of the front wall on both sides of the altar.

"We're going to be working on kata today," said Mike as Katana and Chris walked into the dojo. "Chris, I'm going to give you the higher belts..."

"That means Katana gets Billy!" said Chris, looking delighted with his good fortune. Billy had recently turned seven. Chris had spent many a class this summer trying to keep Billy from running out of the dojo every few minutes.

"He's not that bad," said Sensei Mike. "He's really focusing a lot better now that he's got his orange belt."

"I'll never forget that time he bit you," Katana said with a smile.

"That's not funny!" said Chris. "It hurt!"

After a dozen little kids filed into the room, Sensei Mike started the lesson. He lit a stick of incense on the altar, then had the whole class bow and kneel down. He led them through a series of warm-ups and stretches. Next he had them get into a horse-riding stance and go through their basic punches and kicks.

After basics, he split the class into three groups. He, Katana and Chris each took one group to work on kata. Kata were prearranged forms or patterns of stances, punches and kicks. They represented the "art" of the martial art of kempo. The key to doing a good kata was to execute every move exactly the right way.

Katana had to admit that Billy was doing a much better job of concentrating than he'd been able to do earlier in the summer. She only had to stop him from running out of the dojo once.

At the end of the hour, Sensei Mike lined everyone up again. They bowed, and knelt down to remove their belts. Jenny, a little blond-haired girl who wore a blue belt, raised her hand.

"Yes, Jenny?"

"Today is my birthday!"

"Is it really? How old are you turning?"

"Eight," she said with a big smile.

"That's awesome, Jenny—Happy Birthday!" said Sensei Mike.

"I'm seven!" exclaimed Billy, holding up five fingers on one hand and three on the other. The rest of the class tried to stifle their giggles.

"Raise your hand first, Billy," said Sensei Mike.

Billy promptly raised his hand.

"Yes, Billy?"

"How old are you, Sensei Mike?"

Mike chuckled. "That's a secret, Billy."

The whole class erupted at this point; they all wanted to know how old Sensei Mike was. "Okay, okay, settle down everyone! I'll tell you how old I am, but you have to promise you won't tell anyone."

"We won't," they agreed.

"I am two thousand, three hundred and fifty-four years old," said Sensei Mike.

Chaos reigned again. "You're not that old," Billy screamed, as Jenny broke down in a fit of giggles.

"That's what Osaka always used to say," an older girl at the front of class said accusingly. "You need to get some new jokes."

Sensei Mike calmed them down again, and herded them out of the dojo.

The teens class also worked on kata that night. Katana and Chris had tested for their second degree black belts in kempo the previous month at the Hall of the Dragon. Since their return home, Mike had been teaching them their next kata—they needed two new forms to go from second to third degree.

"That's good everyone, please line up," he said at the end of class. He bowed them out. "Hey, why don't you two come by tomorrow during the day," he said to Katana and Chris as everyone walked out of the dojo. "We can polish up Kata Thirteen a bit, and you can show me some of the stuff you've been doing at the Hall of the Dragon."

"Yeah, that's cool," said Katana. Chris nodded in agreement. "What time?"

"How's one o'clock?" asked Sensei Mike.

"That's good," said Katana. "We'll see you then."

Chapter Two: Private Lesson

Katana found it very difficult to get to sleep that night; it was much too hot. She finally drifted off well after midnight. The heat wave broke a few hours later. Katana had left the fan droning away in her open window, but woke up shivering with cold before dawn. She got up and shut off the fan, closed the window and went back to bed.

It was nearly eleven by the time Katana finally got out of bed the next morning. She found Chris already awake, eating his cereal at the breakfast table. She ate too, then they lounged around and watched television until it was time to go to karate.

Mike was on the phone, standing outside his office door when they arrived a little before one. He was wearing the pants to his karate uniform and a tank top. He waved at them, and they went to change into their uniforms.

"You guys don't have to wear full uniform for this if you don't want. I'm not going to," said Mike as they walked back into the dojo to stretch.

"Oh, cool," said Katana. She draped her uniform top and belt over the half wall. She, too, was wearing her karate pants and a black tank top.

Chris kept his uniform top on. "My back is sunburned," he

explained. "The tatami hurts it when I fall without the top."

They stretched for a while. "I hate you two sometimes," Chris complained. Katana and Mike could both do full front splits on both sides, but Chris was woefully inflexible.

"Do you know where Osaka is now?" asked Katana.

"He was here for a couple of weeks after he came back with you guys," said Mike, "then he went back to the Hall of the Dragon right after he tested me for my fourth degree."

"I didn't know you got your fourth!" exclaimed Chris. "Congratulations!"

"You don't know anything about him going off on some mission, do you?" asked Katana.

"No," said Sensei Mike. "He said he'd be at the Hall for the rest of the summer. Why?"

"We talked to our friend Sara online yesterday," Chris explained. "She said that Master Nash was at her house, and he was talking about someone from the Hall going on some dangerous mission."

"Hmm," said Mike, looking pensive for a moment. "Osaka did say that Jaaku had attacked the Shaolin Temple a couple of times; maybe it has something to do with that."

"Jaaku attacked Shaolin?" Katana and Chris both asked at the same time.

"Well, I guess he sent the Arashi. But they couldn't get in for some reason. Osaka said they tried to break in secretly, late at night, but they couldn't. The headmaster woke up and went to fight them with some of the monks."

"I wonder..." said Katana. "I bet the temple is protected the same way the Hall is. Sam—she's the kempo master at the Hall—she told us that nobody could break into the Hall because of the chi from everyone who's trained there all these years."

"Yeah, Osaka explained something like that," said Mike. "He said everyone's chi leaves an imprint on the building. Nobody can get in if they're trying to hurt anyone inside or steal anything."

"Why were the Arashi trying to get into the Shaolin Temple?" asked Chris.

"Apparently Jaaku's going nuts trying to figure out the Scroll of the Five Masters. Osaka said Jaaku thinks there might be something in the archives at Shaolin that explains it. They have a whole big library there with a ton of old scrolls and manuscripts."

"Maybe that's what the mission is—maybe one of the masters is going to Shaolin," Katana suggested.

"That doesn't sound very dangerous," Chris replied doubtfully.

"I don't know," said Sensei Mike. "I'll call Osaka later and see if he knows anything. All right, are you two ready? Let's start with combinations."

Combinations were self-defense moves that consisted of various strikes and takedowns. They were designed to be used against an untrained attacker. Katana and Chris had learned a total of twenty combinations on the way up to black belt.

Katana went first. Chris stepped in and threw a punch at her head. Katana blocked his punch, wrapped his arm, struck his neck, and swept his leg out, hitting him again after he landed. Each of the combinations had a different kind of takedown—some had flips and throws, and others used different kinds of joint locks.

Chris had his turn when Katana was done. Sensei Mike had them work on attack drills next. For these, they had to do their moves freestyle. One of them would attack—they could punch or kick the other person, grab them, or tackle them. The other person had to defend against the attack. Generally one did not do the combinations exactly as they were taught—instead, the idea was to react without thinking, and do whatever came naturally.

"So you guys can both deflect intent now, right?" asked Sensei Mike.

"Not me," said Chris. "I can do a chi hit, but I haven't been able to deflect intent yet."

"I can do both," said Katana.

"Don't feel bad, Chris," said Mike. "I can't do either of them yet."

"Won't you need to deflect intent to get your fifth degree?" asked Katana.

"No, not exactly. You can get fifth without doing it, but to be promoted to master, you need to have your fifth degree *and* be able to do the chen do," explained Sensei Mike. "Well, let's work on that for a bit. Katana, why don't you show us how it's done? Chris, go ahead and attack again..."

"She can't do the chen do on me," said Chris.

"Why not?"

"Because our chi is mixed," said Katana. "That's why Chris was still able to attack me in the dragon circle last summer. Osaka said that we're so close that our chi has mixed, so we can't use the chen do against each other."

"Wow," said Sensei Mike. "All right, I'll attack for you, and you can help me and Chris get it."

Sensei Mike and Katana bowed to each other and assumed fighting stances. He lunged at Katana to tackle her. She dropped to a low stance and flung out both hands, palm open. Mike's attack seemed to deflate. He fell to the side.

"That's neat," he said. He tried to attack a few more times with the same result. "Tell us how you do it!"

"Well, that's the thing—I just do it. I don't know how," Katana said apologetically. "Sam taught us about auras last year. She said that everyone glows because of the chi flowing through their bodies. If you can see a person's aura, you can read their intent, and block their attack with your own intent."

"Can you see my aura?" asked Sensei Mike.

"No, not really... I was able to see Nash's and Osaka's last year, but not anyone else's. But Sam said even though I couldn't *see* other people's auras, I could still sense them somehow. Otherwise I wouldn't be able to do the chen do."

"Well, what do you think about when you do it?" asked Sensei Mike.

"When I got it the first time, I was feeling overwhelmed, because Osaka called like four people at the same time in the dragon circle. I just wanted it to stop. But I guess that's how I always do it. I kinda wish for the attack to stop, concentrate really hard, and it just happens."

"Okay, let's give it a shot. Come on, Chris," said Sensei Mike. "I'll attack first."

Chris assumed a low stance, held his hands out in front of him and said, "I'm ready."

Sensei Mike lunged in at him. Whatever Chris might have done, it didn't work. Sensei Mike tackled him and they both crashed to the floor.

"You have to focus, Chris! Imagine him falling to the side when he comes at you, and concentrate really hard on it," suggested Katana. Chris tried it several more times unsuccessfully.

"Let me have a turn," said Sensei Mike. But he couldn't do it either; Chris was able to reach him every time. "Well, I'm in no hurry. I've got years before I test for fifth degree. Let's work on some sparring—did you guys bring your gear?"

"Yeah," said Chris. They went to get their gloves and headgear out of their backpacks.

"We'll go with the official rules," said Mike. "Two points for a kick, two for a takedown, and one for a punch. The first person to five points wins." Katana and Chris bowed to each other, and Mike yelled "Fight!"

They circled around each other, each looking for an opening. Finally Katana launched at Chris with a volley of kicks. "Up!" yelled Sensei Mike. "Nice roundhouse kick, Katana—two points."

They started again and this time Chris took the initiative. He drove Katana back with a series of kicks to her head. Katana deflected them, and then countered with another kick to Chris's head. But Chris dropped down and swept out her other leg.

"Nice!" yelled Sensei Mike. "Two to two."

Katana and Chris squared off. Again, Chris took the initiative. But this time, as he moved in with his first kick, Katana dropped and swept out his leg, just as he'd done to her. As Chris landed on his back, Katana turned over and threw a kick to his head.

"Good combo, Kat," said Sensei Mike. "You win, six to two. You guys are getting really good at sparring. What you should work on now is feinting."

"What's that?" asked Chris, getting back to his feet.

"Basically, you fake with one kick, and when your opponent tries to block that, you throw something totally different. Here, watch." He squared off with Katana. "Kat, I'm going to throw a front kick, and I want you to block it like you normally would." Mike threw a kick at Katana's ribs; she dropped one arm to deflect it. But he pivoted on his bottom foot, swinging his leg around to throw a roundhouse kick instead. "See that?" he asked, holding his foot right next to Katana's head. "Two points."

"That's cool—let me try," said Katana, squaring off with Chris. She feinted with a front kick, just as Sensei Mike had done. And when Chris dropped his hand to block it, Katana flicked her foot up to his head.

"Good," said Sensei Mike. "Give it a try, Chris."

Chris tried the same combination, but stumbled and yelled "Ow!" when he tried to swing his leg around for the roundhouse kick.

"What's wrong?" asked Mike.

"That hurts my hip when I move my leg that way," he said, hobbling on one foot.

"Hmm," said Mike. "You may not have the flexibility for that combination. Here, try this instead." He faced Katana. "Start with the roundhouse kick. When she blocks that side of her head, swing your leg around the other way and throw an axe kick, like this." He swung his leg over Katana's head, dropping it in front of her face.

"Whoa!" said Katana. "That's cool."

"I can't lift my leg that high!" Chris exclaimed. "I'm not flexible in that direction either."

"I wanna try it," said Katana. She threw a roundhouse kick at Chris's head, which he blocked. Then she snapped her leg around the other way. Chris tried to duck. Katana slammed her foot down, across the back of his skull. Chris went sprawling on the mat.

"Oh, sure," he said. "Make her even more dangerous than she was already. Thanks a lot!"

"No problem," Mike replied with a smile.

"What happens if I land both kicks?" asked Katana.

"Only the first one counts," Mike explained. "The only time you can get points for more than one element in an exchange is after a takedown—you can get the points for both the takedown and a follow-up strike, for example."

"Got it," she replied.

"All right, me and you," Mike said, pointing at Katana.

"Are you kidding? You're like three feet taller than me!"

"You're exaggerating, Kat," he said, squaring off with her. "Chris, you judge."

"Uh... okay. Go!"

Sensei Mike circled around Katana for a moment, then threw the front kick to roundhouse kick combination he'd shown them. But Katana was ready for it. She dodged both kicks. They went back and forth for a minute, each trying different combinations. Finally, Sensei Mike feinted with a front kick again, and landed his roundhouse kick to her head when Katana blocked the feint.

"Up!" yelled Chris. "Two points, Mike."

They started again, and this time Mike launched directly into a series of kicks. Katana dropped immediately and swept out his base leg, dropping him to the floor. She rolled over to kick him in the head, but Mike rolled out of the way before she could get him.

"Two to two," said Chris.

They began again. This time as Mike advanced on Katana, she dropped into a low stance, threw both hands out, and shot a bright red, glowing ball of chi energy. It hit him square in the chest, throwing him into the wall.

"Uh... how many points for a chi hit?" asked Chris, looking surprised.

"None!" said Mike, and coughed, trying to catch his breath. "That's not fair—we didn't say anything about using chi hits!"

"Yeah," Katana said, grinning mischievously, "but we didn't say anything about *not* using them either!" She squealed as Mike grabbed her, threw her to the floor, and gave her a noogie to the head.

"GAH!" yelled Mike when Chris put his arm around his neck and pulled him back in a chokehold. Katana and Chris proceeded to wrestle with Sensei Mike until they tired themselves out. "Two against one is *not* a fair match," said Sensei Mike, lying back on the floor.

"It is when you're as big as both of us put together," said Chris.

They caught their breath and stretched for a few minutes.

"Katana, how did you get the chi hit the first time?" asked Mike.

"It was during the fight with the Arashi, when they came to steal the scroll the weekend of nationals. One of them hit Sara with a huge fireball—and I threw one back. It just happened."

"Had you been doing anything special to work on it before that?" he asked.

"Yeah, I was," said Katana. "After Thompson kidnapped me, I asked Sam to help me with the chen do. She worked with us for weeks. But I didn't actually get the chi hit until the fight with the Arashi."

"Sam had us working on the standing chi kung exercise, remember?" asked Chris.

"Which one?" asked Mike.

"We learned it in tai chi class. Here, it goes like this," she said, getting to her feet. She stood with all her weight on one leg, and put her other foot in front of her so that only the ball of her front foot was touching the mat. "Hold your hands out in front of you in a circle, like this—pretend you're holding a big beach ball, with one hand going over the ball, and the other underneath."

Mike followed along. Within a few moments, a glowing red ball of energy formed between Katana's arms.

"How are you doing that?!" asked Mike. He stopped doing the exercise himself to watch her.

"You have to relax," she said, "and feel the energy flowing from your fingertips into the ball." She held the pose for a minute, moving her hands around the fireball. It grew a deeper shade of red and little lines of fire danced along its surface.

"Whoa," said Chris. "I've never seen you hold it this long before."

Katana let the energy dissipate. "I've never been *able* to hold it that long before," she said, looking surprised herself.

"So can any of the other students at the Hall do the chen do, or are you two the only ones?"

"A few other kids can do them, but not many," said Chris.

"Our friend Jelly can do levitation," said Katana.

"How'd he get it?" asked Sensei Mike.

"He was doing a double backflip one day when the wushu team was practicing their demo. His foot slipped during his round-off, so he had to fight for the landing—but instead of crashing, he floated. It was totally by accident the first time," explained Katana.

"A *double* backflip?" asked Sensei Mike. "I can't even do a single..."

"I can!" said Katana. She did a round-off, and threw herself over backwards, landing a perfect backflip.

"You're *such* a show-off," complained Chris.

"I thought you could do that, too?" said Mike.

"Well, I can do it sometimes, but I'm not real consistent."

"Try one—let me see," said Mike.

Chris got up and did it, but landed poorly. He stumbled a couple of steps and fell down on his rear end.

"Ouch," said Mike with a grimace. "No offense, Chris, but your body looks kinda... broken when you do that."

"I know!" said Chris.

They goofed around with different tricks, and Katana tried to teach Mike how to do an aerial. He could do a cartwheel and a one-handed cartwheel, but couldn't manage it without using his hands. He gave up after a few minutes as Katana showed off some more.

"Do a flash kick," suggested Chris.

"What's a flash kick?" asked Mike.

"You do a backflip, but you separate your legs as you go over," said Katana.

"Show me," said Sensei Mike.

Katana did a round-off again, and extended her legs almost to a full split as she flipped over backwards.

"That was good," said Mike. "You're getting a *lot* of height on your tricks. But listen—I'm hungry. I gotta get some lunch before my first class starts. You guys wanna get a pizza?"

They ordered from their favorite pizza place—Anthony's, right across Main Street from the dojo. Mike gave them some money and Katana and Chris went to pick up the order when it was ready.

"Hey," said Chris as they sat down in Sensei Mike's office to eat. "I just realized—didn't we come here to work on Kata Thirteen today?"

"Oops," said Sensei Mike as he took a bite of pizza.

"Oh well, who cares," said Katana. "This was more fun anyway."

Chapter Three: Back to the Hall

Master Samantha Malloy was sitting in the den inside her suite at the Hall of the Dragon, her legs folded up underneath her, holding a cup of coffee in both hands. She knew she had a choice to make. Nash expected her decision today.

She took a sip of coffee, then placed the cup on the end table. Rising from the chair, she walked into her bedroom. She pulled a large cardboard box out of her closet and rummaged through it. At the bottom she found what she was looking for.

Sam lifted an old photo album out of the box and curled up in her bed. This album contained pictures from her college years. Most featured herself, Jesse Thompson and Adrian Kahanu—Katana's dad. The three had been best friends at the Hall of the Dragon, and went to school together at the University of Hawaii.

She flipped through the album one page at a time, past photos of parties, luaus on the beach, classes at Osaka's dojo. Finally, she found the section she was looking for. The last several pages of the album contained photos of Adrian and Kristine, Katana's mother. There were shots from their wedding and their new house. And baby pictures of Katana.

Sam gazed at a photo of Adrian holding his daughter, taken only a few days before he died. He looked so happy. Her eyes filled with tears thinking about his unlived life. Adrian never got to see his baby grow up into the young woman she was today.

Not for the first time, Sam contemplated the irony of her situation. Long robbed of her two best friends, Sam was now one of Katana's teachers. One of her mentors. The girl's arrival at the Hall had opened old wounds for Sam. She thought she'd moved past the pain of Adrian's death many years ago. But Katana reminded her of him so forcefully, Sam sometimes felt like she was reliving her own days as a student at the Hall.

Sam had made up her mind. Later that morning, she went to see Nash.

"You've come to a decision?" he asked as she took a seat across the desk from him.

"I have," she said. "And I'm sorry. I can't do it. My place is here."

Nash nodded. "I'll let Hua know."

Sam felt a twinge of guilt. He'd be going alone now. "I'll still help him get ready. I'll keep training with him and everything..."

"Of course," he replied. "And I appreciate that. Shaolin isn't ready yet in any case. This will take some time."

"They'll send someone with Hua?" asked Sam. "When the time comes?"

"Yes. I have their guarantee."

This was reassuring. Hua was a good friend and colleague. Sam felt like she was betraying him by refusing to go on this mission. But at least he wouldn't be alone for the most dangerous part of the journey.

For the rest of the summer, Katana and Chris spent most of their days at Turtle Beach—Katana grew very dark, and Chris very red— and most of their evenings at the dojo with Sensei Mike. They went in for a private lesson once a week and spent a lot of time working on their sparring skills. Mike taught them a number of different kicking combinations and they practiced various ways to transition from kicks to sweeps. They also learned Kata Fourteen, which was the second form they would need to progress to third degree black belt. Katana tried to teach Mike and Chris to deflect intent, but this effort didn't meet with much success.

Mike called Master Osaka at the Hall of the Dragon to ask about the secret mission they'd heard about. Osaka was evasive. "This is not something I can discuss," he said.

"So someone *is* going on a mission somewhere," replied Sensei Mike.

"I didn't say that," said Osaka.

Sara told Katana online that she was trying to get more information out of her dad, but he was being as tight-lipped as Osaka. Katana had the impression that this was unusual—it seemed like Sara's dad usually told her anything she wanted to know.

"We can talk to Sam when we get back to the Hall," suggested Katana. "I'm sure she'll tell us what's going on."

August twenty-eighth arrived on a Saturday, and Mrs. Boyd drove Katana and Chris to the airport for their flight to California.

"I wish we could go in the school jet again," said Chris, as they sat down in their cramped seats on the plane.

Katana looked over at the two little kids in the seats next to them. They were hitting and shoving each other; their mother was futilely trying to break it up. "Me too," she replied.

They landed in Eureka, and went to collect their luggage.

"Is Gerald picking us up?" asked Katana. Gerald was one of the drivers for the Hall. He'd picked up Katana from the airport when she arrived the previous year.

"No idea," said Chris. "Nash picked me up last year."

They walked toward the exit. Katana heard someone yelling their names.

"Katana! Chris—over here!" It was Samantha Malloy, the kempo master. She was the same height as Katana. She had short, dirty-blond hair and piercing blue eyes. "You both got so much taller—I'm going to have to look up at you soon! How was your summer?"

"It was good," said Katana.

"You mean boring," Chris retorted.

They followed Sam out to the parking lot.

"We get to ride in the Porsche!" said Chris as they walked up to a black 911 Turbo.

"I would have come in the Ferrari, but it doesn't have a back seat. One of you would have had to ride in the trunk," said Sam with a wink.

"It doesn't look like this has much of a back seat either," said Katana, looking in the window.

They loaded into the car, and Katana rode in front. "Comfortable back there, Chris?" asked Sam as she put on her sunglasses and started the car.

"No."

Sam pulled out of the parking lot and shot up Highway 101. The road wound up the Pacific coast, and the landscape grew steadily less developed as they traveled north of Eureka. It was a beautiful sunny day and lacked the fog cover that was so common to the area. They had a spectacular view of the ocean to their left.

Katana thought riding in the Porsche was much more fun than taking the limo, as she'd done the previous year. Sam's driving was rather spirited and they made the trip in much less time than usual.

She exited the highway and drove down the long gravel driveway that led to the Hall. She parked in front of an enormous, wooden torii gate.

The main building reminded Katana of the Shaolin Temple in the Chinese kung fu movies she and Chris liked to watch. The long, sloping roof was covered in greenish tile, and two long, lower buildings extended forward at forty-five degree angles from either end. A large stone courtyard sat immediately in front of the Hall, a fountain gurgling away in the middle of it.

Katana and Chris climbed out of the Porsche. They pulled their suitcases out of the compartment in the front of the car. "Here are your keys," said Sam. "I'll see you two at dinner." She got back in the car and drove off to park it in the barn.

Katana and Chris hauled their suitcases across the courtyard.

Two huge and very intimidating foo dogs sat in front of the entrance, one on each side. Chris opened one of the two giant wooden doors. They dragged their luggage inside.

The doors opened into an immense central atrium. The ceiling was covered with a painting of a dragon flying through a torii gate in the middle of the ocean. Directly across from them was the grand staircase. Two balconies ran along each side of the second floor, overlooking the atrium.

As they walked toward the doors that led to the north wing and the student dormitories, Katana heard a voice screech, "Come back here, you midget!" A short, freckle-faced boy with floppy brown hair came running into view on the second floor. A very pretty girl with curly, shoulder-length hair was chasing him.

The boy jumped over the balcony's stone barrier and floated down to the atrium.

"UGH!" shouted the girl. She ran around the end of the balcony and down the staircase.

"Hey guys!" said the boy as he came running up to Katana and Chris.

"Hi Jelly," said Chris.

"What's with the shoe?" asked Katana. She'd just realized that Jelly was holding a white sneaker in his hand.

"Oh, it's Sara's," he said, laughing. "I've been taking her stuff and running off with it all day. It's so much fun pissing her off!"

"Hey Kat," said Sara as she ran up to them, somewhat out of breath.

"Hi Sara," Katana replied, pulling her into a hug.

"Hi Chris," said Sara, tentatively reaching to give him a hug, too. But Chris had reached out to shake her hand. They looked at each other awkwardly for a moment, then Sara giggled, took Chris's hand and pulled him into a hug. Katana thought she could make out a blush through Chris's sunburn.

Sara let go of Chris, lunged at Jelly and shouted, "Now give me that!"

But Jelly was too quick for her. He ran off again. As Sara hurtled after him, Katana noticed that she was wearing only one shoe. Jelly got to the center of the atrium, jumped in the air, and floated back up to the second-floor balcony.

"No fair!" yelled Sara, dashing up the stairs after him.

Katana and Chris walked off through the double doors that led to the north wing and headed up to their rooms. "See you at dinner," said Katana as Chris went down the hallway on the second floor where the boys lived. Katana continued to the third floor, and went all the way to the end. She stopped at the last door on the left.

The room was spacious for only two people. A bunk bed sat in one corner, and two desks lined the wall on the right. A couch and two reclining chairs sat on the left, facing the large television screen mounted on the wall. Heavy drapes covered the far wall. Katana moved these aside to look out the windows. She opened the sliding glass door and walked out on the balcony.

"It's good to be back," she said to herself, looking out across the courtyard. She could see the ocean beyond Highway 101.

Katana busied herself with unpacking her things and setting up her room. She placed her father's samurai sword in its stand on her desk with special reverence. Sara came in a few minutes later, slightly winded, her olive complexion flush from her chase.

"You got it back?" asked Katana.

"Yes!" said Sara, throwing her sneaker on the floor and kicking off the other one. "That kid is *so* annoying sometimes!"

"Yeah, but he can levitate, so I guess he can stay," said Katana.

Sara walked into the bathroom, and fixed her hair in the mirror. Katana followed her. "When did you get here?" she asked, leaning against the doorframe.

"What? Oh, just last night. Gerald picked me up in the limo," said Sara. She turned sideways and seemed to be examining her figure in the mirror.

"Sam picked us up in the Porsche," said Katana. "It was a fun ride—she drives kinda fast. Sara, what are you doing?" Sara had now turned the other way, facing away from the mirror, and was looking at herself over her shoulder.

"Huh? Oh, nothing. Does my butt look big to you?"

"What? No!"

"Ugh. I'm getting so *fat*!"

"Sara, you're *not* fat," said Katana, shaking her head. She walked back into the room. Sara was a little shorter than Katana, and had grown into her body quite a bit more than Katana had had time to do yet.

"Oh yeah?" said Sara, following Katana into the room. She

walked around the couch and picked up a pair of jeans draped over the back of a chair. She held them up to show Katana. "Then what about *these*?"

"A pair of jeans? I don't get it," said Katana.

"My *favorite* jeans, and I can't fit into them anymore because my butt's too big!"

Katana laughed. "It's not funny, Kat!" said Sara. "I wish I had your figure. You're thin and muscular, just like Sam. It's not fair!" She flopped down on the couch with a sigh.

"Are you kidding me?" asked Katana. She held out her arms. "I could still pass for a boy if it weren't for the long hair! I'm the one who should be jealous of *you*—all the boys think you're hot."

"Kat, you could *not* pass for a boy," said Sara. "You're much too pretty for anyone to think that."

"If you say so," said Katana. She went back to her unpacking.

Once Katana had put all her things away, the girls went downstairs and knocked on Chris's door. "Come in," said a voice inside. They walked in and closed the door.

Chris and another boy with short brown hair and an excessive amount of acne were sitting in the chairs watching a baseball game on the television. "Jimmy Lawlor. I didn't know you two were rooming together this year," said Sara. Katana remembered with a pang of sadness that Jimmy had been Robert's roommate the previous year.

"We're going down to dinner; are you two coming?" asked Katana.

"Yeah," said Chris. "This game sucks."

They walked downstairs and through the student lounge, which occupied the front half of the first floor. It was littered with big, comfortable chairs and couches, and tables for doing homework. A huge television screen was mounted on one wall, and several video game systems were set up with projectors along the front of the room. They walked into the cafeteria and got in line for the buffet. "Hey, what's that?" asked Katana.

"It's a sushi bar," said Sara. "Let's go!"

"Ew..." said Chris. He stayed in line with Jimmy.

The cafeteria had begun serving sushi a few days a week the previous year, but it had only been an addition to the buffet. Now there was an actual sushi bar and a real, live sushi chef to go with it.

"Hi," said Sara as she sat down on one of the stools at the bar.

"Konichiwa," said the Japanese man behind the bar. "What can I get you girls today?"

Sara looked at Katana. "You order," said Katana. "I like the stuff, but I still don't know what any of it is."

Sara ordered for them, and they sat in awe as they watched the chef prepare the fish.

"That's so... perfect," said Sara. "I've made sushi with my dad a few times, but it's always a mess when I make it!"

"In Japan, everything has a kata," the man replied. "Just like there is a right way to do your kata in karate, there is a right way to make sushi, serve tea, or anything else. It takes practice and focus to do it just right."

Sam walked over and sat down on the stool next to Katana. "I see you girls have met Terry-san," she observed.

"Konichiwa, Master Samantha," said Terry-san.

"This is Sara Brown and Katana Kahanu," said Sam.

"Oh, yes," said Terry-san. "Master Nash has told me all about you, Katana. Two chen do already, that is very impressive."

Katana could feel her face growing warm. "Do you do karate?"

"Yes," said Terry-san. "But I am not very good—not like Master Samantha," he added with a smile.

"Well, we're very fortunate to have Terry-san with us this year," said Sam. "He may not be a karate master, but he is a master sushi chef. I hear the headmaster of Shaka-In wasn't very happy when he found out Nash was taking him away!"

"No, Master Tanaka was not happy at all. But Master Nash made me an offer I couldn't refuse," he said with a wink to Sam.

"Enjoy your sushi, girls. Remember that you have orientation Monday morning at nine," said Sam. She walked over to talk to Chris and Jimmy. Katana and Sara ate their sushi and chatted with Terry-san, then went to hang out in the lounge for the rest of the evening.

Katana woke up Sunday morning to the sound of someone pounding noisily on the door. "Go away!" yelled Sara, but Katana jumped down to see who it was.

"Get up you two," said Jelly, jumping up and down with excitement. "It's tricking time!"

"It's seven o'clock," said Katana grumpily. "It's sleeping time." She started to close the door in Jelly's face, but he ducked under her arm and ran into the room.

"Come on, fatty, get up!" he said to Sara, prodding her with his foot. Sara tried to grab him, but he jumped out of the way. "Let's go!"

"Why are you so awake this early in the morning?" asked Katana, flopping down on the couch. "You never liked getting up early last year."

"I wanna trick!" he said. "I haven't been able to work on the double backflip all summer."

"Why not?" asked Sara, giving up on getting back to sleep.

"My instructor back home wouldn't let me do it. He said it's too dangerous!"

Sara looked at Katana, who simply looked back and shrugged. "Why not," said Sara. "I'm awake now."

They went downstairs and banged on Chris and Jimmy's door, but they wouldn't wake up. So the three of them made their way down to the kempo dojo.

The room looked almost exactly like Sensei Mike's dojo back in Vermont, only much larger. The floor was covered with the same tatami mats, and there was an altar in the middle of the front wall. A scroll with the character for "Do" hung on the wall behind the altar, and large mirrors ran down the rest of the wall on both sides of the altar. Three enormous scrolls hung, evenly spaced, on the walls at each end of the dojo. They were red with black kanji characters. Sam let her students use her dojo to practice on the weekends. The other dojo were off-limits outside of regular class time.

"Hey," said a shy-looking boy who was already there, stretching out.

"Hi Scott," said Katana. "You're rooming with Jelly again?"

"Yeah," he said with a sigh. "But if he keeps waking me up this early I'm gonna request a room change."

Katana and Sara sat down on the mat to stretch, but Jelly ran across the room and did a backflip.

"Aren't you going to stretch first?" asked Sara.

"Nah," said Jelly. "Stretching is a waste of time. All right... time for a double." He concentrated, then ran across the room again. He did a round-off, and flipped over backwards, completing two full rotations before landing.

"YES!"

"That was really high," said Katana.

"I know," said Jelly. "That was the one thing my instructor let me work on. We did all these conditioning exercises to get my jumps higher. I told him I could levitate and go as high as I wanted, but he wouldn't let me levitate either!"

The other three finished stretching and started working on their tricks. Sara could do aerials and backflips, but that was the extent of her repertoire. She had started working on some of the variations of the backflip the previous year, but had never mastered any of them. Jelly had her start working on a flash kick.

Katana and Scott could both do several variations on the backflip already, so Jelly had them start working on a gainer. "A gainer's just a backflip where you run forward and flip over backwards, without turning around or doing a round-off first."

"I never quite got this last year," Scott complained.

"Yeah, but my instructor showed me a new way to teach it," said Jelly. Katana and Scott spent the next half hour trying a gainer. The last few times they were finally able to do it—it wasn't very clean, but they could at least get over without falling.

"I think I get it now," said Katana. "I love this trick."

"Once you get it down better, you gotta try a gainer *flash*. It's the same thing, but you do it like a flash kick, and kick one leg over before the other," said Jelly.

Katana and Sara got up Monday morning and went downstairs to collect Chris and Jimmy. They arrived in the student lounge to find it crowded and noisy. They sat a table with Jelly and three other students. "Hey," said Sara as they sat down.

"Hi," said Scott.

"Hey guys," said Dana. "So Jelly, guess who I'm doing double whip chain with this year."

"Um... Kelly?"

"No, dummy," said Paul. Dana Arlington and Paul Santiago were both members of the Hall's wushu team. They competed in the team demo division at the tournaments, and had won first place at nationals the previous year. "Kelly graduated last year, so she's gone."

"Oh yeah!" said Jelly. "I remember now. So who are you doing chains with?"

"Donnie," said Paul, rolling his eyes.

"Donnie who did staff with me last year?" asked Jelly.

"Yeah," said Dana. "That's him."

"I didn't know he could do chains!"

"He can't! That's the problem," said Dana.

"He can," Paul corrected her, "but not very well. Dana's pissed because she thinks Hua should let her do it solo."

"I don't want a solo," said Dana, "but Donnie's horrible with chains. I don't think it's gonna be as good this year."

"Hmm," said Jelly. "Wait—if Donnie's doing chains now, who's doing staff with me?"

"Tim's still doing it," replied Paul, "and Hua put Johanna on the team this year—she'll be the third person for staff."

"Who's Johanna?" asked Jelly.

"She's a senior this year—don't worry, she's amazing at staff," said Dana. "Oh, and Scott, you're on the team, too. You're doing broadsword with Paul because Simon's gone now."

"Really?" asked Scott. "Yes!"

At that moment Master Nash—a tall black man with a shaved head—called them to attention. Like all the masters, Nash wore black kung fu pants that were gathered at the ankles, and a white top with black frog buttons down the middle. A dragon flying through a torii gate was embroidered on the left breast of the uniform top. The students wore uniforms just like these, except the tops were black with white frog buttons.

Katana thought that Master Nash looked like he was in his late forties or early fifties. She'd found out the previous year that he was actually in his early seventies.

"Welcome to the Hall of the Dragon," he began. "For those of you who are new here, my name is Jordan Nash. I am the tai chi master and headmaster. Most of you will remember Master Osaka and Master Malloy," he said, pointing them out in turn. "This year they will be switching posts. Master Osaka will be taking over as kempo master. As Master Malloy has recently tested, she will take on the position of tae kwon do master, and head coach of our sparring team." Katana looked at Sara in surprise as everyone clapped for the new appointments. Sara merely shrugged as Nash continued. "Master Hua Xiang will continue as our wushu master and head coach of the demo team," he said, holding his hand out to a short Chinese man with a friendly smile. "And Master Brock Daniels will continue as our aikido master." Master Daniels reminded Katana of a small mountain. He was very large—nearly as wide as he was tall— with short, spiky hair. He gazed around the room with beady little eyes. "Master Daniels would like me to remind you that projectiles such as water balloons, spitballs and the like are not allowed in the student lounge, nor anywhere else at the Hall for that matter. And levitating in the central atrium or over the balconies is definitely prohibited as well," he added with an ironic smile as he looked over at Jelly.

"Aw!" said Jelly. Everyone broke out laughing.

"Your regular martial arts lessons will commence on Wednesday after school, and the competition teams will have their first practices this Friday. Your morning tai chi lessons will begin at five o'clock next Monday morning." At this, the whole room groaned in unison. "Your school uniforms have already been placed in your rooms— remember that full uniform is required for your regular classes, although casual dress is allowed for our morning tai chi practice and the team practices on Fridays. The buses will be here shortly to bring you over to Lincoln Academy for orientation. And I remind you all that you are required to maintain honor roll status at Lincoln to continue training at the Hall of the Dragon. Now, please see Francine for your schedules, and then you may proceed to breakfast," he concluded.

Chaos broke out again as everyone rushed to the back of the room to see Francine. Katana yelled her name, grabbed her schedule and followed the crowd into the cafeteria.

"Wushu on Mondays and Wednesdays, tae kwon do on Tuesdays and Thursdays, and privates with Osaka right after school on Thursdays," Sara read from her schedule a few minutes later as Katana sat down with her food. "I wonder why Sam and Osaka switched positions."

"Osaka was never into competition when I trained with him in Vermont," said Katana. "He probably likes kempo better."

"Yeah, that's true," said Sara. "And Sam has always seemed like she's really into sparring."

"You have privates with Osaka?" asked Dana. "Usually only the juniors and seniors get privates."

"It's probably because she already made her second degree," suggested Paul. "I bet Kat and Chris have that, too."

"Yep," said Chris, looking down his schedule.

"Yeah, me too," said Katana. "And it says I have sparring team practice on Fridays..."

"You made the sparring team?" asked Jimmy. "That's awesome—I'm on it too."

"Wait," said Dana. "I didn't think they had a girls' division for team sparring."

"They never have before," replied Jimmy. "There were never enough girls who wanted to do it. But I guess there must be this year."

"There were a bunch of girls in my sparring ring last year," said Katana.

"Yeah, but not enough to make teams," Jimmy replied. "In the boys' division, each team has to have six people. But most schools only have one or two girls who spar; when I was at Thompson's school, *none* of the girls did sparring."

"I don't know about this," said Katana. "I don't know anything about how the team sparring division works. How can you spar as a team?"

"You don't," said Jimmy. "You just fight in the regular sparring division. But if you place, the points you earn count toward your team. If your team makes it to nationals, everyone on the team goes, even if they didn't make it individually."

"That's cool," said Katana. "I wonder who else is on the girls' team?"

"No idea," said Jimmy. Sara merely shrugged.

They finished their breakfast and loaded onto the buses that had pulled up in the driveway beyond the torii gate. Lincoln Academy was a private college preparatory school for students from sixth grade through high school. It was located about twenty minutes away from the Hall, halfway to Eureka.

Katana walked into the auditorium with Sara and Chris, and they found the table for the ninth-graders. Katana made her way to the front of the line and gave the plump older lady sitting at the table her name. "Kahanu... let's see," she said. "Ah yes, here we go. You are in all honors classes, dear—geometry, English, world history, environmental science, Spanish... oh, wait a minute..."

"What's wrong?" asked Katana.

"There is a note here that says you have a schedule conflict—you cannot take Spanish two *and* honors geometry. You'll have to do regular geometry, or switch to a different language this year."

"I have the same problem," said Sara from the head of the next line.

"What other language can we take?" asked Katana.

"Let's see..." said the woman, perusing a course catalog. "Well, for first-year language, you can take either French or Latin."

"Let's do French," said Sara. "I don't want to drop honors geometry, and I hated Latin when I took it at my old school."

They both finished figuring out their schedules, and then Katana went to talk to Chris. He was a couple of places behind her in line. She told him to switch to French.

"Uh... okay," he said.

The three of them left the auditorium when Chris was done and went to find their classrooms.

"Is geometry hard?" asked Sara.

"It's not as bad as algebra," said Chris. "You do lots of stuff with angles and shapes and stuff. But then there are proofs. Those are hard."

"What are proofs?" asked Katana.

"You have to start with simple rules and definitions," he explained, "and go step by step to show that a more complicated theorem is true. It's kinda confusing." Chris had begun taking geometry at his old school in Vermont before he came to the Hall halfway through the previous year. "Hey!" he said. "This means for once I'm gonna be helping *you* with homework!" For most of his life, Chris had struggled with math. Katana had always had to help him study and get through his homework.

They went back to the Hall after orientation. Katana and Sara hung out in their room the rest of the day. Right before dinner, Chris came to get them. "Sam wants to talk to us in her room," he said.

They walked downstairs, across to the south wing, and up to the third floor where the masters lived. Each master had living quarters and an office in his or her suite. Katana knocked on the door to Sam's apartment. The door opened slowly, but it was dark inside.

"What...?" she said, stepping into the room. "Sam?"

The lights came on, and Sam jumped out from behind the door. "Surprise!" Katana saw that Jimmy, Dana, Scott, Jelly, Paul and Jason Beecher—an older boy on the sparring team—were already there. "Happy Birthday, Kat!" said Sam, closing the door behind them. "You didn't think we'd forget, did you?"

Sam had ordered pizza and birthday cake. They sang "Happy Birthday," and Sam cut the cake for everyone. Katana was thrilled.

She'd forgotten about her birthday in the excitement of returning to the Hall.

"So you guys are going into high school this year," said Sam, taking a bite of cake.

"Yeah," said Sara. "I can't believe it. High school is so cool—formal dances, and pep rallies…"

"And way harder classes," Chris added apprehensively.

"That's true," said Sam. "High school does get a lot tougher. The teachers won't keep reminding you when your assignments are due—you have to stay much more organized."

"It won't be that hard," replied Katana.

"I don't know," said Sam. "I was like you in middle school—I breezed my way through my classes. But high school was a rude awakening. I thought I'd have it easy still, but it was a *lot* harder. Be careful, Kat—you may actually have to study this year!"

"Hey Sam," said Sara. "Nash came over my house this summer, and I heard him and my dad talking about a mission…"

"I was wondering when you three would ask me about this," Sam replied with a sigh. "Nash told me your father caught you eavesdropping."

"Well, I wouldn't have had to eavesdrop if he didn't kick me out!" Sara said indignantly.

"So what's the mission?" asked Katana.

Sam looked around the room. Katana had the distinct impression that she was making sure no one else was listening. "Guys, I'm sorry, but I can't discuss this. And you three have to promise me you won't breathe a word about it to anyone. You know too much already, but if anyone else finds out... Promise me, not a word to anyone. All right?"

"But Sam," Sara protested, "we don't know anything in the first place. What could we possibly tell anyone else?"

"You know that *something* is going on, so just promise me that you'll keep that knowledge to yourselves," Sam insisted.

They agreed, but Chris said, "So there definitely is a mission. Is Osaka going somewhere again?"

"No, it's not Osaka this time—although he may be traveling a bit himself in the next few months. But I really can't talk about this. I promise if everything works according to plan, I'll tell you guys all about it when it's over."

"Does it have something to do with the Scroll of the Five Masters?" asked Sara.

Sam looked at Sara for a moment, then shook her head and laughed. "I *absolutely* cannot talk about this!"

"It does have something to do with the scroll, doesn't it!" said Katana. "Sensei Mike told us this summer that Jaaku was trying to get into the archives at the Shaolin Temple. He said he's going crazy trying to figure out the scroll!"

"And how did he find out about that?!" asked Sam, looking quite exasperated.

"Osaka told him," said Chris.

"Osaka... And he warned me to keep *my* mouth shut!"

Sam refused to say anything more, and went to talk to Jason Beecher about the sparring team.

"I think he likes you," said Sara when they got back to their room later that night.

"What? Who likes me?" asked Katana.

"Are you kidding me? He couldn't keep his eyes off of you the whole night!"

"Who?!"

"Jason Beecher!" said Sara.

"Oh, come on," said Katana, but she was smiling as she said it. "That's what you said last year too..."

"And I was right all along! Katana, I'm telling you, he likes you. Boys don't look at girls that way if they're not interested. You can't tell me you don't think he's hot."

"Yeah, I guess he is kinda cute..."

"*Kinda cute?*" said Sara. "He looks like a movie star, Kat. He's tall, he's muscular," she counted on her fingers, "and he let his hair grow out this summer—it looks *so* good!"

"That's true," said Katana. She thought Jason's wavy, light-brown hair looked much better than the shrub that was growing on Chris's head. "And his eyes, too..."

"I know!" said Sara. "They're that grayish blue... it makes him look kinda mysterious. You two would make a cute couple, Kat."

As she drifted off to sleep that night, Katana found herself unable to stop thinking about Jason. She hoped that Sara was right.

Chapter Four: The Sparring Team

Li Shiao crept around the perimeter of the grounds at the Shaolin Temple in China. It was the dead of night and he could hardly see a thing. He'd heard a noise in the forest—it sounded like someone was out there, behind the temple. Turning back toward the building, he knew other guards watched from the top floor, although he couldn't see them. He gathered his chi to throw a fireball high into the sky— the signal for an intruder. Taking a deep breath, he resumed his course into the trees.

There it was—he heard the noise again. Something was moving behind a thick oak tree. Li Shiao tiptoed closer to the trunk. Suddenly, something jumped out at him.

"Hah!" a voice yelled.

Li Shiao backpedaled, raising one arm to throw a fireball. But he tripped over a root, landing flat on his back.

Looking up, he saw his fellow monk, Choy Mei, laughing down at him.

"Oy! That wasn't funny," Li Shiao shouted, regaining his feet and brushing off his backside. "I almost gave the alarm signal!"

The two had been walking the perimeter in opposing circles for hours. Li Shiao felt anxious—he didn't understand how Choy Mei could make light of the situation. The Arashi had attacked numerous times in recent weeks, trying to gain entry to the temple.

"I had to do something to break up the monotony," Choy Mei complained. "I've been stuck with guard duty every night this week."

"This isn't what I signed up for," Li Shiao agreed. "I came to Shaolin to seek enlightenment, not to risk my life."

"Blame the Americans," Choy Mei told him. "If they hadn't lost their precious scroll, we wouldn't be in this situation."

"Why doesn't Jaaku attack *their* temple? They're the ones who should be dealing with this."

"The Hall of the Dragon has limited archives, and no proper library. Americans care nothing for history or tradition. Every piece of ancient knowledge resides here, as it should," Choy Mei replied, a tone of pride in his voice.

Li Shiao grunted in agreement. Shaolin was the oldest hall of martial arts in the world, and it certainly hosted the most extensive collection of old documents and treatises.

"We'd better keep moving," said Li Shiao. "At least our shift is almost over."

They parted ways, continuing their courses around the temple. Li Shiao contemplated how little sleep he'd be getting this night; he was still required to attend morning meditation at dawn. He could skip it, but the punishment would be hours of extra training. Better to endure the fatigue, he decided.

Coming around the front of the main temple building a few minutes later, Li Shiao spotted something in the far corner of the court. It was difficult to make out in the dark, but there appeared to be a small boulder that hadn't been there before. How did it get there? Choy Mei was probably playing tricks on him again, but Li Shiao moved to investigate anyway.

Approaching the object, he realized it wasn't a boulder at all. It looked like an old man, resting on one knee, holding himself up with a walking stick.

"Hey! What are you doing here?" Li Shiao called out, approaching cautiously.

The old man groaned; he sounded like he was in great pain.

"What is wrong with you?" Li Shiao asked.

"I am lost," the old man croaked. "And so tired. I've been wandering in the forest for hours but I cannot find my village. Can you give me some bread and water? I have no strength left."

Poor peasants often came begging, but never at this hour.

"Come with me," said Li Shiao, grabbing the man by one arm to help him to his feet.

But suddenly the old man reached out and smacked Li Shiao on the back of the neck. He tried to pull away from the old man, but found he couldn't move. A sensation of hot liquid ran down his spine, and the next moment, Li Shiao felt frigidly cold. He was paralyzed, completely unable to move his limbs or turn his head. His breathing continued and he felt his heart hammering in his chest, but he was immobile.

The old man stood up in front of him; in a burst of panic, Li Shiao recognized him. This was Master Lu. The traitor who had left

Shaolin to join the Arashi. Before the Americans discovered that Jaaku was still alive, Shaolin had actually believed that Lu was the new dim mak master. But it turned out he was nothing but a servant of that greater evil.

Lu grinned at him before turning away and striding toward the temple. Li Shiao struggled to move; it was his duty to shoot a fireball and warn those within of the approaching danger. But he was powerless.

Suddenly over a dozen Arashi appeared behind Lu, all clad in samurai armor. Li Shiao spotted a fireball across the courtyard, streaking toward the sky—it must have been Choy Mei. An alarm bell sounded within the temple. But it was too late. Lu and his minions marched up the front steps.

And to Li Shiao's astonishment, Lu opened the door and strode inside. This should not have been possible—the chi that had built up in the structure over the centuries should have prevented such an enemy from getting inside. But suddenly it occurred to Li Shiao— Lu had been a master of the temple for years. His chi must still be imprinted upon the building. He could enter at any time.

Li Shiao's heart sank as he watched the Arashi move inside. He had failed to protect the temple.

***

The students at the Hall of the Dragon boarded the buses to Lincoln on Wednesday morning after breakfast. Katana went with Sara and Chris to geometry, then drama, then world history and French.

"Good day," said their French teacher as they settled down at their desks. "My name is Madame Perry. And from now on, this class will be conducted entirely in French."

Chris raised his hand. "Oui?" asked Madame Perry.

"We don't know French yet. How are we supposed to understand you?"

Madame Perry grabbed an eraser from the chalkboard and threw it at Chris, hitting him in the head. "En Francais!" she said.

"How are we supposed to learn French if she only speaks *French*?" Chris asked dejectedly a little while later when they sat down for lunch.

"I don't know, but I'd like to see her chuck the eraser at you again," said Sara.

"Oh, ha-ha," Chris replied, looking rather sour.

At that moment a tall and lanky boy with sandy hair walked up to their table. "It's Jimmy the cry-baby! I hear you made the sparring team this year over at the freak school. Don't cry too much when you *lose* all your matches!" It was Ed Golia. He and his sidekick, Tommy Cosgrove, took advantage of every opportunity to bully Katana and her friends.

"Shut up, Golia," said Katana, giving him a dirty look.

"I never knew you were a boy, Kahanu," said Tommy. "But that explains a lot; you didn't make a very pretty girl." Ed gave him a high-five and the two of them walked away, giggling at their own cleverness.

"What was that about?" asked Sara.

"I don't know..." said Katana. "Is their school still open?"

"I think so," said Jimmy. "I went by it a few times over the summer, and it seemed like it was still running."

"Who's teaching there now?" asked Sara.

"That Sebastian kid was when I went by," said Jimmy.

"Sebastian who goes to Lincoln?" asked Sara. "He's a senior in high school—he can't be *running* the place."

"I wonder who the master instructor is..." said Katana.

"No idea," said Jimmy.

After school that day, Katana went with Sara and Chris up to their wushu class. The dojo occupied the entire north side of the second floor. A large springboard floor, elevated a few feet in the air like a giant stage, occupied one half of the enormous room. There was a foam pit at the end of the springboard floor that the students could jump into when they were learning new tricks. The other half of the room was covered with tatami mats—this was where they practiced most of their routines.

Weapon racks, which held a variety of staves, swords and spears, lined the wall on the right. Giant mirrors covered the front wall and they made the room look even bigger than it was. And like the kempo dojo, this room had an altar in the middle of the front wall, and three giant scrolls evenly spaced along the walls on each end.

"Line up!" called Master Hua. Katana and Sara went to the back row with the other students who were new to wushu this year. Jelly, Scott, Paul and Dana were in the front row.

"Bow," said Master Hua. The whole class bowed in unison.

"Jump!" he yelled. He began jumping up and down on the balls of his feet, keeping his knees straight. Katana looked at Sara, who shrugged. They started jumping.

"Stay on balls of feet," yelled Master Hua.

The entire class jumped up and down, over and over, for what felt like an eternity. Katana's calves began to burn, but they kept going. Hua went over to the stereo equipment in the corner, and put on some techno music with a strong beat, then continued jumping with the rest of the class.

Katana noticed that Jelly was jumping as high as Dana and Paul even though he was much shorter. But Master Hua was jumping the highest of all—he seemed to float for a moment before he came down each time. Katana wondered if he was using levitation.

Katana's calves started to cramp. But she wasn't alone; several of the newer students stopped to rub their legs. "Keep jumping!" admonished Master Hua.

After several more minutes, he finally gave them a break. He had them sit down on the floor and took them through some stretches. "Calves are most important muscle for jumping," he said. "You should bounce on feet thousand times every day. Do this and get very high on tricks."

"A *thousand* times? Is he kidding?" whispered Chris.

"Good, now do front splits," said Master Hua. He dropped down with his legs flat on the floor. Most of the students could do a full split as well, including Katana and Sara. Those who could not were close—except for Chris. He seemed to be the only one in the whole room unable to get his legs close to the floor. And much to his embarrassment, Master Hua came over and tried to push him down farther.

After they were done with stretches, Master Hua taught them a short form. It consisted entirely of high kicks and low stances. He walked though it with them a few times, then called off the moves as they did it again. Finally he left them to do it on their own. The more experienced students walked around to help the beginners.

Katana remembered the form on her own—she'd always had an excellent memory for movement. She helped Sara and Chris with it the first couple of times.

"This called 'Short Form One,'" Master Hua announced once everyone had it. "This form build stances and kicks we use in harder forms."

Next, he had them make four lines at one end of the springboard floor in order to run through their tricks. Everyone did cartwheels and aerials on their first two turns, gradually working up to harder tricks. Katana and Sara were the only two beginners who could land a backflip consistently. Chris was able to do it once but fell every other time he tried it. "Jump higher!" said Master Hua.

Finally, he had everyone take a seat along one edge of the floor. "Please come up, Jelly," he said. "In wushu, you learn how to extend chi, and bounce off ground."

"Or off the wall!" said Jelly.

"Yes," Master Hua said with a grin. "Or off wall. This is chen do of wushu. Jelly, please demonstrate for class."

"Yes!" said Jelly. He jogged to one corner of the floor. He ran across the room, did a round-off and executed a perfect double backflip. But at the end of his second rotation, he didn't land—he sailed up from the floor and completed a front flip before finally hitting the ground.

The class cheered except for Sara who yelled "Show-off!"

"Very good," said Master Hua, clapping for Jelly. "In wushu, you will learn weapons form. You can start with staff, broadsword, straight sword or spear. Paul, please come up."

Paul ran to one corner of the room, and showed the class the broadsword form he'd competed with the previous year. The broadsword was sharp on only one side and had a slight curve to the blade.

Next, Master Hua had Johanna demonstrate her staff form. She was an older girl he was adding to the competition team. A wushu staff was as tall as the person using it. Made of waxwood, it was cream-colored, flexible, and slightly tapered at one end.

Hua had two older students demonstrate how to use the straight sword and spear. The straight sword was more slender than the broadsword, totally straight, and sharp on both sides. And the spear was like the staff, except it had a sharp metal dagger with a red tassel at one end.

"This week we work on short form. Next week we start weapons, so please decide what weapon you want to learn," said Master Hua. He dismissed the class.

"Why can't we start with whip chains?" asked Katana as they sat down for dinner a few minutes later.

"Whip chain is *much* harder," said Dana. "Usually you start with one of the four you saw today—those are the basic wushu weapons. Once you have one of those, you can learn chains, or three-section staff, or double broadsword... There's a ton of different weapons."

"I wanna do staff," said Sara. "It looks cooler than the other ones."

"Me too," said Chris. "Staff is my favorite weapon. With my luck I'd stab myself if I tried one of the swords."

"So there's no way I can start with chains?" Katana persisted.

"Well... if you already knew how to use them a little, Hua might let you do it," said Dana thoughtfully.

"But I've never done *any* weapons before," said Katana.

"I'll tell you what," replied Dana. "Let's get together this weekend and I'll show you how to do some of the stuff."

"That's awesome," said Katana. "We can use the kempo dojo..."

"You mean the tae kwon do dojo," Sara corrected her. "Sam and Osaka switched, remember?"

"Oh yeah," said Katana. "Do you have an extra set of chains?"

"I'm sure Hua will let us borrow a set. I'll ask him on Wednesday," said Dana.

"You should come too, Jelly," suggested Sara. "You can show me and Chris how to do staff."

***

Katana walked into the tae kwon do dojo the next day with Sara, Chris and Jimmy. Sam took them through some warm-ups and stretches, then divided them into four groups to work on sparring. Four red squares were painted on the mats of the tae kwon do dojo—

which otherwise looked identical to the kempo dojo. They used the squares for sparring rings.

Katana went with Sara and Chris to the first ring. She put on her headgear, gloves and shin pads. Sam had her assistants—all members of the sparring team—run the matches. Jason Beecher ran Katana's ring.

He picked Katana and Chris to spar first. "No chen do, you two," he said as he started their match. Katana and Chris looked at each other and smiled—apparently Jason didn't realize they couldn't use the chen do against each other.

Katana won the match 5-4. Jason called Sara and Jimmy next. Jimmy beat Sara easily, with five points to her one, and Jason called up the next match. Once everyone had a couple of turns, Sam called them back together to have a seat on the mats.

"Today we're going to start working on feinting," she said. She showed them some of the same combinations Katana and Chris had worked on with Sensei Mike, then had them break up into four groups again to practice. Once they'd practiced each of the combinations several times, she had them sit down again. "Katana and Jason, please come up."

Katana looked over at Jason. Walking into the ring, she felt her face grow warm with a blush. "Katana and Jason will demonstrate the chen do you will learn in tae kwon do," said Sam. "We don't have time to start working on the chi kung exercises today, but these two will show you what you'll be working toward. Are you ready?" she asked. "I won't call points." Katana and Jason bowed to each other and Sam said "Fight!"

Jason launched in immediately with a flurry of kicks to Katana's head using a couple of the combinations they'd just practiced. Katana dodged each of these, then dropped to a low stance and threw her hands out to deflect his intent.

Jason fell to the side, but then he dove into a front roll. He sprang up, turned around and threw a fireball at Katana. She was expecting this—she held her hands out and started to deflect the fireball, but gathered it into herself instead. She spun around and threw it right back at Jason. It hit him in the stomach, knocking him through the air.

"Nicely done," said Sam. Jason got up and bowed to Katana. They took their seats on the mat.

"We'll be working on several different chi kung exercises this year that are designed to help you learn how to extend your chi beyond your body," Sam explained to the class. "As Katana demonstrated, you can use the chen do of kempo to deflect someone else's chi hit, and you can even throw the fireball back at them."

"Why didn't her chi hit knock him out?" asked a small freckle-faced boy, whom Katana didn't recognize. "My old instructor told me that's what happens when you throw a fireball."

"That's right, Dennis," said Sam. "If you put enough energy into your chi hit, you can render someone unconscious. It's easier to do if the other person's chi is weaker than yours, or if you catch them by surprise. But Jason's chi is flowing pretty good right now. Besides, Katana wasn't exactly trying to kill him."

"Coulda fooled me," Jason muttered, and everyone laughed.

"Okay, nice job today," said Sam. "Class dismissed."

On Wednesday Katana had wushu again. Hua let Dana borrow an extra set of whip chains so she could start working with Katana over the weekend. Sara and Chris each borrowed a staff. On Thursday Katana had her private lesson with Osaka before their tae kwon do class and he worked with them on their new kata. Katana and Chris had already learned both of their new forms over the summer, but Sara had only learned Kata Thirteen. Osaka started her on Kata Fourteen and worked with them on the details in their forms.

"Second degree is essentially an extension of first degree," he explained at the end of the lesson. "You must refine and sharpen your movement in both your kata and your combinations to get second degree. But third degree represents a major step forward. That rank is the first step to becoming a master. You three advanced very quickly from first to second, but it will take longer to make it to third. You must start to internalize everything we do in kempo before you will be ready for that test."

"What do you have to do to get fourth degree?" asked Katana.

"By that time you'll know all the forms and external skills that are taught in kempo. But much like second degree, fourth is mostly an extension of the previous level. Fifth degree is the next big step," Osaka explained.

"And to get that you have to be able to do the chen do," said Sara.

"Not exactly," said Osaka. "You can be a fifth degree without being a master. To become a master you must be able to do the chen do. But there is more to it than that. You have to *totally* internalize the concepts in the art. Your body should *become* the art—your very movement must be an expression of its principles. True mastery in the martial arts is very subtle—not everyone will attain it, regardless of how long they train."

"Does it work that way in all the arts, or only in kempo?" asked Chris.

"At the Hall of the Dragon, all of the arts work that way."

"What about the Shaolin Temple? Do they use the same guidelines?" asked Katana.

"Not precisely," said Osaka. "They use the degrees, but at the other temples you are either a disciple, a monk, or a master. Chow moved away from the disciple system when he founded the Hall. He was a master at Shaolin, but he didn't always see eye to eye with the other temples. In fact, the headmaster of Shaolin was very much opposed to his founding this school."

"Why?" asked Sara.

"In those days, many masters from China and Japan felt that they should keep their arts to their own people. They didn't want foreigners to learn what they considered their family treasure. But Master Chow found this attitude closed-minded. He believed that anyone who had the discipline and dedication to train should be able to learn martial arts. So he left Shaolin and founded the Hall of the Dragon against the wishes of the headmaster. This school was independent of the temple network the entire time that Chow was headmaster."

"What other schools are in the temple network?" asked Sara.

"Oh, there are quite a few," said Osaka. "Originally they were only in China—there were over a dozen Shaolin temples at one point. They spread to Japan next. Master Kosho was a samurai warrior in the 1400s, and he traveled to China to learn from the headmaster of Shaolin. He went back to Japan and founded the Shaka-In temple, which survives to this day. There are also temples in Korea, Indonesia and Thailand. Most are in East Asia, although there are some in other parts of the world."

"How is the Hall of the Dragon affiliated with the temples now if it was independent when Master Chow was here?" asked Chris.

"Well, Master Chang, Chow's successor, went to Shaolin when he became headmaster. The old headmaster at Shaolin had died, and his replacement was a little more open-minded. Master Chang convinced him to allow the temples to accept foreigners. He was able to bring the Hall of the Dragon back into the temple network because of that decision," explained Osaka. "But the Hall has retained some measure of independence ever since."

"What about people who have degrees higher than fifth?" asked Sara. "My dad told me that a lot of arts have ten degrees of black now."

"That is a very recent development," said Osaka. "Even Master Funakoshi, who brought karate from Okinawa to Japan in the 1920s, used only five degrees. When he died in the 1950s, he was a fifth degree black belt. Only after his death did anyone in karate add the higher levels. Today most schools and styles outside of the temple network use ten degrees. But for the most part, the degrees beyond fifth are honorary in nature. They are not awarded for new skills or knowledge."

"Do other schools require the chen do to become a master?" asked Chris.

"No, most do not," said Osaka. "Some of the first schools that split with Shaolin, over a century ago, did so for precisely that reason. They felt that since most people are never able to do the chen do, it was not reasonable to require them for rank.

"However, there are many schools throughout the country which are affiliated with the Hall—like Sensei Mike's dojo, for example. Those schools follow our guidelines for the degrees of black belt.

"That is enough for today. I want the three of you to practice both of your new kata for next week."

***

On Friday Katana had to hurry to her room to change into her uniform, then back down to Sam's dojo. The sparring team practice began immediately after school.

"Hey, Kat," said Jimmy when she walked in.

"Hi!"

"Do you know everyone yet?" asked Jimmy.

"No, just Jason."

"Okay, the shorter stocky kid is Matt Kennedy, and the big kid with the brown hair is Jeff Smith," said Jimmy. "And that tall black kid over there is Bobby Wellington—he's the team captain this year."

"What does the captain do?" Katana asked.

"Sometimes he coaches the team," said Jimmy. "And he helps out at the tournaments, making sure everyone gets to the right ring and stuff. But there are some special privileges, too."

"Like what?"

"Like driving the Porsche!"

"Are you kidding me?"

"Nah, I'm serious," Jimmy said earnestly. "The team captain gets to use any of the Hall's cars, just like the masters."

"Wait a minute. Where are the other girls?" asked Katana.

"Um... I don't know," said Jimmy, looking confused. "I didn't think of that."

Sam arrived a minute later. She was red-faced and sweaty. "Sorry I'm late," she said. "My lesson with Master Nash ran over."

"I thought the masters trained with Nash in the morning?" asked Katana.

"We do, but I'm doing some extra training this year. Take a seat, everyone; we have a lot of work to do."

"Sam," said Katana as she sat down, "where are the rest of the girls?"

"There aren't any, Kat," Sam said with a mischievous grin. "You'll be sparring with the boys this year."

"WHAT?"

"Well, there have never been any girls' sparring teams. There aren't ever enough girls to put a team together. But after I sparred with you on your test last term, I decided I wanted you on the team. I ran it by the tournament committee, and they said you could compete with the boys. I'm hoping you'll get some publicity from this, and then more girls will think about doing it," explained Sam. "If you're not comfortable with it, I can get someone else to take your spot," she added with a shrug.

"Yeah," said Jason. "We'll understand if you think the boys' division is too tough."

"Psh, whatever! Count me in," Katana said defiantly, sounding more confident than she felt.

"Good, I thought you'd be up for it," said Sam with a wink. "All right. Katana and Jimmy, you two will be in the fourteen- and fifteen-year-old division. Bobby, you, Matt and Jeff will be in the sixteen- and seventeen-year-old division. But Jason, you have a choice to make. You don't turn sixteen until December. The season starts this month, and the rules say you can compete as the age you are when the season starts, or you can jump to the next age bracket. But if you jump to the sixteen- and seventeen-year-old division, you can't go back. Which way do you want to go?"

"Um…" said Jason, glancing at Katana, "I'll stay with the fourteen- and fifteen-year-olds for now."

"Good," said Sam. "That will give us equal numbers in each division. All right, let's get started."

Sam had them pair off. Katana worked with Jimmy to work more on the feinting combinations they'd been learning in class all week. Katana was getting quite good with these. She had the flexibility and muscle strength to snap her front leg from any one spot on Jimmy's body to any other point. Jimmy had a very difficult time blocking the second kick in each of her combinations.

When they switched partners, Katana worked with Bobby next, which was difficult considering how much taller he was. Sam had them sit down afterwards. She brought them up one pair at a time to run some actual matches. "Keep it to kicks and strikes tonight—no takedowns," she said.

The first match was Bobby and Matt. Katana thought Bobby must be unbeatable. He was as tall as Sensei Mike, and almost as muscular. And he had his flexibility as well. Bobby beat Matt 6-0.

Sara and Chris walked in at the end of that match and Sara asked quietly, "Can we watch?"

"Sure," said Sam, "but no distracting Katana!"

Katana and Jason went next. Katana was determined to beat him after his comment at the beginning of practice. Sam started the match and Katana took the initiative. She did the front kick to roundhouse kick combination they'd been working on. Jason blocked each of these with ease but then she snapped her leg up and dropped an axe kick on the back of his head. Not expecting a *third* kick, Jason had lunged in at the wrong time.

Sam gave Katana a strange look when she stopped the match to award the points.

"What?" asked Katana.

"Nothing... that was a great combo," said Sam. "Well Jason, do you still think the boys' division will be too tough for her?"

Jason merely grunted.

The match continued. Katana won 6-4. Sam dismissed them for the night once everyone had had two matches.

"Where are the other girls?" asked Sara as she walked upstairs with Katana and Chris to watch the wushu team practice.

"There aren't any," said Katana. "I have to spar in the boys' division."

"You're joking," said Chris. "That's not exactly fair, is it?"

"You're right," said Sara. "That's not fair to the boys at all. Katana's gonna beat their butts."

"That's not what I meant..." said Chris.

"I know what you meant!" said Sara. "You don't think Kat can handle herself in the boys' division!"

"I didn't say that!"

"Enough, you two!" yelled Katana. "You sound like an old married couple."

Sara said, "Hah!"

"You know, I just realized something..." said Katana.

"What?" asked Chris.

"That must be what Tommy was talking about at lunch the other day."

"What did Tommy say?" asked Sara.

"He made that comment about me being a boy. He must've known that I was on the sparring team."

"So whoever their new master is must have told Ed and Tommy about it. We gotta find out who's running that place now," said Sara.

Master Hua had already started the practice by the time they arrived. He always welcomed spectators because he felt the team worked harder for an audience. They were practicing tricks when

Katana, Sara and Chris walked in. They took turns doing everything from aerials to backflips and variations on the backflip.

"Jelly's really getting much higher this year," Sara commented.

After tricks, Master Hua had the team split up to work on their weapon sets. Katana saw Dana roll her eyes as Donnie tried to untangle his chains. Dana and Donnie went through the set together. It was apparent to Katana that Dana had to slow down so Donnie could keep up.

Master Hua went around to each group to watch them perform together. Katana thought he'd made it to Dana and Donnie in the nick of time—Dana was becoming extremely frustrated and seemed like she might lose her temper at any moment.

"Faster, faster," Master Hua demanded as they ran through the set again.

"Thank you," muttered Dana, and started going full speed. Donnie fell behind.

"Donnie, you must practice every day," Hua admonished when they were done. "We have a lot of work to win nationals again. Practice, practice!"

Dana was not in a very good mood at the end of the practice. "Hua should let me do a solo," she said as they walked to their rooms to get ready for dinner.

"Don't worry," Sara said, "Donnie'll get there." But it didn't sound to Katana like Sara believed that.

"Hey, you guys should come with us to Hua's tonight," suggested Paul.

"What's going on at Hua's?" asked Sara.

"He's having the whole team up for a movie night," said Paul. "We're getting pizza and we're gonna watch the demos from last year."

"Oh, cool," said Katana. "He won't mind it if we show up?"

"Nah," said Dana. "He said we could invite friends."

Katana, Sara and Chris went up to their rooms to shower, then headed to Master Hua's suite in the south wing. "Come in, come in," he said with a smile when they knocked on the door. The older members of the team were there, and the pizza had already arrived. Master Hua's suite was every bit as spacious as Sam's, but with all the kids there it felt a little crowded. They sat down to eat, and Hua started the video of their first demo from the previous year.

"Oh no! I forgot about this..." said Jelly. He'd been doing a particularly difficult move, where he'd had to throw the staff up in the air, perform a backflip, then catch it again. He'd done it successfully, but as he spun the staff around for the next move, it had slipped out of his hand, hitting two of the judges in the head.

"Don't worry," said Dana, giving him a little push. "We'll *never* let you forget it!"

"Here it comes..." said Sara. "Yes! Wow, that third judge would have gotten hit too if he hadn't ducked!"

"Hah! Check out the look on your face!" said Chris. "That's great."

"Judges not happy," said Master Hua.

"Can we fast forward now?" asked Jelly.

"Why?" asked Dana. "The rest of the demo was fine after your little improv!"

Next they watched the demo from the Golden Gate Classic. "At least we didn't assault any judges at this one," said Paul.

"This demo very strong. Watch Dana. Very focused. Must all look like that this year," Master Hua said with pride.

"Oh, it's nationals!" said Sara when the third clip started. "We never got to see this last year."

Katana thought the team looked even sharper at nationals than they had at Golden Gate. The whole routine was more polished.

"Did that kid from Supernova ever get the double back?" asked Paul. Master Hua had taught Jelly how to do a double backflip the previous year, and they'd added it to the demo for Golden Gate. At nationals, one of the members of Supernova, the team that had been the reigning champions, had tried the same trick but wasn't able to land it. That mistake had allowed the Hall of the Dragon to win first place.

"No, no," said Master Hua, shaking his head. "I talked to coach of Supernova this summer, and he not allow double back. He think too dangerous. But maybe someone from some other team get it this year."

"I hope not," said Jelly.

***

Sam sat up late that night, flipping through her old photo album again. She stopped at a picture of herself sparring with Adrian. It was uncanny how closely Katana's style of movement resembled his. From her flexibility when she kicked, to the way she held her hands in her fighting guard, Katana was her father's daughter.

But it was her intensity that made Sam feel like she was channeling Adrian's spirit. That look of ardent focus when she sparred was exactly like his.

Sam closed the album and placed it on her nightstand. Turning out the light, she curled up to go to sleep. Adrian was dead, no matter how much Katana might remind her of him.

Disturbing visions invaded Sam's dreams that night. The Arashi penetrated the Hall, killing students who got in their way. Sam ran downstairs to find Katana lying on the floor of the atrium, a puncture wound in her chest. Blood was everywhere. Sam dropped to her knees beside her, tried to talk to her. But Katana was dead.

"NO!" Sam screamed, sitting up in bed, her heart beating wildly. But it was only a dream, she realized, taking a deep breath. The Arashi had not infiltrated the Hall; Katana was still alive.

But would the Arashi try to get inside again? They'd managed it once—to take the Scroll of the Five Masters. It stood to reason that they might attempt it again in their search for information to explain the meaning of the document. The Hall had hosted the scroll for many long years; did it also hold the secret to understanding it? Would Jaaku send his forces here as he had to the other temples?

Sam had been unable to shake the feeling of guilt over her decision not to accompany Hua on the mission. As much as she knew her place was here, sending him alone felt wrong. The thought of the Arashi attacking the Hall strengthened the sentiment. Their success would likely remove the threat of such an attack.

Sam gazed at her alarm clock. It was five in the morning. Nash was certainly awake by now. She climbed out of bed and left her apartment, not bothering to change out of her pajamas. At the end of the hall, she knocked on Nash's door. No answer. But she knew where to find him.

She went down to the atrium and up to the big dojo on the third floor. Sure enough, Nash was here, practicing tai chi.

"Good morning, Samantha," he said with a bemused grin. "What brings you here so early on a Saturday?"

"Do you think the Arashi will attack the Hall?" she asked.

Nash's smile faded away. "Looking for information about the scroll, you mean?"

Sam nodded. "They've attacked the other temples. I know their archives are far more expansive than ours, but still. It would make sense to look here, too."

"We do not possess the knowledge Jaaku is seeking," he told her. "But you're right. The attacks against the other temples have intensified. In fact, Master Lu recently showed up at Shaolin with a band of Arashi. He was able to walk right inside."

"What? How?"

"He was a master of Shaolin for many years," Nash replied. "His chi is still imprinted upon the building. The connection will fade eventually, but it will take time."

"What happened? Did the Arashi acquire anything important?"

Nash shook his head. "Liang and a team of monks turned them away before they reached the archives. But they're certain to try again. And it's probably only a matter of time before the Arashi attempt to get inside the Hall of the Dragon."

This was exactly what Sam feared. And it changed everything. She knew what she had to do.

"Count me in," she said.

"What are you talking about?" asked Nash.

"The mission. I'll go with Hua."

Nash regarded her in silence for a moment. "What changed your mind?"

Sam recalled the image of Katana lying dead from her dream, but said only, "It's the right thing to do."

"This is no small commitment," Nash reminded her. "The whole mission will be planned around you. There's no backing out of this decision. Are you certain?"

Sam nodded, feeling determined. "I have to do this."

Chapter Five: Beecher's Question

On Saturday afternoon Katana and Sara went downstairs to get Jelly, Scott and Chris. They headed to Sam's dojo to work on tricks. Jelly had shown Katana how to do an aerial the very first weekend she'd arrived at the Hall the previous year, and the weekend tricking sessions had become a tradition.

Once they'd stretched and warmed up, Sara worked on her flash kick, and Chris tried to get his backflip more consistent. "Hua's right," said Jelly, "you just have to jump a little higher."

"That's easy for you to say," Chris muttered.

Katana and Scott both did several backflips and flash kicks to warm up, then tried the gainer again. Katana's was better than it had been the previous weekend, but she didn't feel comfortable enough to try the gainer flash yet.

"You should try levitation," suggested Jelly.

"Are you kidding me?" said Katana. "What makes you think I'm gonna be able to do *that*?"

"I dunno... You can already do two chen do, why not go for three?" said Jelly. "I was thinking about it, and I bet you can trick yourself into doing it. Can you do a wall flip?"

"Um... no," said Katana apprehensively.

"It's not that hard. Here, try running up the wall first." Jelly showed them how. He was able to get three steps up the wall.

Katana surprised herself by getting two steps on her first attempt, but Scott took a few tries. Jelly made them keep doing it until they could both get a third step. "Okay, now push over on your second step and do a backflip." He demonstrated for them. "Try it! You can put your hands down if you get scared and do a back handspring instead."

Sure enough, Katana did a back handspring. But at least she didn't crash—Scott landed on all fours the first time.

Once they had it, Jelly brought them to the corner of the room. "Now do this." He ran up one wall, taking two steps, then used his third step to push off the adjacent wall.

"Okay..." said Katana. She got it after a few tries.

"Good," said Jelly. "Now keep going." He ran around the corner again. This time he ran a dozen steps up the wall before jumping to the floor.

"Yeah, right!" said Scott. "And how are we supposed to do *that*?"

"I dunno, just do it!"

Neither Katana nor Scott could get more than one step on the second wall. Dana walked in a minute later. Katana went over to talk to her.

"Jelly's trying to teach you how to levitate?"

"Yeah, but I'm not getting anywhere," said Katana with a sigh.

"Me neither. I've been working on it for like two years now. Oh well. You ready to work on chains?"

"Why not," said Katana. "Hopefully *this* is something I'll actually be able to do."

The chains consisted of nine thin, metal sections, linked together. They had a handle on one end and a spike on the other. Katana had seen Dana do her double whip chain form a million times the previous year. She always started with one chain folded up in each hand. At the beginning of the form, she'd throw them out, holding on to the handles. And because they were flexible, unlike the other wushu weapons, Dana always kept the chains moving once she'd started the form.

"I'm gonna show you some of the basics with one chain first," said Dana. "Most of the stuff you do with two chains is based on single chain work, but it's easier to learn without the second chain at first."

She handed Katana a chain. They worked together for the next half hour. Dana showed her how to redirect the weapon using an arm or a leg, or even her neck. "Okay, time for body jumps," she said finally. "This is wicked hard at first."

Katana had seen Dana do this move in her double whip chain set. She would lie down flat on her back, spinning one chain in a circle above her, the other underneath—jumping off the ground with her entire body on every circle to clear the bottom chain. "It's easier with one chain," said Dana, "because you don't have to worry about what the other hand is doing."

Dana showed her how to do it. Katana didn't think she'd ever get it. The chain kept getting stuck under her legs. But finally, twenty minutes later, she managed to pass it underneath herself once.

"Yeah, that's it!" said Dana.

"I think I get it," said Katana. "You have to jump at exactly the right time—but how do you do more than one?"

"That's the hard part," said Dana. "You gotta keep the chain going in a circle, and jump every time it goes under you."

Katana discovered that getting additional jumps was significantly more difficult than doing just one. She took a break eventually to watch Sara and Chris.

Sara was working with her staff. Jelly had taught her how to do flowers—essentially a figure eight with an extra circle on each side of her body. Sara could even spin in a circle, keeping the staff going the whole time.

Chris wasn't having as much luck.

"No," said Jelly. "You have to keep this end on your right side for one more circle before you go to your left."

"Oh, I get it," said Chris. He did the move again. Katana didn't think he was any closer.

"No," said Jelly. "You're going to the left too early."

This went on for a few more minutes, and Chris became steadily more frustrated. Dana looked at Katana and shook her head. "You wanna try some stuff with two chains now?" she asked.

"Yeah, I do," said Katana.

They returned to where they'd left the chains. Dana showed her how to do flowers first. "It's almost the same as staff," she explained. "You make circles, and when you can't go any farther, you switch to your other side."

Once Katana had it, Dana showed her how to turn in a circle while she did it, just like Sara was doing with the staff. Katana kept working with the chains for the rest of the afternoon. She was determined to get good enough for Hua to let her start with this weapon.

"Hey, are we going to Sam's for sushi tonight?" she asked Sara once everyone had finished working out. "I forgot to ask her at practice last night."

"Yeah," said Sara. "I talked to her at breakfast this morning and she asked if we were coming."

"I hope she remembered to order me a sandwich," said Chris. Despite how many times Katana had tried to get him to eat sushi, Chris couldn't get beyond the fact that the fish was raw.

The three of them walked up the stairs to the third floor of the south wing and knocked on Sam's door. "Hey guys, come on in," she said. "Gerty just brought everything up." They went inside and sat down on the floor around the low table in Sam's sitting room.

"Ooh, what are these?" asked Sara.

"Terry-san specializes in putting together some really creative rolls," Sam explained. "This one is spicy tuna and seaweed salad..."

"You're gonna eat seaweed?" asked Chris with a look of utter disgust.

"It's good, Chris—you should try some," said Sam with an amused twinkle in her eye.

"No thanks. I'll stick to my sandwich."

Sam pointed out the rest of Terry-san's creations.

"Sam, how does levitation work?" asked Katana.

"Well, it's similar to the chi hit," said Sam. She thought about it for a moment before she continued. "When you project your chi, you throw a ball of energy away from your body. When you levitate, you also extend your chi, but not as far; it only reaches just beyond your body, far enough to hit the chi of whatever you're bouncing it against."

"I thought only living things had chi?" said Chris.

"No, not exactly," said Sam. "Everything has chi. The difference is that in living things it flows through meridians. In inanimate objects, chi is static—and it doesn't change. In living beings, it grows.

"Say for example you're using levitation to jump off the floor. What you're doing is extending your chi through your feet, just enough to bounce it off the chi in the floor."

"But I don't see a fireball or anything when Jelly levitates," said Sara.

"No, you wouldn't," said Sam. "When you throw a chi hit, you have to throw a huge amount of energy to make anything happen, and it separates from your body entirely. When you levitate, it's a short pulse—and it doesn't separate from you."

"That makes sense," said Katana. "How about fading?"

"That's a little trickier," said Sam. "Think about the chi hit, and how you can deflect it. Those two skills are like yin and yang. To throw a chi hit, you have to extend your chi beyond your own body—that's the yang, or active skill. When you deflect a fireball, you extend your intent, or your shen, to redirect the chi into the surrounding energy field. That's the yin, or passive skill.

"Levitation and fading are similar. When you levitate, you bounce your chi off the energy in a solid object. But when you fade, you insert your chi into the energy of the air around you—instead of bouncing off of it, your energy fades into the surrounding field."

"So when you do the chen do in kempo or tae kwon do, you're using your chi against someone else's. But when you do the chen do of aikido or wushu, your chi is interacting with the chi of everything else around you?" asked Sara.

"Yes, precisely!" said Sam. "And that's why fading and levitating are usually harder to get. The chi of living things is easier to sense because it's stronger in a way—it is always moving and flowing. It's harder to feel the chi in the ground because it's much subtler. And fading is harder than levitating because the chi in the air is even more difficult to sense than the chi in the ground.

"Why do you ask? Has Hua got you working on levitation already?" asked Sam.

"No, I was working on it with Jelly today," said Katana.

"Oh, I see," said Sam. "It would be pretty amazing if you got it. Three chen do at the age of fourteen? I don't know if anyone has *ever* done that before."

"Yeah, she's the wonder kid, and I can't do *any* of the chen do!" said Sara.

"Well I can only do two of them myself," said Sam.

"You can't levitate?" asked Chris.

"Nope. I've never been much good at wushu," said Sam. "Kempo and tae kwon do are more my thing. I've been able to do a chi hit and deflect intent for ages, but that's it. I've been working with Nash recently on fading, but I haven't been able to get it yet."

They finished their food. "Do you think Gerty can bring up some more of that tuna and seaweed roll?" asked Sara.

"Sure, I'll call it in," said Sam. "But I don't see how you can still be hungry. I'm stuffed!"

Gerty brought up more sushi a few minutes later.

"So Kat, are you feeling a little better about sparring with the boys?" asked Sam. "You looked pretty nervous about it when you first found out the other day."

"Yeah, I'll be fine," said Katana. "I was thinking about it and I realized it's not a big deal. I spar with Chris all the time, and I sparred a lot with Sensei Mike this summer. This shouldn't be any different."

"You're right, it's not," said Sam. "But once some of the other girls see you doing it, it *will* be a big deal to them. Hopefully we can generate enough interest to get some girls' teams started next year."

Sara had a couple more rolls, and then they said goodnight. Katana, Chris and Sara walked back up to their rooms.

"Ooh, I'm not feeling so good," said Sara.

"Yeah, no wonder after that extra sushi," said Katana as she flopped down on the couch. But Sara ran to the bathroom and closed the door. A moment later Katana could hear her vomiting. "Are you okay in there?" she called out. Katana thought vomiting was disgusting.

"Yeah, I'm better now," said Sara when she came out of the bathroom. "I probably just ate too much."

"Ya think?"

***

On Monday morning, they had to get up horribly early for their first tai chi lesson with Master Nash. Katana thought that holding a class at five in the morning could qualify as cruel and unusual punishment. But she had to admit, doing tai chi in the morning last year had given her a lot of energy throughout the day.

Katana woke Sara and they drudged their way through the Hall. The tai chi dojo occupied the entire third floor of the main building—it was twice as large as any of the other dojo. To get to it, they had to go up the grand staircase from the atrium, and walk along the balcony to the front of the building. One set of stairs on each side of the central atrium led up to a hallway that ran along the front of the building behind the tai chi dojo.

Katana sat down in the hallway. The door to the dojo was open. Katana could see that inside, Sam and Master Hua were taking a lesson with Master Nash. They were working on pushing hands. Sam was in a stance with her front foot next to Master Hua's. She held her hands in front of her, wrists in contact with his. They didn't seem to be doing much beyond standing there. But Katana knew that each was trying to push the other over. They made only slight adjustments to their stances or to the positions of their hands.

Katana thought she could make out a faint glow around the two of them, and knew she must be sensing their auras. She'd been able to see Master Nash's aura the previous year, and had seen Osaka's as well during the battle with the Arashi.

Suddenly Sam shifted her weight forward and pushed. Master Hua fell to the ground.

"Well done, Samantha," said Master Nash. "Good work today, both of you. We'll continue this afternoon."

The students filed into the dojo. The entire school did the morning tai chi class, but the dojo was so large that it didn't feel crowded.

The tai chi dojo had two features that set it apart from the others. The first was the second altar along the wall on the left side of the room. It contained only one item: a jade sculpture of the Hall's main building. Katana knew that marked the spot where they'd kept the Scroll of the Five Masters until Master Sato stole it the previous year.

In addition, a set of portraits lined the back wall of the room. Katana had learned the previous year that these were the pictures of all the headmasters—from Master Chow on one end down to Master Nash on the other.

"Good morning everyone," said Nash as he started the class. "Please have a seat. As you know, the first tournament will be taking place in Eureka at the end of November. And as always, we will be attending the Golden Gate Classic in early March."

"Why is he announcing the tournaments already?" whispered Sara.

"This year, the Hall of the Dragon will be hosting the U.S. nationals at the end of May," said Master Nash. The room broke out in a wave of chatter. "Quiet please," he continued. "We will be holding the event at the Pacific Hotel in Eureka, which is the same location as the Eureka Challenge in November. Hosting nationals is quite an honor, but it also involves a tremendous amount of work. You will all be allowed to attend as spectators even if you do not make the tournament as competitors. But we will be asking some of you to volunteer to help us organize the event. We will, of course, discuss this more as we get closer to May. Now, please rise," he said, and began their class.

They started with the same standing chi kung exercise Katana had taught Sensei Mike. Like she'd done that day, Katana formed a fireball in her hands very quickly. She could feel the energy flowing up from her feet, through her body and down her arms, finally extending to her fingertips.

Some of the students right around her were staring, whispering to each other. Only a couple of the students from Master Nash's regular tai chi class were able to hold a fireball like this. Master Nash had them switch legs. Katana was able to hold the ball as she shifted her weight.

They did a few more chi kung exercises, then Nash had them begin the tai chi form. They practiced a short form of twenty-four postures in the morning class. Katana had learned the previous year that the students in the regular tai chi classes learned a much longer form of 108 postures.

Master Nash had some of his senior students walk around and teach the first few postures to the beginners. He worked with those who already knew the form. Katana hadn't practiced tai chi all summer, but unlike some of her peers, was able to remember the whole thing.

Nash came over to Katana as she finished the form. "Katana, can you sustain the energy ball as you do the form?"

"Um... I don't know. I've never tried," said Katana. She'd never talked much with Master Nash; she found him rather intimidating up close. His aura was very strong—Katana could see it clearly.

"Follow me," said Master Nash. He stood next to her in the opening position of the form. Katana assumed the posture as well. As Master Nash began the form, he formed a strong ball of glowing red energy between his hands. Katana followed him. By the third posture, she'd formed a fireball as well.

Katana moved through every posture with Master Nash, maintaining the ball the entire time. She realized that the postures in the form all seemed designed to do this very thing. Some of them required shrinking or elongating the ball, but every move allowed her to continue holding it. They finished, and Katana realized to her great embarrassment that the entire room had stopped to watch.

"Holding the energy ball through the form is the first part of the chen do you will learn in tai chi," Master Nash said to the class. "Some of you have been able to form the ball when you do the standing chi kung exercise. Keep practicing that. Ultimately, you will be able to maintain the ball through the entire form, as Katana and I just did."

"Katana, that was incredible," said Sara as they walked back to their room to shower and get ready for their day.

"It was amazing," Katana agreed. "I could feel the energy flowing through my whole body. I've never experienced anything like that before."

"You've gotta teach me how to do some of this stuff. I'm tired of being the only one around here who can't do any of the chen do!"

For the rest of the day, Katana felt much more alive and alert than usual. She had no problem staying awake during her classes. She could feel her chi flowing through her body all day, and a few times, almost thought she could feel the chi in the air around her.

Her energy lasted all the way to their wushu class that afternoon. Master Hua had them start with jumping again. Katana wasn't hyper like she was when she had too much sugar, but felt like she could keep doing the exercise forever.

After warm-ups and stretches, Master Hua had everyone start working on their weapon sets. He came around to the new students to find out which weapons they wanted to learn. Chris and Sara both told him they had decided to work on staff.

"Katana, you do work with Dana on chains already?" he asked.

"Yes," said Katana, feeling nervous about screwing up the moves in front of him.

"Good, please show me."

Katana picked up the chains she'd used over the weekend with Dana. She showed him everything she'd learned.

"Very good," said Master Hua, looking surprised at how much she could do already. "You start with chains. Dana, please work more with Katana." He went off to teach the students who were learning staff.

For the rest of the lesson, Katana worked on double whip chain with Dana and Donnie. She was already able to do some of the basic spins faster than Donnie, much to Dana's distress. By the end of the lesson, she could do a few moves with two chains that Dana had shown her with only one. She also worked more on the full body jumps—with one chain—and was able to complete three or four in a row.

Sara made good progress with staff, but Chris didn't fare as well. He still couldn't do the flowers correctly, and hit himself in the head a few times when they tried to swing the staff in upward circles.

"I gotta sit down for a minute," said Sara near the end of the lesson.

"What's wrong?" asked Katana.

"I don't know... I feel lightheaded and dizzy all of a sudden. I've been tired all day," she said, sitting down against the wall at the back of the dojo. But Master Hua lined them up and finished class a minute later.

"So Hua's letting you start with chains?" Chris asked as they walked out of the dojo.

"Yeah!" said Katana. "I love this weapon so far."

"I wish I could get staff," said Chris. "This is what I've always wanted to learn, but it's a lot harder than I thought it would be."

"We'll get Jelly to keep teaching us this weekend," said Sara. "Don't worry, you'll get it."

"I'm definitely not giving up on it. I don't care how long it takes me, I'm gonna get good with this weapon," he said.

Master Nash continued doing form work all week during their morning tai chi lessons. Katana found it was getting easier and easier to hold the fireball all the way through the form. And she was amazed at how much energy she had. She didn't even feel tired or groggy when she woke up anymore.

Sam and Master Hua seemed to be training very hard before the tai chi class every day. They were doing pushing hands again on Tuesday, and sparring—with both external techniques and chen do—for the rest of the week. And it sounded to Katana like they were coming back to train with Nash again every afternoon.

In fact, when Katana got to the sparring team practice that Friday, she saw that Sam must have come directly from a lesson again. She was very sweaty, had a cut on one cheek, and looked like her lip had been bleeding.

"Sam, are you getting ready for another master's exam or something?" asked Katana. Sam had taken the exam in tae kwon do at the end of the previous term, and Katana remembered how hard she'd trained for that.

"Huh?" asked Sam, looking confused for a moment. "Oh—no, I'm not testing again. Master Hua and I have just been doing a lot of extra training lately. Okay everyone, get your gear on, we have a lot of work to do today." She seemed very eager to change the subject.

Sam had them pair off and work more on feinting, then brought them up in pairs to run a few matches. "We're going to work more on takedowns today," she said after the last match. "The rules say you can't grab your opponent with your hands, so that's why we rely mostly on leg sweeps. But there is one takedown you can do where you grab your opponent with your legs—and there's nothing in the rules that says you can't do *that*!"

"I know that takedown!" said Jimmy. "We saw you do that against Van Heldon last year."

"And that Becca girl did it on you at the tournament, remember Kat?" added Sara, who'd just walked in with Chris.

"Yes, that's the move I'm talking about," said Sam.

She had them pair off. Katana worked with Jimmy again. "I want you to stand off to the right side of your partner—no, *Katana's* right side, Jimmy."

"Oops," said Jimmy, moving over to Katana's right side.

"Good, now stand facing away from them, squat down like this and put your hands on the floor." Sam was demonstrating the move on Bobby Wellington. "Now you're going to kick out with your feet. You want your left leg in front of their waist and your right leg under their rear end. Then right away you have to grab onto them with your legs, and twist over hard to your left, like this." She dropped Bobby to the mat.

Jimmy kicked his feet out and tried to copy Sam. He grabbed onto Katana with his legs, but slid down her body until he was lying on the mat.

"I don't think that was right, Jimmy," said Katana.

"No duh."

"You have to twist harder," said Sam. "Try it again."

Jimmy repeated the move. This time he twisted hard and knocked Katana down.

Once everyone could do it, Sam had them try it a little differently. "Now I want you to stand facing away from them, but don't squat down. You're not going to use your hands this time—instead, jump in the air, kick your legs out, and grab on. But be careful—make sure you don't kick them in the face."

Jimmy went first again. He did exactly what Sam had said not to do—his left leg went high, and he caught Katana in the cheek with the back of his ankle.

"Oh Kat, I'm sorry! Are you okay?" he said.

"Yeah, I'm fine," said Katana.

Jimmy completed the move perfectly the second time. Everyone tried the takedown this way a few times, then Sam had them square off as if they were sparring. "Now, when you use this in a match, you're going to set it up by throwing a side kick at them. When you throw the kick..."

"The person is going to sidestep to get out of the way," said Katana, recalling how Becca had used the move against her at the tournament.

"Exactly," said Sam. "And now they're behind you, so you can throw your other leg in the air, grab them with your legs and drop them. Everyone pair off again and give it a shot."

They spent the rest of the practice working their new takedown into their sparring matches. Katana felt pretty comfortable with it by the end of the lesson.

Sam wrapped up the practice a few minutes early. "That's good for today everyone. I have a meeting with Nash so I have to run. Practice that takedown; I'll see you next week." She ran out of the room.

Katana walked over to Sara and Chris as the crowd began to filter out of the room.

"That's such a cool move," said Chris. "I gotta try it this weekend."

"It looks like it's hard to defend against, too," added Sara.

Just then Jason Beecher walked over to them. "Katana? Can I talk to you for a minute?"

"Uh..." said Katana, her face instantly growing hot. "Sure!"

"Um—alone," said Jason. He looked at Sara and Chris, who apparently had no intention of moving.

"Oh, I guess," said Sara. "Come on, Chris. We'll catch up with you at wushu practice, Kat." She gave Katana a big smile as the two of them walked away.

"What's up?" asked Katana.

"Oh, um, I was thinking. Well, I was wondering if you'd like to go to the Fall Ball with me..." Jason stammered.

"Oh!" said Katana, feeling awkward and happy at the same time. "Yes, sure! I'd love to go! Um... when is it?"

"Really? It's the first weekend in October, on Saturday night," said Jason. "Okay, well cool. So I'll talk to you later?"

"Yeah, definitely," said Katana. Once he was out of sight she ran up to the wushu dojo.

"*What* was that about?" asked Sara excitedly when Katana sat down next to her and Chris.

"Did he ask you to the Fall Ball?" Chris asked with a devious smile.

"How did you know?"

"He talked to me about it a couple of days ago. I guess he was worried that you and me were going out. I told him we're just friends."

"So did he ask you?" asked Sara.

"Yeah, he did," said Katana with a smile.

"No way!" Sara squealed. She lowered her voice when Master Hua gave her a dirty look. "Oh my God! Katana, that's awesome. The Fall Ball is only for juniors and seniors!"

"Wait, so I can't go?"

"You can go if an upperclassman asks you. And Jason's a junior. Kat, you're so lucky!" said Sara, but Chris rolled his eyes. "What, you mean you wouldn't *love* to go to a formal dance, Chris?"

"Um… no, not exactly," he said. "I hate dressing up. And I'm not crazy about dancing either."

Katana felt her heart drop into her stomach. "It's a formal…" she said. "I don't have a dress."

"You don't?" asked Sara in complete surprise. "I brought one this year because I was hoping someone might ask *me* to one of the formals!"

"No," said Katana. "I don't even *own* a dress. I haven't worn one since I was five."

"Hmm," said Sara thoughtfully. "Well, I'd let you wear mine, but I don't think it would fit you. Don't worry. We can talk to Sam tomorrow. I'm sure she'll think of something. Kat, this is so exciting!"

***

On Saturday afternoon, Katana went down to Sam's dojo with

her friends. They worked on tricks for a while first. Chris could land the backflip more consistently, but still didn't look clean doing it. Katana and Scott worked on their gainer and tried wall flips again. Katana was able to get over this time without putting her hands down. Jelly said he was certain Katana would get levitation, but she didn't understand what made him think that. She tried running up the wall and around the corner again, but didn't feel any closer to levitating than she'd been the previous weekend.

Sara and Chris both tried the leg scissors takedown that the sparring team had worked on the previous night. It took them a few tries. "Watch where you're kicking," said Sara when Chris kicked a little too high and caught her in the chest.

They worked on weapons, too. Katana felt much more comfortable with the chains now. She'd realized that she was being overly cautious because she was afraid of smashing herself in the face with the spikes. But now she could do all of the moves more fluently.

Sara was getting good with staff very quickly. Jelly was now teaching her the beginning of the form he'd competed with the previous year. But Chris continued to struggle. Katana thought he was making *some* progress, but then he smashed himself in the head again.

"That's enough staff for today," said Sara. "Katana, you gotta teach me how to do the chen do."

"I can try," Katana said with a sigh, "but I haven't been able to teach anyone how do them yet. I don't know how to explain it very well."

"I don't care. I'm working on this every day until I can do one,"

Sara replied. "It's *so* not fair that you and Chris and Jelly can do one and I can't."

"I wanna do this too," said Jelly, walking over to them. "I wanna be able to throw a fireball at Daniels next time he yells at me for levitating!"

"Oh, that's a great idea," said Chris.

Katana suggested that they start with the standing chi kung exercise. "I can feel my chi the strongest when we do this," she explained. Katana and Chris could both form the glowing ball of energy between their hands.

"I don't get how you do that!" said Sara.

"It's like when we do the unbendable arm," said Katana, looking at the ball of energy in her hands as she spoke. "Like you told me last year; you have to relax, like totally relax, and feel the energy flowing from your fingertips into the ball."

"Okay, relax," Sara mumbled to herself. Suddenly Katana saw the faintest spark of energy between Sara's hands.

"Sara! That's it!" she said.

"Whoa!" said Sara. She lost it a moment later. "Oh, man! I had it!"

They worked on the exercise for a while longer. Sara was able to get an indistinct ball to form a few times, but couldn't sustain it for more than a few seconds. Chris could form a much stronger ball, but Jelly couldn't do it at all.

"Oh well," he said. "At least I can levitate."

Katana went with Sara and Chris up to Sam's room for sushi after they'd thoroughly tired themselves out.

"You're never going to guess what happened," Sara told Sam as they sat down to eat. "Jason Beecher asked Kat to the Fall Ball!"

"You know, I figured he might," said Sam thoughtfully.

"Did everyone know about this but me?" asked Katana, feeling quite exasperated.

"I didn't know for sure," Sam explained, "but I overheard him talking to Bobby. It sounded like he wanted to ask you."

"We need to get Kat a dress," said Sara. "She doesn't have one, and there's no way she's gonna fit into mine."

"No problem," Sam replied with a smile. "When's the ball?"

"The first weekend of October," said Katana.

"We have plenty of time. I'll have Gerald take you into Eureka this weekend to go dress shopping."

"Why can't you take us?" asked Sara.

"Me? Shop for a dress? No, I don't think so, Sara. I don't do dresses. I hate formal occasions."

"Me too!" said Chris, looking relieved.

"No, trust me, you'll be much better off with Gerald," said Sam.

Suddenly Katana had a horrible thought. "Sam, I don't have any way to pay for a dress. How much is it going to cost?"

"It depends on where you get it."

"I can talk to my mom if you want, Kat," said Chris. "I'm sure she wouldn't mind buying you a dress. She always says you're like the daughter she always wanted."

"Or I can talk to Master Nash. I'm sure he'll let Gerald put it on the school account," said Sam.

"Where is the Fall Ball?" asked Sara.

"The last I knew," said Sam, "they held it at Eureka Gardens. It's outside of the city, right on the water. It's a huge banquet facility. Lincoln usually reserves the big room on the second floor overlooking the ocean."

"Did you go to the Fall Ball when you were at Lincoln?" asked Katana.

"Actually, I went with your dad our senior year," said Sam with a smile. "Neither of us wanted to go, but Jesse wouldn't leave us alone. 'It's the *Fall Ball*,' he said, 'You *have* to go.'"

"You went out with Katana's dad?" asked Sara. She looked shocked.

"Oh, no," said Sam. "Adrian, Jesse and I were best friends back then. Jesse went with his girlfriend, but Adrian and I went together because we were only going to placate Jesse. We went as friends.

"I think Jesse regretted talking us into it, though. We didn't like his girlfriend much. She was a real girly girl—all the makeup, and the nails, and the big hair," said Sam, shaking her head. "Oh, we gave her a hard time that night. I think she broke up with him right after that."

"It's too bad Jesse turned out to be such a jerk," said Katana.

"Yes it is," agreed Sam.

"I wanna know who asked Ed and Tommy to the ball," said Chris.

"WHAT?!" Katana and Sara said at the same time.

"The moron twins are going to the Fall Ball?" Sara added.

"According to Jimmy," Chris said with a shrug. "I guess they were gloating about it the other day. They said they both had hot dates."

This was not good news. Katana was sure Ed and Tommy would find some way to ruin the dance for everyone.

Chapter Six: The Fall Ball

The following Saturday, right after breakfast, Gerald met Katana and Sara in the atrium. "Ready, girls?" he asked.

"Chris, are you *sure* you won't come with us?" asked Katana, with a pleading look on her face.

"No. No way," said Chris. "Katana, you're my best friend, and I'd do almost anything for you. But going shopping for a dress is where I draw the line."

"He must think it would hurt his macho image if he were seen in a dress shop," said Sara as they walked outside to get in the limo. Gerald had left it running in the driveway beyond the torii gate.

"Psh, what macho image?" said Katana.

They got to downtown Eureka and Gerald pulled over next to a long line of parked cars. "That's Zelda's. She runs the best dress shop in the area," said Gerald. "I'll let you two out here. I'm going to park in the garage around the corner. I'll be right back."

"Thanks, Gerald," said Katana as they got out of the limo.

They joined the crowd strolling along the sidewalk and made their way up the street to Zelda's. But suddenly Sara stopped, grabbed Katana by the arm, pointed across the street and said, "Katana, look!"

"What?" asked Katana, confused for a moment. She looked across the street. The sign at the top of the building read "U.S.A. Tae Kwon Do." It was Thompson's old school. Katana had only been here once before—when Thompson kidnapped her from the Hall of the Dragon. The memory of that experience seemed like a nightmare.

"Let's go!" said Sara, running across the street. Katana followed apprehensively.

The front of the space was made of plate glass. They crept up to the edge of the first window and peered inside. "Yep, that's Sebastian," said Sara as they watched the class. Sebastian was tall and gangly, with bright red hair.

"It's Ed and Tommy!" said Katana. Most of the students were sitting along the opposite wall. They all wore full sparring gear. Sebastian was running a match in the ring that was drawn out on the carpeted floor.

"Where?" asked Sara.

"The last two on the right over there against the wall," said Katana.

"You're right," said Sara. Sebastian finished the match, and gestured to the students sitting along the wall. He must have called on Ed Golia, because Ed stood up, took off his gear, and walked into the ring.

Everyone else stood up, removed their gear, and stood in a circle around the two. Katana and Sara had to shift position to keep their view of Ed and Sebastian.

Sebastian placed one hand on Ed's shoulder, the palm of his other hand to the left of Ed's sternum. "Isn't that the move we saw Van Heldon learn on the beach with Thompson last year?" said Sara.

"I don't believe this!" said Katana, as she watched Ed Golia double over and wince in pain. The class spread out and broke into groups of two. Each group began to attempt the move Sebastian had demonstrated on Ed. "He's teaching them dim mak!"

Katana and Sara watched in shock for a few minutes longer, until Gerald came up to them. "I wondered where you two had disappeared to!"

"Oh, sorry Gerald!" said Sara.

Sebastian lined up the class, and bowed them out. The students filed out of the dojo.

"Let's get out of here before they see us," said Sara.

They walked back across the street with Gerald and went into Zelda's dress shop. Zelda was an older woman who seemed to have boundless energy. "Ah yes, Lincoln Academy's Fall Ball. They're holding it at Eureka Gardens again, you know," she said.

She immediately brought out a dress for Katana. It was pastel peach and rather poofy looking. Katana went to try it on, but when she came out, Gerald and Sara both looked at each other and shook their heads.

She changed into a green dress next. It was less poofy than the first, but Gerald and Sara both rejected this one as well. Zelda brought out an endless stream of them. Sara liked a few of them and Gerald a couple of others, but they couldn't agree on a single one.

Katana soon grew weary of this process. "I'll tell you what," she said finally. "Why don't the two of *you* go to the Fall Ball together, and you can each wear the dress you like the best."

Katana herself rejected the next one without even trying it on. "That looks like a wedding dress!" she said. "I'm *definitely* not getting married!"

But Zelda finally found something that Gerald and Sara both liked. It was simple, elegant and black.

"You're both sure?" asked Katana.

"Well, turn around again," said Sara. She and Gerald nodded to each other. "Yep, that's the one, Kat." Zelda had Katana try on shoes next, but now that they had the dress picked out, this was much simpler.

"I can't walk in these!" Katana complained.

"Don't worry," said Sara. "You'll get used to them. You just have to practice."

Zelda took Katana's measurements. "Okay dear, I'll take this in for you and have it sent up to the Hall by the end of next week."

They left the shop and stopped at an old-fashioned diner for lunch. After that, they returned to the Hall.

"Are you gonna come down and work on tricks and stuff?" asked Katana when they got to their room.

"I don't think so..." said Sara, flopping down on her bed. "I'm not feeling so good."

"That sucks," said Katana. "Well, I'm gonna go down. I wanna try that gainer flash today. I'll see you at dinner."

Chris, Jelly and Scott were already in Sam's dojo when Katana arrived.

"Finally!" said Jelly. "What took you so long? You *have* to try a gainer flash today. Scott just got it!"

"Oh, cool!" said Katana. "Show me!"

He ran forward a few steps and jumped up, kicking one leg over before the other. He flipped over backwards, landing a perfect gainer flash kick.

"Yeah, I'm gonna get this today," said Katana. She stretched for a few minutes, then warmed up with some regular flash kicks. "Here it goes," she said finally.

She ran forward then sprang into the air, kicking one leg over as hard as she could. She stumbled a bit on the landing, but she'd done it. "Yes!" she yelled. "I *love* this trick!"

They worked exclusively on tricks that day. Within a few minutes, Katana could land the gainer flash perfectly. It was easier than she'd thought it would be, probably because she'd practiced a regular gainer so many times.

Sara came down later. Katana and Chris went with her up to Sam's for sushi.

"So how'd the shopping go?" asked Sam as they sat down around the table in her sitting room.

"Really good," said Sara. "Katana got this elegant black dress—she looks so beautiful in it. Jason's not going to be able to take his eyes off her!"

"Aw," said Sam, "that's great."

"Oh!" said Sara suddenly. "We saw Thompson's old school! This kid Sebastian was teaching the class. But there's no way he's running the place. He's still in high school."

"Hmm," said Sam thoughtfully. "Well, it's a great location. I'm not surprised someone else opened up there. Is Sebastian the tall kid with the red hair?"

"Yes," Sara replied.

"You don't know who's actually running the school?" Katana asked.

"No," Sam confirmed. "But Sebastian was at all the coaches meetings over the summer. Whoever owns the place must not have much interest in the tournaments."

"Sam, Sebastian was teaching the students dim mak!" said Sara.

"Dim mak?" said Sam, looking totally surprised. "Are you sure?"

"Yes," said Katana. "He was showing them one of the moves we saw Van Heldon do last year."

Sam looked very troubled at this news. "That's not good..." she said. "I'll talk to Nash about it next time I see him."

Katana woke up early on Monday morning. She was waking up at quarter to five now without her alarm clock. She dragged Sara out of bed for their tai chi class.

As they had been every morning since the start of term, Sam and Master Hua were there for a lesson with Nash. But this time Master Daniels was present as well. Sam and Master Hua were taking turns attacking Daniels. Sam lunged to tackle him, but Daniels disappeared, rematerializing right behind her.

"Fading a very short distance is the easiest way to learn," he said, "because you can see where you want to be. Simply visualize yourself stepping forward. But don't actually step—instead, relax and insert your chi into the field around you."

Katana watched in amazement as Sam and Master Hua continued attacking Master Daniels. He would fade out as they moved in, and reappear only inches from where he'd started. He was gone only for the instant it took Sam or Master Hua to pass through the space he'd been occupying.

"It's amazing that someone that large can disappear like that," whispered Sara.

"That's enough for this morning," said Master Nash. "Brock has agreed to continue helping us, so we will see you again this afternoon. I'll feel better about this mission if one of you can fade consistently by the time it begins." He bowed them out of their lesson, and the students filed into the dojo.

"Sam and Hua are the ones going on the mission!" Sara whispered to Katana. But just then Master Nash began their lesson. For a moment Katana was surprised that Nash would talk about the mission so openly with everyone hanging out in the hallway, watching through the doorways. But she realized that other than herself, Sara and Chris, no one would think twice about what Nash had said. They were the only ones in the whole school who knew something was up—and even they knew next to nothing.

They started with chi kung exercises, then worked on pushing hands. Katana paired up with Chris. After a while they stopped to watch Master Nash, who was working with one of the older students from his regular tai chi class.

"Whoa!" said Sara. "He's glowing! I can see it!"

"So now you know I'm not crazy," said Katana. She'd been the only one who could see Nash's aura the previous year. This time, it was more than a faint glow. She could see a large field of energy around him, with tendrils that branched out toward his opponent. Suddenly there was a flash. A pulse of light shot along one of the tendrils. It hit the student in the chest and knocked him over.

"What was that?" asked Sara.

"It looked like Nash hit him with his chi," said Katana uncertainly. "But it wasn't nearly as bright as a fireball." Katana wasn't sure what she'd just witnessed, but she was growing very curious about the chen do of tai chi.

They continued working on pushing hands for the rest of the week. After that, Master Nash switched to form work. Sam and Master Hua were there every morning. Master Daniels showed up half the time to help them work on fading. The rest of the time, they did pushing hands or sparring.

In their free time, Sara taught Katana how to walk in high heels. Some of the other students gave Katana strange looks as she walked delicately up and down the stairs, trying to improve her balance. "I feel like I'm walking on stilts!" she complained.

Katana hadn't talked to Jason much since he'd asked her to the Fall Ball. They saw each other at tae kwon do class twice a week, but he was usually busy assisting Sam. Katana found out he was doing private lessons with her for his own training.

Katana worked with him every Friday at the sparring team

practice as well, but they spent the entire time training. Sam reminded them every week how soon the first tournament was, so they didn't waste any time socializing. Katana was able to hold her own against the boys—except Bobby Wellington, who was way too tall for her.

The school year at Lincoln was well underway. Chris derived great satisfaction from being able to help Katana with geometry. She wasn't having much trouble with it anyway, but picked it up more quickly with Chris's help than she would have otherwise. But Katana had to help Chris with French. "I don't know why you're having such a hard time with it," Sara said to him one evening in the student lounge as they did their homework. "It's just like Spanish... only different."

"It's that different part I'm having the problem with," said Chris. "And she keeps throwing that stupid eraser at me every time I ask a question! How am I supposed to learn?"

"You have to ask it *en francais*!" said Katana.

Dana started teaching Katana her double whip chain form. Katana was able to do nearly all the moves with two chains now—even the body jumps. "I wish Donnie could do it this well," said Dana with a sigh.

Chris finally made some headway with staff. He wasn't smashing himself in the head as frequently. But Sara far outstripped his progress. Jelly had taught her the entire form by the time the Fall Ball arrived. Sara could even do the flash kick with the staff in her hands.

Katana had to agree with Dana: the wushu team didn't look as sharp as it had the previous year. She felt bad blaming it on Donnie, but the fact remained that Dana had to slow down for him. And they'd taken out the moves that Master Hua had added for nationals the previous year because Donnie couldn't properly perform them.

They asked Sam about the mission again—the mission they now knew involved her and Master Hua. While Sam did not deny that she was taking part in whatever was going on, she wasn't willing to discuss the subject with them. Chris began asking her about it at the most random moments. It seemed to Katana that he was trying to surprise her into giving them more information.

"So where are you and Hua going?" he asked in the middle of a sparring match one day. Sam simply gave his opponent two points and ended the match.

September seemed to fly by and the weekend of the Fall Ball arrived much more quickly than Katana had thought it would.

"I'm feeling nervous now," she said while Sara put her hair up in an elaborate arrangement.

"Don't be nervous, Kat, you're gonna have a great time," said Sara. "I'm so jealous. I wish someone had asked me, too."

"Do you wanna go for me?" asked Katana tentatively.

"Katana! Don't be ridiculous. Okay, I think we're done." Katana got up to look at herself in the mirror. "Wow, Kat, you look stunning," said Sara.

Sara walked downstairs to the atrium with her, and whistled when she saw Jason. "You sure clean up nice," she said. Jason was wearing a tuxedo, looking quite nervous himself.

"Hi," said Katana. She had to agree with Sara that Jason looked very handsome.

"Hi," he replied. "Um… Gerald said he'd be waiting for us out in the limo."

"Have fun, you two!" said Sara as Jason offered Katana his arm. They walked outside.

Gerald got out of the limo and opened the back door for them. "It may not be a sports car, but it's quite comfortable."

"Don't rub it in," Jason replied with a scowl.

Katana and Jason got in the car. "Did Bobby take the Porsche?" she asked.

"Sure did," said Jason. "I hope I get to be sparring team captain someday."

As Gerald pulled away from the school Katana and Jason rode in awkward silence for a few minutes.

"So you're getting good at sparring," he said finally.

"Oh, thanks," said Katana, grateful for the opportunity to break the ice. "Osaka never did any sparring with us in Vermont, but I like it."

"It sucks that they don't have any girls' teams."

"I know," said Katana. "I kind of like fighting with the guys, though. And Sam thinks that once everyone sees me doing it in the boys' division, more girls might participate next year. She's hoping to get the tournament committee to start a girls' division."

"You know, it would be so cool if they allowed the chen do at the tournaments," Jason said.

"Oh, I know!" Katana agreed. "They should have a separate division for it or something. But it's never going to happen. The chen do are supposed to be a secret."

"Yeah, that's true," said Jason. "And it would be totally unfair unless everyone who competed could throw a fireball *and* deflect intent—otherwise the people who could do both would automatically win!"

"Yeah, good point," said Katana. "Have you been able to deflect intent yet?"

"Nah," said Jason. "I got the chi hit on my test at the end of last term, but I can't deflect intent yet. You wanna teach me?"

"Sure," said Katana. "Actually, a bunch of us have been working on tricks and stuff every Saturday, but we work on the chen do a lot, too. Sara can form the ball now when she does the standing chi kung exercise. You should come with us next Saturday."

"I think I will," said Jason.

The limo pulled up in front of Eureka Gardens. Gerald came around and opened the door for them. "Have fun, kids. I'll see you in a few hours."

Katana took Jason's arm again and they walked into the banquet hall. "Lincoln Academy?" asked a man in a tuxedo standing inside the door.

"Yes," replied Jason. The man pointed them up the stairs at the end of the hallway.

They walked up the steps, into a large room in the back of the building. "Everyone's out on the deck," said Jason. He led Katana past the DJ, through the sliding glass doors.

"This is beautiful," she said. The sky was clear. Katana could hear the waves breaking on the beach below.

"Hey, Bobby," said Jason. Bobby Wellington and a very pretty girl with long blond hair came over to them.

"Hey," said Bobby.

"Katana?" said the girl. Katana realized suddenly who it was.

"Becca!" she said, giving her a hug.

"You two know each other already?" asked Bobby, looking puzzled.

"Yeah," said Becca. "We competed against each other at the tournament last year. I still think you would've made nationals in kata if you weren't forced to withdraw from Golden Gate."

Moments later the staff at the banquet hall called them inside for dinner. "You guys are at table five with us," said Bobby.

Two other couples were already seated at their table. Katana and her friends greeted them as they sat down.

"You don't go to Lincoln, do you?" Katana asked Becca.

"No, I'm a sophomore at Eureka High. But I've been going out with Bobby since nationals last year."

"Where do you train?" asked Katana.

"I go to a traditional karate school in Bayview," said Becca. "But my instructor is into sport karate, too."

"Oh, cool," said Katana. "Are you competing in sparring and kata again this year?"

"I'm not going to do sparring," said Becca. "I'm doing weapons though. I've been working on this really cool nunchuck form. It wasn't where I wanted it last season, so I decided to wait until this year. But I'm ready now. I'm hoping to give Dana Arlington a run for her money."

"Dana's good," said Katana.

"I know," said Becca. "Double whip chain's a hard weapon, though; it's tough to add tricks to the form because you have to keep the chains moving the whole time. But with the nunchucks I was able to add a ton of tricks."

"I didn't know you could trick!" said Katana.

"I used to do gymnastics," explained Becca, "so I can do backflips and flash kicks and stuff. Do you trick?"

"Yeah, I only started last year when I got to the Hall. I just got a gainer flash last..."

"You can do a gainer flash!?" asked Becca, clearly impressed. "I've tried a gainer but I can't get it. That's a tough trick."

"You two should eat before it gets cold," said Bobby. He and Jason had already dug into their food, listening in amused silence as the girls talked.

"What?" asked Becca.

"Nothing," said Bobby. "It's just that usually you yell at *me* for talking too much."

They finished their dinner, and the DJ turned up the volume. The crowd moved out to the dance floor. Katana silently thanked Sara for dragging her to the school dances the previous year. She would've been mortified if her first time dancing was in front of Jason.

After a while they went back to the table to take a break. "So what events are you competing in this year?" asked Becca.

"Kata and sparring," said Katana.

"Kat made the sparring team," Jason said with pride.

"What?" said Becca, looking confused. "They have a girls' team this year?"

"No. She's sparring in the boys' division," said Bobby.

"You're joking!" said Becca. "I tried *so* hard to get my instructor to let me do that last year. None of the other girls at my school would spar, so I tried to convince him to put me on the boys' team. But he refused!"

"Do you two ever talk about *anything* besides karate?" asked one of the other girls at the table. Katana and Becca looked at each other and laughed.

"No, not usually," said Becca.

Just then there was a loud disturbance by the top of the stairs. Katana turned to see what was happening. Two boys wearing jeans and T-shirts ran into the room, followed closely by a man in a tuxedo.

The boys were Ed Golia and Tommy Cosgrove. Ed was holding a large bottle of clear liquid in one hand. He stopped for a moment, threw both hands in the air—sloshing the bottle's contents all over the floor—and shouted, "We're here! Let the party begin!"

The maitre d' tried to grab Ed, but Tommy shoved him out of the way. The man slipped in the liquid and fell flat on his back.

Ed and Tommy ran right past Katana to the center of the dance floor. The crowd moved away in surprise, forming a circle around the two. Ed took a swig from his bottle, and although a fast song was playing, he and Tommy began to slow dance with each other. Everyone roared with laughter.

"Drunken idiots," Jason mumbled, as the maitre d' and two other men tried to grab Ed and Tommy. But the pair managed to evade their grasp and bolted across the room.

"I'm going to give them a hand," said Bobby, getting to his feet with a scowl. Becca was right behind him.

Katana got up to follow them, but Jason had other ideas. "Let's go for a walk," he said, grabbing her by the hand.

Everyone else returned to the dance floor as a small crowd followed Ed and Tommy out of the room. Jason led Katana out to the deck. They walked beyond the edge of the building, into the far corner. The beach extended into the distance beneath them.

"Chris said those two would be here," Katana said as they came up to the railing and looked out over the water. "I should've known it would be something like this."

Jason was silent for a moment. "Chris told me you've never had a boyfriend," he said finally. "But that can't be right."

Katana turned to face him. She could feel her face growing very hot. "And why not?" she asked with a smile.

Jason took her hands in his. Katana saw that he was blushing, too.

"Because the prettiest girls always have boyfriends."

Katana rolled her eyes and glanced down for a moment. When she lifted her gaze, his face was much closer. Katana panicked. She'd never kissed a boy. She had no idea what to do. But one heartbeat later, Jason pressed his lips against hers. Katana felt her panic evaporate, replaced by a combination of exhilaration and joy. Her whole body started tingling, from head to toe.

"So are you my first boyfriend?" she asked.

"I don't know," Jason replied teasingly. "Do you want me to be?"

Katana leaned in and kissed him again.

They stood for a few minutes, looking out over the ocean. Jason was behind Katana, his arms around her waist. She held his hands in her own.

"So what actually happened last year," he asked quietly. "With Jaaku and Sato and all that? Everyone knows the basic gist of the story, but not the details. Nash told everyone to leave you alone about it."

Katana hesitated for a moment before telling him everything— how she had gone with Sara, Chris, Jimmy and Robert up to the tai chi dojo that night. They'd expected to see Van Heldon helping the Arashi take the scroll, and had been shocked when it turned out to be Sato.

She told him how she'd tried to keep the scroll from Sato, and how he'd ended up taking her and Robert to Jaaku. She fought back tears as she described the brutal way Jaaku had ended Robert's life. Jaaku had taken his prenatal chi; using that connection he'd been able to steal the rest of Robert's chi, too.

"Sato saved you," Jason said quietly when she was done. "How was he able to do that if Jaaku was controlling him?"

"Osaka said that Jaaku needed Sato to be normal at the Hall. If he looked like a zombie, the other masters would've known something was up. So I guess Jaaku couldn't take him over all the way, like he did with Robert. But Sato died for trying to save me.

"When my dad was a student at the Hall, he trained with Sato. I guess he was Sato's star pupil—they were really close. I wish I could've trained with him."

Suddenly Katana heard voices from below.

"This sucks. I can't believe they called the cops on us!" someone shouted.

Katana and Jason looked at each other, then down at the beach. Two figures stumbled a short distance across the sand, then sat down on a large rock.

"Ed and Tommy," Jason whispered.

"At least they didn't arrest us," muttered a voice that Katana was pretty sure belonged to Ed Golia.

"Screw the Fall Ball. We shoulda gone to the Arashi meeting instead," Tommy replied.

Katana gasped. What Arashi meeting?

"Hah!" Ed exclaimed. "They woulda *killed* us if we showed up there. I'd rather get arrested."

"It's so unfair, though," said Tommy. "How come Sebastian gets to go and we don't?"

"Because he's gonna join the Arashi, dumbass."

"They're not gonna let him join. They're just pissed cuz he was teaching everyone dim mak. They don't want him giving away their secrets. They're probably just gonna scare the crap outta him and make sure he doesn't do it again."

"He *told* me the master's bringing him so the others can decide if they wanna let him join," Ed retorted.

"Our new master sucks. He won't let us learn anything. At least Thompson used to teach us stuff sometimes."

"Yeah, but Sebastian's gonna be an Arashi. He'll keep showing us everything. It's *us*."

"What time is it?" asked Tommy.

"Almost eleven. Why?"

Tommy got to his feet and stumbled up the beach. "The meeting's at eleven. We can still make it."

Ed followed him. "You got a car I don't know about? Pavilion Park's about ten miles away. We're not getting there in five minutes."

"It's not *ten miles*," Tommy yelled. "Come on!"

"No way! I'm telling you, we're dead if we show up there. That's a secret meeting, you idiot! We're not even supposed to *know* about it." But Ed got up and followed him anyway.

Jason looked at Katana, his eyes wide. "Sebastian's joining the Arashi?"

"Let's go!" Katana said, pulling Jason by the hand.

Jason looked confused. He stood his ground.

"Go where?"

"Pavilion Park!"

"You want to go to an Arashi meeting?" Jason pulled his hand out of Katana's. "That's nuts—after everything that happened to you last year?"

"Whoever the new master is at Thompson's old school, he's

an Arashi! And he's gonna be at the meeting. We've gotta find out who it is!"

Katana strode away from him. "Kat, wait!" she heard Jason call out as she walked into the banquet hall. She ran to their table. Bobby and Becca weren't there. She went to the edge of the dance floor, scanning the crowd until she spotted them.

"I need to talk to you," she yelled over the music when she got to Bobby. Jason caught up with her. Katana pulled Bobby out on the deck, Becca and Jason close behind.

"What's up?" Bobby asked. Becca looked concerned.

"Do you know how to get to Pavilion Park?"

She told them everything she and Jason had overheard.

"Bobby's told me about the Arashi," Becca said. "Barging in on one of their secret gatherings sounds pretty dangerous."

Bobby looked at Becca for a moment, then back at Katana.

"This is insane," said Jason. "We should go back to the Hall and let Sam know. The masters can go find out who it is!"

"It'll be too late," Katana insisted. "Even if I call her, it'll take them half an hour to get to the park."

"Can't they just fade there?" Becca asked. Bobby had told her quite a bit, Katana noted.

"I doubt it," said Bobby. "They can only fade somewhere they know really well. Pavilion Park's in the middle of nowhere. I don't think any of the masters ever go there."

The three stood there, staring at Bobby. He was the one with the keys to the Porsche, so clearly the decision was his.

"Okay," he said finally. "Becca, I'm going to drop you off, then..."

"What? Hell no! I'm going with you!"

"You said it yourself. This is going to be dangerous."

"That doesn't mean I don't want to go!"

The four of them ran out the front door, into the parking lot. Katana and Becca climbed into the tiny back seat of the Porsche. Katana found herself wishing she'd brought a change of clothes. This excursion wasn't going to be any fun in a dress.

Bobby tore out of the parking lot. They raced down a couple of side roads and merged onto the highway. They passed only a couple of exits before finding the one they needed. Bobby turned up a long, deserted road through a forest and into a gravel parking lot. A narrow drive led farther into the woods.

"Kill the lights," Jason suggested.

"Good call," Bobby said. They were plunged into darkness. "Actually, I'm going to park here. If we get any closer they might hear the engine. We can walk the rest of the way."

They got out of the car and made their way up the road. There were no lights, but once Katana's eyes had adjusted, there was enough light to see the path. They moved along warily for a minute or two until Katana was able to see several large structures looming out of the darkness ahead.

The road ended at a large clearing in the woods. There, several pavilions looked out over the Pacific. Three of them were open, but stone walls enclosed the rest.

"That one," Bobby whispered. The other structures were dark, but a faint glow flickered inside of one of the closed buildings, as if someone had lit a fire inside. Bobby led the way. They crept up to a window.

Katana peered inside. The pavilion was long and rectangular. There was a fire pit at the far end, a group of people huddled around it. Most of them were wearing samurai armor. All but one—Sebastian's red hair stood out like a flame of its own amidst the black figures.

Katana could hear voices, but wasn't able to make out what they were saying.

"Let's go around," Bobby whispered. There were wide, open entrances on each side of the pavilion. Katana led the way this time. They went around the corner of the building, past piles of firewood, and tiptoed up to the opening.

Katana looked inside.

"And remember, once you join us, boy," one of the Arashi was saying, "you will be sworn to secrecy. You may only teach dim mak with your master's permission. The consequences for breaking that oath will be... severe."

"I know," Sebastian choked out.

"That is the final matter of business," the Arashi said to the group at large. "If Jaaku approves our new recruit, the boy will go to Shanxi. Until then, he is your responsibility, Sato."

Katana was stunned. Sato? That was impossible. Jaaku had killed Sato; Katana had seen it with her own eyes. But the Arashi closest to them replied, "I understand."

Katana turned back to her friends, and whispered, "Let's go."

When Jason turned around to run he tripped over the nearest woodpile. Several logs came crashing down.

"Who's there?" yelled someone inside.

"Sato, Epstein, with me," a voice commanded. "The rest of you fade away! Take the boy!"

Katana and her friends bolted out of the clearing. Katana's high heels were hindering her progress. When they got to the road, she took a bad step, twisting her ankle. As she stumbled, trying to recover her balance, she felt one of her high heels break off. She fell to the ground, scraping her hands and knees in the gravel. She heard her dress tear as she regained her feet.

But this was the least of her worries. Her friends had stopped in their tracks—three Arashi had appeared directly in front of them. One was much shorter than the other two.

Becca screamed.

"A group of teenagers on prom night," the short Arashi observed. Katana could hear the amusement in his voice. "I can only imagine what they were doing at the pavilions," he added sarcastically. "Let's get out of here."

"Wait," said one of the other men. "Sato, do you recognize them? Are they Jordan's brats?"

Sato hesitated.

"Hit them, Kat! Now!" Jason yelled. He threw a huge fireball at the leader. Katana didn't need to be told twice. She hit Sato with the brightest fireball she'd ever thrown. The leader fell to the ground, unconscious—clearly they hadn't been expecting an attack. Katana's fireball sent Sato flying, but he faded away, vanishing mid-flight.

The short Arashi moved to grab Becca. Bobby wrapped his arm around the man's neck and threw him to the ground.

The four of them ran down the drive. But the short Arashi faded directly in front of them. He grabbed Bobby in a bear hug as Bobby tried to run around him.

Becca came from behind and ripped the Arashi's helmet off. Jason lunged in and elbowed the man in the temple. The Arashi fell to the ground.

"Thanks," said Bobby. They ran the rest of the way to the Porsche. Jason and Becca ended up in back this time.

The engine roared to life, and Bobby slammed the car into reverse. All four tires spat gravel everywhere as Bobby threw the car in gear and gunned it.

They were almost back to the main road when a lone Arashi appeared in front of them.

"Run him over!" Jason yelled, but Bobby slammed the brakes instead. The Arashi had his hands up, ready to throw a fireball. Katana didn't want to think about what would have happened if Bobby had been knocked out while he was driving.

Katana got out of the car and strode toward the Arashi.

"KAT!" Jason yelled. "GET BACK HERE!"

The Arashi threw a fireball. Katana was ready. She raised her hands in an instant, deflecting the shot easily. But the Arashi faded, appearing directly in front of her. He grabbed Katana by the neck with one hand, and slammed his other hand against her sternum.

"Don't come any closer, or Katana dies."

It was Sato. He was walking her backwards, toward the Porsche. Katana stared directly into his eyes, but could see her friends in her peripheral vision. They had run forward to join her, but stopped when Sato grabbed her.

"What are you doing here?" Sato demanded.

Katana only whimpered in reply.

"Who told you we would be here?"

Katana stared unblinkingly into his eyes, and Sato stared right back. She felt like he would bore into her skull with the force of his gaze.

But what Sato could not see was Bobby sneaking up behind him with a large tree branch.

"Answer me now!"

Katana flinched—she expected to feel great pain at any moment. She knew Sato could use dim mak to disrupt her chi. But for whatever reason, Sato did nothing. And an instant later it was over.

Bobby slammed the branch into the back of Sato's knees. He crumpled, and Katana dove away from him. Jason slammed Sato with another fireball. When Sato hit the ground, he didn't move.

Chapter Seven: Halloween Scare

Katana sat in Nash's conference room with Bobby and Jason. She stared across the table at Nash, Osaka and Sam. They'd just finished telling the masters everything that happened.

When they'd arrived back at the Hall, Katana had been worried that she'd be expelled. After all, this hadn't been the first time she'd strayed out of bounds. But the masters had been much more concerned with the Arashi's activities than the transgressions of Katana and her friends.

Gerald had arrived at the Gardens only to hear from some of the other students that Jason and Katana had gone racing off somewhere with Bobby and Becca. He'd gone straight back to the Hall. Sam and Gerald had been running out the front doors to go looking for them when they pulled up in the Porsche.

Gerald had left to drive Becca home, while Sam had escorted Katana, Jason and Bobby up to Master Nash's office. Nash and Osaka had been waiting for them.

"Sato?!" said Sam. "How can that be?"

"I don't know," said Nash, looking troubled.

"We don't fully understand the connection Jaaku establishes when he takes someone's prenatal chi," said Osaka. "Perhaps he was able to use that link to keep Sato alive."

Nash looked at Osaka. "This changes things."

Katana didn't understand it any better than the masters, but she was glad to get out of there. She kissed Jason goodnight on the landing to the boys' dormitory and ran up to her room. Sara wasn't there.

Katana changed out of the tattered remains of her dress into her pajamas, and ran downstairs. She was pretty sure she knew where Sara would be. She knocked on the door to Chris and Jimmy's room, and heard Chris yell, "Come in!"

"Hey guys," she said. She walked in and sat down at the end of one of the couches. Sara, Jelly and Scott were there with Chris and Jimmy; they were watching *Fighters of Shaolin.*

"How'd it go?" asked Sara with a smile. Chris looked up, interested in her reply.

"I don't know where to begin," Katana answered with a sigh.

"Shut up!" said Jelly. "I wanna watch this!"

"Let's go," Sara said. Katana, Chris and Sara walked outside on the balcony and sat down. Katana told them the whole story.

"Sato..." Sara whispered, and looked like she was in shock for a minute. "So he's the one who took over Thompson's old school."

"You know, I had a feeling something bad was happening," said Chris.

"Really? Why?" Katana asked.

"I dunno..." Chris hesitated. "I had this picture in my head of the Arashi showing up at the ball..."

Sara rolled her eyes. "So did he kiss you? Jason, I mean?"

"Sara!" said Katana. She knew it was pointless to try to hide anything from Sara, though. Other than Chris, she was her best friend in the whole world. "Yeah, he did," she said with a smile.

"Aw... your first kiss," Sara said. "How was it?"

Chris turned red. "I don't wanna hear about this."

"Sara, it was amazing," said Katana. She couldn't find the right words to describe what she'd felt. "Actually, it was weird. I could feel my chi flowing like *crazy*..."

"You're unbelievable!"

"What?"

"You're in the middle of your first kiss and all you could think about was your *chi flowing*?!" said Sara. "No, I know what you mean, though. It is kind of magical. So did he ask you out?"

Chris made a retching sound.

"Yes!" said Katana. Despite everything that had happened that night, she couldn't help but giggle.

***

Katana spent the rest of the weekend trying to wrap her mind around Sato's being alive. She had seen Jaaku hit him with that jet of fire. When he crashed into the wall, she'd heard a horrible crunching sound. How could Sato have survived that?

Ever since she'd come back with Osaka that terrible night, she hadn't had to worry about the Arashi, or Jaaku. She'd heard the stories about Jaaku attacking Shaolin, but that was on the other side of the world. Sato's presence in Eureka, and the fact

135

that the Arashi were recruiting, brought the problem much closer to home.

Katana and Sara went up to tai chi Monday morning. Master Daniels was already there with Sam and Master Hua.

"Blend with their energy," Daniels was saying. "Do not resist. Absorb the attack, and redirect it. Watch." He gestured at Master Hua to attack him. Master Hua lunged at Daniels with a hook punch. Daniels shifted his weight, picked Master Hua's fist out of the air, and turned. He sent Master Hua flying.

"Easier said than done," Sam muttered. Sam and Master Hua both tried the same technique. They could do it, but lacked Daniels' fluency.

Master Nash bowed them out of their lesson a few minutes later, and waved the students into the dojo. They worked on pushing hands that day. Sara and Chris had paired up together, so Katana went with Jimmy.

As they began the exercise, a thought occurred to Katana. What if she used the chen do she'd learned in kempo during pushing hands? She decided to try it. When Jimmy shifted his weight to push, Katana deflected his intent. Sure enough, she sent Jimmy crashing to the mat.

"What the..." said Jimmy, looking confused. "I didn't even feel you move that time!"

"I didn't," said Katana with a mischievous smile.

"Then why am I on the ground?" asked Jimmy.

"Well... I wondered what would happen if I deflected intent

during pushing hands. Now I know," she said with the most innocent look she could manage.

"Oh…" said Jimmy as they resumed the exercise. Katana tried to relax more, and feel where Jimmy was going to push. Suddenly something very strange happened. She could see the faintest wisp of energy coming toward her from Jimmy. She focused, and tried to deflect his intent again. He fell over to one side.

"I have a question," said Katana when Nash came over to work with them. "When you were doing pushing hands a couple weeks ago, I could see… Well, I don't know what I could see, but it looked like little tentacles reaching out from your aura…"

"What you are seeing is the shen," said Master Nash.

"So I was *seeing* your intent?" Master Nash regarded her for a moment. "Yes, Katana. When you deflect intent, you can only do so because on a subconscious level you can *sense* intent. As your skills advance, you gain the ability to see it consciously. Eventually you will learn to send very small amounts of chi through your shen."

"I could see it when I was doing pushing hands with Jimmy just now, too. I saw it before he even pushed, so I deflected his intent like I do in sparring and stuff," said Katana.

The way Nash was looking at her made Katana feel like she'd done something wrong. "Although you may not see it yet, when you do pushing hands, you are reaching out with your own shen, and yes, you can detect your opponent's intent to push *before* he pushes," explained Master Nash.

All day at Lincoln, Katana kept thinking about what she'd done in tai chi that morning. She realized she didn't know very much about the chen do of tai chi. She tried to recall everything she'd ever learned about it and didn't pay much attention in any of her classes.

When she got to wushu class that afternoon, she went to talk to Dana. "Do you remember that Becca girl from the tournaments last year?"

"The one who won grands in kata at nationals?" asked Dana.

"Right, that's her," said Katana. "Well, she's apparently going to compete in weapons this year. She's doing a nunchuck form with a bunch of tricks, I guess. She waited a whole year to compete in weapons because she wanted to get her form good enough to go against *you*."

"Wow..." said Dana. "How'd you find this out?"

"She went to the Fall Ball with Bobby Wellington. We talked about the tournaments and stuff."

"Well, that's cool. If she's as good at chucks as she is in kata, she should do well."

Master Hua had them practice weapons that day. Katana worked with Dana and Donnie for the whole class. Master Hua had taught her how to do butterfly kicks with the chains last time. Katana could do the kick, but found that doing it with the weapon was much more difficult. She tried it again, but succeeded only in tangling herself in the chains.

"Try it with one chain first," Dana suggested. "Hold it in your right hand, and spin it underneath you as you do the kick." Katana found it was easier that way. Once she'd got the hang of it, she tried it again with both chains.

"I like that move," said Dana. "It's not as flashy as backflips and stuff, but it looks cool with both chains like that."

"Why don't you do this move in the demo?" asked Katana.

"There's not enough room on the stage for two people to do it at once. But I'm keeping it in my individual form. You're almost up to that part now—you wanna add it in?"

"Yeah, sure," said Katana. Dana taught her the next couple of moves, which led into the butterfly kicks.

"That's pretty much the whole form," said Dana. "You gotta add the body jumps at the end, and the final salutation—but that's easy."

Once Katana had tired herself out, she went over to watch Paul and Scott. They were practicing with an older black girl named Sasha, who was on the team with them. They were working on a new broadsword set for the demo. Paul could do a lot more tricks than he'd been able to do the previous year, and Scott and Sasha were trickers as well. Hua had put together a new form that took better advantage of their repertoire. Katana couldn't wait to see it in the demo.

Katana accompanied Jimmy to their sparring team practice on Friday. As usual, Sam walked in at the last minute and looked like she'd come from a tough workout.

"Let's get started," she said. "We're only six weeks away from the Eureka Challenge, and we still have a lot of work to do. You're doing well with the feinting combos we've been working on, you're transitioning well from kicks into sweeps, and you've got the leg scissors takedown now," she counted off on her fingers. "I want you all to focus on getting another kick in after you do a sweep or the leg scissors though. Four points are better than two.

"I'm going to run matches," she continued. "Bobby and Jason, you're first. I want the rest of you to grab a partner, go to one of the other rings, and go half intensity while you're waiting your turn."

Katana had a chance to spar with everyone that night. They'd finally moved beyond the novelty of having a girl on the team once they realized that she was a formidable opponent. They'd held back in the beginning, but went all out against her now. But she was still able to pull out a win in each of her matches, except when she went against Bobby Wellington. "He's so *tall*," she said after he beat her 6-1.

"Don't worry, Kat, nobody in your division is Bobby's size," said Sam. She wrapped up the practice, and had to leave right away for a meeting with Master Nash again.

"Hey Kat," said Jason, "are you guys still gonna be working out tomorrow?"

"Every Saturday," she replied. "Are you gonna join us?"

"Yeah, I think I am," he said. "You really think you can teach me to deflect intent?"

"I can try," said Katana. "Hey, I'm going up to watch the wushu team practice. Do you want to come?"

"Nah, I can't. I'm hanging out with Bobby and Matt tonight, and I gotta get a shower first. But I'll see you tomorrow, okay?"

"Yeah, cool," said Katana. She ran up to the wushu dojo. As she walked in, she saw Dana throw her chains down and storm off toward the door. Katana thought for a moment that she was going to walk right out of the practice, but she sat down instead and stretched, muttering to herself.

"What's going on?" asked Katana.

"She's pissed because Donnie can't do chains," said Sara.

"That's nothing new."

"No, but I mean he's extra bad tonight. He *dropped* them and all they were doing was flowers."

Katana could tell the situation was throwing off the whole team. They performed best when they supported each other. Hua worked with Donnie for a few minutes while everyone else practiced their weapon sets. Then he went over to Dana. "You okay?" he asked.

"Yeah, I'm fine," she said.

"We have to work with Donnie. He is getting better," said Master Hua.

"I don't see why I can't do a solo!" said Dana. "We've already taken out half the moves, and now he can't even do flowers!"

"No, no solo Dana," said Master Hua. "We are team, not solo. You and Kelly best with chains, very hard weapon, most people cannot do like that. We need Donnie."

"Why don't we put Katana on the team? She's almost got the whole form, and she can do it way better than Donnie!"

Katana wished Dana would leave her out of this. Master Hua looked over at her, but said, "Come on, more practice." Dana looked rebellious for a moment, but got up and went back to work with Donnie.

"She's right," said Sara. "He should let her do it solo." Katana had to admit that as much as she felt bad for Donnie, she agreed with Sara.

When Katana and Sara went down to Sam's dojo the next afternoon, Jelly, Scott and Chris were already there. Chris was chasing Jelly with his staff, and Jelly was running up the wall to get away from him. Scott was sitting on the mat, laughing at the scene.

"Get back here you midget!" yelled Chris, pointing his staff menacingly at Jelly.

"What's going on?" asked Katana.

"Jelly imitated Chris trying to do staff," said Scott. "It was hysterical—he looked just like him. He did the goofy expression on his face perfectly."

"Hey, I thought Jason was coming today?" asked Sara.

"Yeah, he said he was," replied Katana.

Chris had given up the chase. Jelly came over and said, "it's time to levitate."

"Psh, whatever," said Scott. "I can't levitate. That's your special skill."

"You've gotta help us," said Katana. "You just do it and expect us to get it. What does it *feel* like when you do it?"

"I don't know," Jelly said, furrowing his brow. "It's like I've got little trampolines under my feet. Just do it!"

Katana spent a little while doing wall flips, and running from one wall to another. But Jelly's feeble advice hadn't helped; she was no closer to levitating. She gave up and practiced the gainer flash instead. Jason Beecher walked in a few minutes later and watched her work.

"Look who finally decided to grace us with his presence," Sara said sarcastically.

"Hey, everyone."

"Hi!" said Katana.

"Gainer flash, huh? Looks good," said Jason.

"You gonna trick with us?" asked Sara.

"Nah, I can't trick to save my life. Katana's gonna show me how to deflect intent."

For the next thirty minutes, Katana did her best to teach Jason the chen do. Chris and Sara worked with her, too, and Jelly and Scott even gave up tricking to join them. Katana started to feel like one of the masters, teaching a class on the chen do. She had them start with the standing chi kung exercise. Chris could form a strong fireball, and Sara was getting better at it, too. With Katana's help, Jason did it as well.

After a while, they paired off. Chris and Sara worked together, Jelly went with Scott, and Katana attacked for Jason. They all tried to deflect intent. Katana tackled Jason one time, sending them both crashing to the mat.

"I don't think I focused hard enough," said Jason.

"No," Katana agreed. "Definitely not."

He tried it several more times. Finally Katana stepped in to throw a kick. But as she cocked her knee, her other leg slipped out from underneath her. She fell flat on her back.

"Are you all right?" asked Jason, reaching out to help her back to her feet.

"Yeah. Jason, you did it!"

"Really?" he asked, looking puzzled. "But it didn't feel like I did anything..."

"Here, try it again," said Katana. She lunged in to tackle him. He threw his arms out. Katana felt like she'd run into a wall. She fell over to one side. "That's definitely it."

"You got it?!" asked Sara. "That's *so* not fair! I've been working on this for *ages* and I can't do it!"

Sara and Chris both took turns attacking Jason. They couldn't touch him.

"Let's spar," said Katana with a mischievous look on her face. "And chen do *are* allowed."

They hadn't brought their sparring gear, so they went light. But Katana mostly wanted a chance to fight with the chen do. They threw a couple of halfhearted kicks at each other. When Jason threw a fireball at Katana she deflected it with ease. "I'm gonna throw one at you now. You can deflect it the same way you did the regular attacks. Ready?"

"I was born ready," Jason said. His confident tone belied the look of apprehension on his face, but he deflected the fireball that she threw at him. They spent the next several minutes fighting with the chen do. Katana was much more proficient than Jason. He failed to deflect her fireball a few times, but she didn't miss a single one of his.

Jason joined them again the following weekend. He could deflect intent consistently, so Katana had him try catching her fireball. "You have to take the edge off of it, and not deflect it completely," she said. Jason found this much more difficult than deflecting it entirely. He gave up after taking a couple of her chi hits full force.

Dana showed up again as well, along with Donnie. She'd promised Master Hua she'd help him out as much as possible. "I didn't want to do chains," Donnie said apologetically. "I'm way better with staff and sword, but Hua says I'm the only other one he's got who can do them."

Soon their weekend sessions became rather crowded; in addition to Katana, Sara, Chris, Jelly, Scott, Jason, Dana and Donnie, Jimmy began attending as well. He worked with Katana, Chris and Jason on sparring. Jason thought Chris was getting good. "We should put you on the team next year," he suggested. Chris was thrilled that someone thought he was good at something, but he continued to struggle with his staff form.

"Maybe wushu isn't your thing," Sara suggested delicately. "You seem like you're a natural at sparring though."

Katana looked forward to the chen do practice the most. She and Jason fought using their powers every weekend, and the matches became steadily more intense.

***

Halloween was fast approaching. Sara tried to convince her friends that they should go trick-or-treating. "Aren't we getting a little old for that?" asked Katana.

"Absolutely not!" said Sara.

"But we don't have costumes," complained Chris. "Halloween's this Sunday. We can't go trick-or-treating without a costume!"

"No problem. I talked to Gerald, and he's agreed to take us shopping."

"You've got this all figured out, don't you?" asked Chris, shaking his head.

That Saturday, Katana went to Eureka with Chris, Sara, Jelly, Scott and Jason. Gerald took them to a huge store that sold anything and everything having to do with Halloween.

"Yes! I'm gonna be a ninja," said Sara, showing Katana the costume she'd found.

"I think I'm gonna be a pirate," said Katana.

"Cool!" said Sara. "Jelly can be your parrot—he's small enough to sit on your shoulder!"

"Hey!" said Jelly. "Shut up fatty!"

Chris came up the aisle to them, holding up his costume. "I'm gonna be a samurai. It even comes with a fake sword!"

"Great, Chris," said Sara looking at him askance. "You can look like an Arashi!"

Once they had their costumes, they decided to stop at the diner for lunch. On the way there, they walked right by Sato's school.

"Hey!" said Sara. "I wonder if they're working on dim mak again."

"It doesn't look that way," said Katana. "They're just sparring."

Ed Golia saw them. As they watched, Ed Golia made eye contact. He walked toward the window, making a rude gesture. But as he walked by Sebastian, Sebastian grabbed him by the throat, holding him back. Ed pointed at the window and Sebastian turned. He looked right at Katana, giving her a wicked smile.

"I hope you get to spar with Ed at the tournament," said Sara.

They returned to the Hall after lunch, put their costumes away and went to Sam's dojo for their usual practice session. Katana and Jason put on their sparring gear.

"Ready?" asked Katana.

"Bring it," said Jason. They bowed to each other, and Jason launched at her with a flurry of kicking combinations. Katana dodged, then dropped down to sweep his leg.

Jason fell, but regained his feet immediately. He threw a fireball at Katana. She caught it, spun around and hurled it right back at Jason. Even though she did this nearly every time Jason threw a chi hit, he was never quite ready for it. The fireball hit him square in the chest, lifting him right off his feet. He crashed to the mat. "I wish I could learn that trick."

They started again. This time Katana launched at Jason with her own barrage of kicks. He was only barely able to get out of the way. Katana finished with a side kick. Jason sidestepped, and Katana jumped into the leg scissors takedown. But Jason deflected her intent. She fell to the ground.

Katana sprang to her feet and threw a fireball. Jason deflected it, then came at her with a series of kicking combinations. They went back and forth for several more exchanges. Both were sweating and breathing heavily when they backed off to circle around each other.

Suddenly Katana had an idea. She was able to see Jason's shen, and could tell when he was getting ready to throw a fireball. So as Jason gathered his energy, Katana formed a giant ball of energy between her hands. Jason hesitated, unsure what she was planning, but threw the fireball at her anyway.

Katana used her own ball of energy to catch Jason's. She spun around and threw the whole glowing mass back at him.

She knew instantly she'd gone too far; the fireball was unlike anything she'd ever seen. It looked like a comet streaking through the night sky—it was enormous, with a tail of fire streaming off of it. For a split second, Katana could see a look of terror on Jason's face before the fireball slammed into him. He'd raised his arms to deflect it, but it knocked him halfway across the room, into the far wall. He fell to the mat with a heavy thud and didn't move.

"JASON!" Katana screamed, running over to him. Sara, Chris, Jelly and Scott ran over as well. He was unconscious.

Katana knelt down next to him, taking his hand in her own. "Oh, Jason... are you okay?"

"I'm gonna go get Sam," said Sara nervously, and ran out of the room. A minute later she came back with Sam, Master Nash and Master Daniels.

Nash knelt down next to Jason, and placed two fingers on the side of his neck. "Brock," he said, "give me a hand. We need to get him up to the infirmary. I don't want to fade him—the disruption to his energy could cause further harm. Sam, find out what happened here and meet us upstairs." Nash and Daniels removed Jason's sparring gear, then hoisted him up and carried him away.

"Katana, stay here," said Sam. "The rest of you... I don't know, go to your rooms or something. Practice is over for today."

Katana explained what she'd done. "I'll go tell Nash," said Sam. "Don't worry, Kat, he'll take care of Jason. Come up for sushi tonight and I'll let you know how he's doing."

***

Sam went up to the infirmary and joined Master Nash. Jason was lying in one of the beds, which was pushed away from the wall. Master Nash was standing at the head of the bed, inserting acupuncture needles into various points along Jason's neck and chest. Sam felt a wave of anxiety at the sight. What had Katana done?

"It's not too severe," said Nash, noticing her grim expression. "His meridians were overloaded. He'll be unconscious for a little while, but he'll wake up once his chi flow is restored. What were they doing down there?"

"They were sparring. Apparently Kat taught Jason how to deflect intent a couple of weeks ago, and they've been fighting with the chen do. I guess Kat can see other people's shen now?"

"Yes," said Master Nash, as he inserted another needle. "She was able to see Jimmy Lawlor's shen during pushing hands recently."

"Well, she sensed Jason getting ready to throw a chi hit. So she formed a ball of energy, caught his chi with it, and threw the whole thing back at him," said Sam.

"That would explain it," said Nash, placing two fingers on the side of Jason's neck again. He inserted another needle.

"Is this something you taught her how to do?" asked Sam. "I've never heard of that move before."

"No, I didn't teach her the technique. To be honest, I'd forgotten about it. We practiced it at Shaolin ages ago when I was training there, but I haven't used it in years."

"That sounds pretty advanced," said Sam. "How did she learn it?"

"I don't know," said Master Nash. He appeared satisfied with Jason's progress. He came over to the side of the bed next to Sam. "It's no more advanced than catching someone's chi hit and throwing it back at them. If you can deflect intent and form a ball of energy, then what Katana did is only one step beyond those skills. But it's remarkable that she figured it out by instinct alone."

Yet again, Sam was reminded strongly of Adrian. Like Katana, he'd possessed a prodigious command of his own chi. "What is it about her?" asked Sam, shaking her head. "Two chen do at the age of fourteen, and now this."

"I've never seen anything like it," said Master Nash. "I don't think Katana realizes how powerful she is becoming. Her aura seems to grow brighter every time I see her. I've never heard of anyone becoming so strong so quickly."

"Well, her dad was the same way. He was able to do three of the chen do by the time we graduated. Maybe she inherited her gift from him?"

"Hmm, I wonder..." said Master Nash uncertainly. "We inherit our prenatal chi purely from our mothers. Thus in theory we should inherit our gifts from our mothers, not our fathers."

"Really?" said Sam. "Her mom never trained, so she never cultivated her chi."

"That's not unusual," said Nash. "I suspect there are many people like that—people who have very strong chi, but never train in any martial arts, and thus never develop the chen do. But no one understands the genetics involved. Western medicine doesn't recognize the existence of chi. So who knows, perhaps Katana did inherit her power from Adrian."

"Katana's hit Jason with her chi plenty of times," said Sam. "But it's never knocked him out before."

"When you catch someone else's chi hit with your own energy, you produce the strongest possible fireball," explained Master Nash.

"Jaaku's jet of fire is stronger," said Sam.

"Yes, Samantha. That is correct. Although I still don't understand it—somehow Jaaku is able to manipulate the chi of the surrounding energy field. Theoretically, that shouldn't be possible. Nobody else can do it."

"Well, if Kat can do this much damage now, she's going to be lethal by the time she grows up," said Sam.

Nash stared at her for a moment. "We should talk to her about the responsible use of her power," he suggested.

"I'm sure she didn't mean to do this," said Sam.

"No, I don't believe so either," said Nash. "She doesn't have a cruel bone in her body—that's not what I meant. But she needs to understand how powerful she's becoming, and the potential danger that entails."

"I'll talk to her," said Sam.

"Perhaps Osaka should speak with her as well. He has known her the longest."

"That's a good idea," Sam agreed. "But he's away, isn't he?"

"He's due back any minute. I'll discuss this with him when he returns."

**

"Kat, that was... scary," said Sara when Katana returned to their room.

Katana sat down on the couch. She couldn't hold back the tears. "I'm sure he'll be okay," said Sara, coming over to sit next to her.

"I didn't mean to hurt him," said Katana. "Oh Sara, what did I do?"

Sara did her best to calm her down. A little while later, they collected Chris and went to Sam's apartment for dinner.

"Please tell me Jason's okay," said Katana as they sat down around the table.

"Yes, Kat, he's going to be fine. Nash says his chi was overloaded. He's going to be groggy for a day or two, but he'll recover."

Katana felt a huge wave of relief wash over her. As they ate, Sam explained to them how Katana's technique had worked.

There was a knock at the door a few minutes later. Sam got up to answer it. "Osaka!" she said. "You're back. How did everything go?"

"Very well," he said, glancing around at the other three. "But we can discuss that more later."

Sam looked over at them herself. "Oh, right. Sorry." She retook her seat. "Do you want me to call up some more sushi?"

"Oh, no," said Osaka, "I've eaten already. Katana, have you finished?"

"Yeah, I'm done," she said.

"Let's take a walk."

Katana looked at Chris, who merely shrugged. She followed Osaka out the door. They walked in silence down to the main atrium, and out the back doors to the Zen rock garden. Osaka led her halfway around the garden and took a seat in one of the benches along the path. Katana sat down next to him, pulled her feet up on the edge of the bench and hugged her knees to her chest.

"Master Nash told me what happened today," Osaka began. "Are you okay?"

"Am *I* okay?" asked Katana, surprised at the question. "I'm fine, but I almost killed Jason!" She could feel her eyes beginning to well up. She stared at the boulder in the middle of the garden. Sara had told her the previous year that it was supposed to represent an island in the ocean.

"No, Katana, there was no danger of that. But you do need to be careful," said Osaka quietly.

"Osaka, I swear I didn't mean to hurt him..."

"I know; nobody thinks you did. But the simple fact is that your chi is growing extremely powerful—much more so than that of your peers. And it is for this reason that you must be careful. Had you used that same technique on me, or Samantha or Master Nash, it probably wouldn't have had the same effect. But Jason's chi is not strong enough to withstand that kind of shock. Neither is that of any student here."

"I don't know if I want that kind of power if it means I'm going to hurt my friends," said Katana, wiping a tear from her cheek.

"You just have to be careful. You are going to grow more powerful than this. I have no doubt. I think you are destined for great things, Katana. But in the meantime, you have to realize how much power you do possess and learn to control it. And I would suggest that you refrain from using that technique unless you are sparring with one of the masters," said Osaka with a smile. "Boys don't like being knocked unconscious by their girlfriends."

Katana giggled. "No, definitely not."

***

Katana and Sara changed into their Halloween costumes after an early dinner the next afternoon, then went to visit Jason in the infirmary.

"Hey," said Katana as she came up to the side of his bed. "Oops, I mean, 'ARR!'"

"Hi," Jason replied with a weak smile. "Make sure you two bring me back some candy."

"Don't worry, we'll share the loot," said Sara.

"So what exactly did you do to me?" asked Jason.

"Ninja magic," said Katana with a grin.

"I'll give you ninja magic." he said. "Well, next time we spar, we're doing it *without* the chen do!"

"When are you getting out of here?" asked Sara.

"Nash says I can go to school on Tuesday."

"Why is Nash taking care of you instead of Doctor Hubble?" asked Katana.

"I guess because fireballs only affect chi flow," said Jason. "They don't do anything that regular doctors can fix. But it was kinda freaky having those needles sticking out of me."

Katana and Sara went back downstairs to meet Jelly, Scott and Chris in the atrium. "Aren't you coming with us, Jimmy?"

"Nah," he said. "We're too old for this."

"Whatever," said Sara as they walked out the door. "More candy for me then."

They piled into the limo and Gerald drove them around some of the residential neighborhoods in Westerly. They collected an enormous amount of candy, and Sara dug into it on their way back to the Hall. "You're gonna finish it before we get back!" said Katana.

Katana and Sara went up to their room, and dumped the contents of their bags on the floor. They traded their favorite candy, and made a separate pile of the stuff that neither of them liked. "We'll be nice and give that to Jimmy," said Sara.

Jimmy knocked on the door a few minutes later. "Come on— we're playing hide-and-seek in the tunnels!" He rushed off again.

"He's too old for trick-or-treating but hide-and-seek is acceptable?" Katana asked sarcastically.

"This is mad fun, Kat," said Sara. "We did it two years ago—you can get lost down there. Let's go!"

For the next couple of hours they played hide-and-seek in the expanse of tunnels under the Hall. They'd used some of the rooms for their academic classes the previous year, after Thompson kidnapped Katana. Katana had never explored beyond that area. But now in addition to the classrooms, she found storage closets, offices that still contained desks and bookcases, and even an old dojo whose mats were worn and frayed.

Katana hid in a large storage room one time. As she slid the shoji screen door closed behind her, she looked around for somewhere to hide. The place was loaded with shelves and wooden crates, and was only dimly lit. She made her way through the shadows and suddenly her heart skipped a beat—she saw someone crouching down next to some boxes at the other end of the room, right next to another door. He was wearing a samurai costume.

"Chris!" she hissed. "You're gonna have to hide better than that!"

Chris stood up and looked at her. But he turned and walked out the door without answering.

"Be that way," whispered Katana.

She ran behind one set of shelves, and ducked down behind the crates. When no one came to look for her after a few minutes, curiosity got the better of her. She walked over to the crates where Chris had been hiding. They were already open, so she rummaged around inside a couple of them. They contained old scrolls and manuscripts. But they were in Chinese. Katana couldn't read them.

Finally, Jimmy charged into the room and said "Gotcha!" before Katana had a chance to hide again. Eventually they grew bored of hide-and-seek, and everyone retired to Katana and Sara's room. They went out on the balcony to hang out and eat their candy.

"We were nice, Jimmy," said Sara, handing him a bag. "We saved some for you, even if it is just the stuff that we don't like…"

"Aw, thanks—you shouldn't have," said Jimmy sarcastically, scanning its contents. "Oh, Jelly Bellies! I love these!"

"Hey!" yelled Jelly.

"He wasn't talking about you, moron," said Scott.

"Sara, you're gonna be sick if you keep eating all that chocolate," said Katana.

Sara rolled her eyes. "Whatever."

"So Jason's gonna be all right?" asked Chris.

"Sounds that way," said Katana. "Nash said he can go back to school on Tuesday."

Sara got up to go inside a few minutes later.

"You're not going to bed already, are you?" asked Chris.

"Nah, I just have to use the bathroom," said Sara.

Katana felt suspicious. She followed a minute later. As she suspected, Sara was vomiting in the bathroom. Katana was becoming worried—it seemed like Sara was overeating intentionally. "Sara, are you okay?" she asked when Sara emerged from the bathroom.

"I'm fine," said Sara, surprised to see Katana standing there. "You were right. I ate too much candy."

"Sara..." Katana began hesitantly. "It seems like you're eating too much on purpose. You're not doing this to try to lose weight or anything, are you?"

"No, that's crazy, Kat. I wouldn't do that," said Sara, walking away quickly. Katana decided she needed to keep a closer watch on her.

"Hey, what do you think was in those scrolls and manuscripts?" Katana asked Chris when she got back outside.

"Huh? What are you talking about?"

"All that stuff in the boxes in that storage room we were hiding in," said Katana. "I tried to read a couple of the scrolls, but they were in Chinese."

"I don't know what you're talking about," said Chris, confused.

"When we were playing hide-and-seek—that storage room I found you in."

"I never went in any storage room..." said Chris.

"Wait, I know what you're talking about," said Jelly. "I hid in a place one time that was loaded with boxes and crates and stuff, but I didn't look inside any of them."

Katana looked at Chris for a moment longer. "Well I did," she said to Jelly. "Some of the scrolls looked really old. I wonder what they're about."

"Hmm..." said Sara. "We know the Shaolin Temple has a library of old archives; maybe the Hall of the Dragon does, too."

"Yeah, I guess," said Katana. She felt very anxious now. If that wasn't Chris she'd seen down in the tunnels, who was it? The only other, frightening possibility did not seem very likely.

Chapter Eight: The Eureka Challenge

Katana woke up to the sound of her alarm clock the next morning for the first time in weeks. She'd stayed up much too late with her friends the night before. She dragged Sara out of bed, and they made their way up to the tai chi dojo.

A few students were there already, waiting for class to begin. Jelly was sitting against the wall in the hallway, his eyes only half-closed. A line of drool was dripping out of his mouth onto his chest.

"He's sleeping with his eyes open again. I *hate* it when he does that!" said Katana.

"Yeah," said Chris. "It's especially freaky when he starts drooling like this."

"Guys, shut up and listen—Nash is talking about the mission," hissed Sara.

"...will be useful if you encounter any Arashi," Nash was saying. "Are you ready, Master Hua?"

Hua nodded, and formed a ball of energy in his hands. Nash threw a fireball at him. Hua caught it with his own ball of energy, then threw the whole thing back at Master Nash. Like it had for Katana, the fireball looked like a comet.

"It's gonna hit him!" squealed Sara, but Nash simply held up one hand, and dissipated the energy.

"Well done," said Master Nash. "Samantha, it's your turn. Master Hua, if you will?"

Sam formed a ball of energy in her arms, and said, "I'm ready." Master Hua threw a chi hit at her. Sam caught his energy with her own. She spun around and hurled it back at him. Hua was unable to deflect it. He raised his hands, but it hit him full force, knocking him back several feet. He crashed into the mats with a thud.

Sam and Master Nash ran over to him. Master Nash held out his hand to help him up. "Are you okay?"

Master Hua looked a little dazed, and shook his head for a moment. "Very strong," he said, "hard to deflect."

"Yes," said Master Nash. "That's the greatest amount energy you can throw at someone. If you catch one of the Arashi unawares with this technique, there is a good chance you'll be able to knock him unconscious, as Katana did to Mr. Beecher." Katana felt a wave of guilt at these words.

"How is Jason?" asked Sam.

"Oh, he's fine," said Nash with a grin. "I had to argue with him last night to keep him in bed. I anticipate he'll be fully recovered in time for school tomorrow."

Nash dismissed them, and the students filed in for class. They were working on pushing hands, and Katana paired up with Sara. "I'm not feeling this today," she complained.

"No, me neither," said Sara with a yawn. "We're definitely not staying up that late on a school night again."

After a few minutes, Master Nash came over to Katana and Sara. He assumed the stance for pushing hands, held out his arms and said, "Ready, Katana?"

"Um... no... I don't know. You want me to do pushing hands with... with *you*?" she stammered. She felt that she was getting in way over her head. Nash merely smiled. They started the exercise. Katana could see faint, wispy tendrils of energy extending toward her from every direction. She tried to deflect one. A pulse of energy shot along another one, knocking her over.

"Whoa!" she said, quite startled. "How'd you do that? I thought I deflected your intent..."

Master Nash smiled. "Just as you can feint in sparring, so too can you feint in tai chi," he said. "You seem to be a natural at this, Katana. I think we'll have to put you into the regular tai chi class next year."

"What did he do?" asked Sara after class, as they walked up to their room to get ready for school. "I saw that flash of light again, and then you fell over."

"I'm not sure. But I know he can send a pulse of chi through his shen. I think that's what he did. I didn't feel anything when it hit me, but it knocked me totally off balance." She was certain she wanted to learn how to do that someday.

***

With the Eureka Challenge fast approaching, the masters went into tournament mode for the rest of that week. Nash switched to form work, as some of the students were planning to compete with the tai chi short form. Master Hua spent extra time working with the students who were competing in the weapons division, and Sam devoted every class to sparring.

"Osaka," said Katana on Thursday during their private lesson, "you don't seem like you're into the tournaments as much as the other masters."

"I think tournaments are good for you, Katana," he replied. "It is useful to gauge your skills against others in a friendly, competitive atmosphere. But you are correct. I believe that ultimately, we are each our own greatest foe. And in their highest form, the martial arts help us conquer that foe, and develop ourselves into better people."

"What?" asked Chris, looking like he hadn't understood a single word.

Osaka chuckled. "Don't worry, Chris—we'll prepare your kata for the tournament." They spent the rest of the lesson working on their forms. Katana, Sara and Chris had decided to compete with Kata Thirteen.

The last few sparring team practices were particularly intense. Sam even got in the ring and took a turn sparring each of them. Katana thought she should've taken notes when Sam went against Bobby—Sam was no taller than Katana, but had no problem beating him. "It's all in the timing," Sam said at the end of the practice. "You'll get there."

The wushu team had improved tremendously. Dana had spent hours every weekend helping Donnie with chains, and Katana thought their hard work was definitely paying off. Donnie was still no Kelly, but he could finally do the form well enough to keep up with Dana during the demo. And this seemed to have a profound effect on team morale; they were looking stronger than ever. They were doing nearly the same demo they'd done the previous year. They'd removed the moves from the whip chain set, and added the new broadsword form. But Jelly was still doing his release skill during the staff set—throwing a gainer flash while the staff was in the air—and finishing the demo with his signature double backflip.

The next couple of weeks seemed to fly by. When the day of the tournament arrived, they went downstairs for a good breakfast, then piled into the school buses for the trip to the Pacific Hotel in Eureka.

The weapon divisions were up first, so Katana went with Chris and Sara to watch Dana, Jelly, Paul and Scott. Dana was in one ring with the other fourteen- and fifteen-year-old girls, and Paul was in the corresponding boys' ring. But Jelly and Scott were still in the thirteen and under division, so they were in a third ring.

"This isn't going to work," complained Sara. "There's no way we're gonna be able to watch all three rings, and Dana's way over on the other side of the room this time."

"Hmm," said Katana, looking back and forth at the rings. "Becca's competing in Dana's ring this year, too, and I really wanna see that. Let's go—the boys will understand."

They went across the room to Dana's ring, and wished her luck. The center judge started roll call, so they got out of the ring and sat down along the edge.

"Hey," said Katana when Becca came over and sat down nearby. "You ready?"

Becca looked so focused that Katana almost thought she was angry. "Yeah. I've got this," she said as she started stretching. Katana thought she'd better leave her alone.

Two girls went first—they were both doing straight sword forms—and then they called Dana.

Dana walked up to the judges and yelled "Representing the Hall of the Dragon. My name is Dana Arlington." She backed up to the rear corner of the ring and began her form. Katana was amazed; she'd never seen Dana look so fierce or spin the chains so fast. She had the impression that Dana was letting out her frustration from the past couple of months with Donnie. She nailed every move, finished strong, and bowed to the judges on her way out of the ring.

The crowd went wild, but almost everyone looked over at Becca to see her reaction. It appeared a lot of people knew that Becca was competing in weapons this year specifically to go against Dana. But Becca got up and gave Dana a high-five. "That was awesome."

"Thanks," said Dana, and sat down with Katana, Sara and Chris.

Several more girls took their turns. Some did wushu weapons like broadsword or staff. One girl did spear, but she lost her weapon in the middle of the form. She'd thrown it in the air to catch it behind her back with the other hand. The spear landed in the next ring—nearly hitting the girl competing there.

The judges called Becca. Katana thought she could feel the tension in the air. Dana started fidgeting.

Becca began her form and right away Katana could tell this was something special. She hadn't seen very many nunchuck forms, but Becca did things with the weapon that Katana would not have thought possible. She was able to flip them around her fingers, and had several release skills, where she threw them spinning into the air, catching them flawlessly. She also had some amazing tricks in the set including a flash kick, an aerial, and something that Katana hadn't seen before. It started like a butterfly kick, but she twisted around, rolling sideways in the air before landing on her feet again.

"What was that?" asked Katana.

"A butterfly twist," said Sara. "Jelly can do those."

Becca finished the form, and the crowd went wild again—the ring was clearly down to her and Dana. And like Becca had done, Dana got up and gave Becca a high-five when she left the ring.

"It's gonna be close," said Sara, adding the scores in her head. "I think they might be tied."

A few more girls went, then the judges gathered together with the scorekeeper to figure out the standings. Finally they were ready. They asked the competitors to stand. They called two girls Katana didn't know for third and fourth place.

"We have a tie for first place. Becca Stratton and Dana Arlington, please come up."

"No surprise there," said Chris. The two girls walked up to the judges.

"Call!" yelled the center judge. He and two of the other judges pointed at Dana, while the last two judges pointed at Becca.

"She did it!" yelled Sara. Dana turned to give Becca a hug.

Katana went with Chris and Sara to congratulate them both,

then she and Sara went off to find their kata ring. "Good luck, Chris," said Katana as he headed to the ring next to theirs.

"Hey," said Becca a few minutes later when she came over and sat down next to Katana and Sara.

"Hi," said Sara.

"That form was incredible," said Katana. "I've never seen anyone work nunchucks like that."

"Well, Dana was *amazing*," said Becca. "She's even better than I remember from last year."

"She's been kinda stressed out lately," Katana explained. "I think she let it out in her form."

Their center judge started the ring. The event was somewhat smaller than it had been the previous year. It went by quickly. Katana wasn't paying too much attention—she spent most of the time trying to watch the boys' ring to see whom she might be sparring against. But she managed to pull out a first place win despite her distraction; Sara and Becca finished second and third.

The sparring divisions were next, so Katana went with Chris to find their ring. Sara had decided not to compete in sparring this year, so she tagged along too. They found Jimmy and Jason and sat down next to them.

"Here we go," said Jason when the center judge lined them up. A wave of people muttered and pointed when the judge called Katana's name. "Isn't this the boys' division?" people asked. But the center judge apparently didn't feel an explanation was required; he continued with the roll call.

The first couple of matches went up, and Katana could feel herself growing nervous. "Calm down," she told herself. This was no different than team practice.

The judge called Chris up next. "Go Chris!" yelled Sara.

Chris's opponent was a taller boy who used his long legs to superb effect in his kicking combinations. But Chris was used to this from sparring with Katana; he knew what to do. He lunged in with a punch every time the judge started the match. Chris's opponent relied exclusively on his kicks, but Chris kept jamming him. He was able to pull out a win, 5-2.

"Good job," said Katana. She gave him a high-five.

Katana went next. She was up against a tall boy from team Strike Force. The judge bowed them in. The boy launched at Katana with a series of kicks, almost before the judge had said "Go." But Katana was ready. She dropped down and swept out his other leg, landing a kick to his face when he hit the mat. They'd drilled this combination during the sparring team practices; Katana felt like she could do it in her sleep. She scored with a kick in her next round and won the match easily, 6-0.

Jason and Jimmy each won their first matches as well, so they advanced to the next round. Chris lost his next match against a boy who was nearly as tall as Bobby Wellington. "I thought Sam said nobody in our division was that tall!" said Katana when he came back to sit down.

Katana's next opponent was the same height as she was, but much bulkier. She decided to stick to feinting combinations for this match. She wanted to use the leg scissors takedown, but decided to save it for finals.

Her strategy paid off. She was able to snap her lead leg like lightning from one kick to the next. The boy walked into her second kick every time. She won the match 6-0.

"Awesome!" said Jason. "That means you go to finals!"

Jimmy was next—against Ed Golia. "Go get him, Jimmy!" Sara yelled as he went into the ring.

"Ed's gotten a lot better," said Katana after the first exchange. Jimmy had beaten Ed easily the previous year, but the two were an even match now.

They went back and forth, each throwing a vicious barrage of kicks at the other. The score went to 2-2 very quickly. When they started again, Jimmy dropped down and swept Ed's leg out from underneath him—getting two points for the takedown—then tried to turn over and land a kick for the win. But Ed rolled out of the way too fast—it was 4-2.

Ed swept out Jimmy's leg next, and landed a backfist to his head right as Jimmy hit the floor. Ed won the match 5-4.

Jason won his next match 6-3. "Looks like we're going to finals together," said Katana when he sat down.

"Yeah," said Sara, "you two, that tall kid who beat Chris, and Golia. This should be fun."

The judges took a few minutes to get organized. At last, they started finals.

They called Jason and the tall boy first. Katana thought the two of them were very evenly matched. The other boy had a height advantage, but Jason moved around more quickly. They took turns throwing kicks at each other, and the match went to 2-2. But they went back and forth for the next few rounds without anyone scoring. They both threw many of the same feinting combinations—but it was evident they'd both had a lot of practice defending against them, too. Finally Jason threw a side kick, and did the leg scissors takedown when the taller boy sidestepped. They hit the ground. Jason turned over and dropped a kick on the boy's head before he could roll away.

"YES!" yelled Katana. Jason had won the match 6-2.

Katana was next, against Ed Golia. Katana could feel her energy flowing as the match began: she was ready.

Ed was very aggressive; he lunged in with a series of kicks, but Katana was able to dodge each of these. Then she went to work. She faked with a front kick, and when Ed blocked this, she snapped a roundhouse kick to his face. But as the judge was about to stop the match, she brought her leg around and dropped an axe kick down on the back of his head, sending him sprawling on the mat.

"UP!" shouted the center judge. "Call!" All the judges pointed to Katana.

"GO KAT!" Sara screamed from the sideline.

When the match began again, Ed was out for blood. He came at Katana wildly, flailing his arms at her. Katana dropped down and swept his legs out. Ed stumbled out of the ring, landing on his back in the middle of the adjacent match.

"Call!" yelled the center judge. The judges indicated that Ed had gone out of the ring before he fell. Katana didn't get any points.

They began again, and Ed seemed a little more focused. They circled around each other, each of them throwing a couple of kicks to test the other's reaction. Katana threw a side kick—which Ed barely dodged—and did the leg scissors takedown. She slammed him down to the floor, and turned over to kick him in the head.

"YES!" yelled Sara. But Ed reached up and grabbed Katana by the hair with one hand. He jammed the open palm of his other hand against her chest, just to one side of her sternum.

Katana had never felt pain so severe in her entire life. It felt like someone was stabbing her in the heart. She tried to pull back, but Ed was still holding her hair. She couldn't get away. Her vision started to go black, and she was dimly aware of voices shouting. The pain was spreading—it felt like shards of metal were traveling into her abdomen.

Finally it stopped. Someone pulled her away, and Katana collapsed to the floor. The darkness subsided, but everything was blurry. She was shaking.

"Katana! Kat, are you okay?!" someone yelled. She thought it was Sara.

She felt someone hook their arms under hers, pulling her out of the ring. Her vision started to clear, and she realized it was Master Nash. "Katana," he said, "can you hear me?"

"Yeah," she said, surprised that her voice was barely more than a whisper. She tried to sit up, but Nash said, "Not so fast. Just lie here for a moment."

She could feel Nash push some pressure points on her neck. Slowly her vision cleared. "Feeling better?" he asked.

"Yes," she said. She realized there were a whole lot of concerned faces staring down at her. This time Nash let her sit up all the way, and the people around her cheered. "What happened?" she asked.

"We were hoping you could tell us," said Master Nash, a look of worry on his face. "You won your match against Mr. Golia, then you crumpled over on top of him."

"He was pulling me down!" said Katana, suddenly remembering. "He used dim mak on me! He grabbed me, and put his hand right here," she said, pointing to the spot. "And it *hurt*, and I thought I was going to black out..."

Master Nash stood up and yelled out, "Someone get Ed Golia over here, NOW!"

But Golia was nowhere to be found. He had slipped out of the room in the confusion.

"I gotta finish this ring, Nash," said the center judge. "What are we doing?"

"She can't fight anymore..." said Master Nash.

"Yes I can!" said Katana, and tried to get to her feet. But her vision started to go black around the edges again, and she sat back down. Nash was right.

She was pretty sure Ed had performed the same move on her that she'd seen Van Heldon learn on the beach with Thompson. She'd had no idea at the time how much pain it could cause.

Sam came running over, and Nash said, "Keep an eye on her—

don't let her get up." He went to speak with the judges.

"What happened?" asked Sam.

Sara explained. "I think it was the same technique we saw Sebastian teaching that day in Eureka."

The center judge called the remaining competitors to the ring. "Kahanu cannot continue, so she finishes in second. Beecher takes first. Golia is disqualified for using an illegal move in the competition. So Johnson automatically takes third, and there is no fourth place."

"You beat him, Kat," said Sara. "You got four points when you took him down—it was awesome!"

"I know I did the leg scissors," said Katana, "but all I remember after that is the pain."

"I'm going to kill him if I get my hands on him," said Jason angrily.

Katana started to feel better. With help from Master Nash and Jason, she was able to get up and walk outside. Gerald had come down in the limousine to bring her back to the Hall of the Dragon.

"I have to stay here until the event is over," Nash said to Sam as they got in the car. "Make sure she goes straight to the infirmary, and I'll be up as soon as I can."

Sam, Jason, Chris and Sara rode back with Katana. Doctor Hubble met them at the front doors, and she and Jason helped Katana up to the infirmary.

"Sam," said Katana once she was settled in bed, "when we saw this move before, it didn't look like it hurt that badly. But I almost passed out."

"No one else held it that long," Sara replied. "Sebastian only held it on Golia for like a second—he let go as soon as Ed doubled over. But Golia kept doing it until the center judge pulled you away."

Sam nodded. "I think she's right, Kat. I've never seen the move myself, but it would make sense that the longer he held you, the worse it would be."

Master Nash arrived a little while later, and kicked everyone else out. "What she needs now is sleep. You can come back in the morning."

He pressed two fingers to Katana's neck again. "The dim mak move disrupted your chi flow, but it seems to be normal now. With a good night's rest, you should be fine. Doctor Hubble will keep an eye on you tonight. I'll be back first thing in the morning to check on your progress."

"Thanks, Master Nash," she said.

"Goodnight, Katana."

***

Long after Katana had fallen asleep, Osaka entered the infirmary and walked up the aisle to Katana's bed. He looked down at her, the expression on his face severe. He reached down and touched two fingers to the side of her neck. After a moment, relief washed over him, and he smiled.

"So strong," he whispered, bending down to kiss her on the forehead. A smile lit Katana's face, and Osaka walked away. She didn't wake up, and never found out that Osaka had visited her that night.

Chapter Nine: Fading

Katana woke up the next morning to the sound of voices. She opened her eyes and looked over to see Master Nash and Doctor Hubble standing halfway down the aisle between the beds. "She seems to be perfectly healthy," she could hear Doctor Hubble saying.

Master Nash walked over to her. "How are you feeling?"

"Hungry," said Katana, sitting up in bed.

"Doctor Hubble and I are in agreement that you are well, so you're free to go," said Nash with a smile. "But if your vision gets blurry again, or anything feels off, I want you to march straight back here and tell Doctor Hubble."

"I will," said Katana, getting out of bed to find that she was a little stiff. "Thanks, Master Nash."

She went up to her room, and Sara sat up in bed when she walked in. "Hey," she said groggily, rubbing the sleep out of her eyes. "You're better?"

"Yeah," said Katana, "but I'm starving; I wanna go down to breakfast. I need a shower first, though—I feel disgusting."

Katana and Sara both got ready, then went down to the cafeteria. Everyone else was already there.

"Hey, Kat. Are you okay?" asked Paul as she sat down. "Chris was just telling us what happened."

"I'm fine," said Katana. "Hey, how did you guys do? I left before team demo."

"We did pretty well," said Dana. "We won first, if only barely. We had a couple of little mistakes, but so did Strike Force."

"So Donnie didn't drop the chains or anything horrible?" asked Sara.

"No, the extra work he's been doing with Dana really paid off," said Paul. "He nailed it."

"How'd you do individually?" asked Katana. "We went to watch Dana and Becca compete, and we couldn't see any other rings from there."

"Well, I took first, thanks to the new set Hua put together for us," said Paul. "And Scott, you got second with it, right?"

"Yeah," said Scott.

"That's awesome," said Katana.

"Isn't anyone gonna ask how I did?" asked Jelly. Katana almost thought he looked hurt. But when Sara said, "You got first like always," Jelly said, "Yeah!" with a smug smile.

They arrived in the tai chi dojo the next morning, and Katana saw that Master Daniels was there again. Sam and Master Hua were working on fading.

"Think about stepping forward and turning around, but don't physically step," said Master Daniels. "You can trick yourself into inserting your chi into the surrounding field that way."

Master Hua tried it first, but actually stepped. "No," Hua said, sounding quite frustrated.

"Your mind is attached to the idea that your body is a solid object," said Daniels. "You must realize that you are made *entirely* of chi. Your living chi flows through your meridians, but even the cells, the molecules in your body are ultimately made of chi. As such, you can insert that chi into the energy around you. You can fade as easily as you can walk."

"Right," said Sam, and closed her eyes. She lifted her foot slightly as if taking a step. But then she disappeared. She faded forward a few inches, as if she actually *had* taken the step.

"Yes!" said Master Daniels. "That's it!"

"I did it?" asked Sam.

"Very good, Samantha," said Master Nash. "That's enough for now—we will continue this afternoon. Once you feel more confident, we'll try it over a greater distance. This is a big breakthrough—you should have time to master the skill before you leave."

Their tai chi lesson began, but Katana's thoughts still lingered on what they had just witnessed.

"Well, whatever the mission is, it sounds like it's going to happen soon," said Sara when they went back up to their room to shower.

"I know," said Katana. "And they're going to need to be able to fade over a long distance. I wish I knew what was going on."

For the rest of the week, they saw Sam and Master Hua trying to fade every morning before their tai chi class. Sam wasn't able to do it on Tuesday, but she had it again on Wednesday. Katana thought it must be like the other chen do, and she would get more consistent over time.

Chris started trying to surprise Sam into telling them what the mission was again, but Sam didn't fall for it. "I can't talk about it. I'm sorry," she would say every time, although it seemed to Katana like she *wanted* to tell them.

Nash had gone back to pushing hands in the morning tai chi class now that the tournament was behind them. He paired off with Katana on a few occasions. Each time, Katana could see faint wisps of shen extending from his aura. But no matter which one she tried to deflect, Nash would always send a pulse of chi along a different one to knock her down.

On Friday, Sam called everyone over to take a seat at the beginning of the sparring team practice. "Well, I have some good news," she began. "The tournament committee has disqualified Ed Golia for the rest of the season."

Everyone cheered, but Katana said, "Sam, Sebastian can still teach his students dim mak. What's to stop them from doing it in a sparring match again?"

"I wasn't done," said Sam, shaking her finger at Katana. "The committee also decided that if any of Sato's students ever use dim mak at a tournament again, his school will be permanently barred from competition. Don't worry, Katana, I don't think anyone will be trying *that* again.

"Now for the bad news. Well, it's not *that* bad. Apparently Sebastian, not Sato, is registered as the head coach for that school.

And Sebastian is filing an official complaint about Katana."

Everyone shouted in dismay.

"Settle down," said Sam. "He's claiming that it's against the rules for a girl to compete in the boys' division and that that's the reason Golia used a dim mak technique in the first place."

"That doesn't make any sense..." said Jason.

"He says that Ed held back during his match because he was taught 'never to hit a girl,'" Sam explained, rolling her eyes. "So he got upset when he realized he'd lost the match, and did the dim mak technique in the heat of anger."

"That's insane," said Jimmy. "Golia was definitely going all out against Kat—she beat him fair and square."

"I know," said Sam. "And more importantly, the coaches had an opportunity to contest this decision before the season started. I initially approached the tournament committee about Katana right after the end of last term. Sebastian had all summer to protest, and chose not to do so. Only after Kat beat one of their competitors did he decide to file his complaint.

"Don't worry; he's not going to win this—especially now, with the committee up in arms about the incident with Golia."

Sara and Chris walked in after Sam had started the practice. Katana told them the news on their way up to watch the wushu practice.

"Sebastian's a jerk," said Sara. "I'm so glad you beat Golia."

Katana and Sara went down to Sam's dojo on Saturday for their usual practice session. Katana felt like she wanted a break from sparring and the chen do for a little while, so she and Sara went with Jelly and Scott to work on tricks. Chris and Jason worked on sparring though, and Jason helped Chris with some of the feinting combinations they'd been working on during the team practices.

"Katana, you gotta try to levitate again," said Jelly.

"No way," she replied. "Not today. I've had enough of anything having to do with the chen do or dim mak or whatever. I just wanna trick."

Jelly looked at Sara, clearly stunned that anyone would choose *not* to work on levitating. Sara just shrugged.

They worked on tricks. Katana practiced the backflip variations she knew—like the flash kick and the X-out, which entailed kicking her legs out in a V-shape as she went over—then worked on the gainer and the gainer flash.

Once she'd tired herself out, Katana sat down to watch Chris and Jason. They were sparring for points, and they'd asked Sara to judge for them.

Katana thought about all the tricks she could do, and wondered if they were allowed in sparring. She considered it more, and realized that if they were, she could probably get a gainer flash to work. Why not? It was called a flash *kick* for a reason. She had to kick her legs over to do the trick—she could probably land one of them in a match.

"Hey Jason," she called out when they'd finished. "Are tricks allowed in sparring?"

"I have no idea. Why, you wanna try a backflip in a sparring match or something?"

"Yeah," said Katana, getting up to walk over to them.

"I was kidding..." said Jason, looking confused.

"Can I borrow your gear?" she asked; Chris handed it to her. She put it on and said to Jason, "Watch—just square off with me..."

"Okay..." he said, not knowing what she was up to.

"Don't move." She took one step forward with her left foot, then swung her right leg up toward Jason, into a gainer flash.

"I think I see where you're going with this," said Jason, looking thoughtful. "You're going to have to tilt sideways a little—throw the first leg over more like a roundhouse kick instead of a front kick."

She thought about it for a moment. "Okay, don't move." She tried it again, and did as Jason had suggested.

"You're right," she said. "That way I can get over faster, too. All right, let's try it for real."

"Wait a minute—I thought that was for real!" said Jason, backing up uncertainly.

"No, dummy, I have to try to kick you with it now. I was too far away that time."

"This is gonna hurt..." said Jason.

"Stop being a wuss," said Sara.

"You stand here while she does this!" said Jason.

"Shut up," said Katana. "I have to concentrate."

"Yes, please, concentrate!"

"I want you to block the first kick," said Katana, "and if this works, I should be able to get you in the ribs with my other foot."

"Right..." said Jason. "I'm ready... I guess."

Katana took a deep breath. She threw her first leg at Jason's head, like a roundhouse kick. He blocked that, but she was already going over. She caught him square in the ribs with her second foot. The kick knocked the wind out of him. But Katana had lost too much momentum to get over all the way. She ended up doing more of a back handspring—she had to put her hands down to avoid crashing.

"Hmm…" she said. "That didn't quite work."

"Looked good from here," said Sara with a shrug.

"Kat, that definitely worked. You got me really hard in the ribs," said Jason.

"Yeah, but I had to put my hands down," said Katana with a frown.

"She had to put her hands down…" muttered Jason in disbelief. "You *poor* baby!"

Katana wasn't satisfied. She talked to Sam about her idea at sushi that night. "I did it," she said, "but I had to put my hands down."

"You know, that might work," replied Sam pensively. "Nothing in the rules says you can't use tricks, but I don't think anyone's ever tried this before. There *is* a rule that says you can't put your hands on the floor while you're throwing a kick, though. So you're going to have to change that before you can use it in competition."

"Why do they have that rule?" asked Chris.

"There was this guy back in the seventies who would turn around and put his hands on the floor, and kick back with both legs like a donkey. He launched a few competitors right out of the ring with that move, so the tournament committee banned it the following year," said Sam. "I'll tell you what. We'll play with it more at practice this week. If you can get it consistently without hands before the next tournament, we'll go with it."

They ate their sushi in silence for a few minutes, then Katana asked, "Sam, how much do you know about the chen do of tai chi?"

"Not a whole lot, I'm afraid. Why?"

"Well, I did the form with Master Nash one day back in the beginning of the term, and I was able to hold the ball of energy the whole time. Nash said that's part of the chen do in tai chi. Then I tried deflecting intent when I was doing pushing hands with Jimmy one day—I could see his shen—and Nash said *that* is part of the chen do, too."

"Nash mentioned that," said Sam. "Go on."

"He's paired up with me a few times for pushing hands, and I can see his shen too—but it's way more complicated. There are like a bunch of wisps coming from him," said Katana, waving her arms around, "and he can... well, I'm pretty sure what he's doing is sending a pulse of chi along his shen. So that must be part of the chen do, too... right?"

"I think so," said Sam. "The chen do in tai chi is much more involved than any of the others. I know that."

"Is there anything else that's part of it? That seems like a lot more stuff than the other ones," said Katana.

"I think that's everything," said Sam uncertainly.

"Nash doesn't show you the chen do when you do tai chi lessons with him the way the other masters always do at the start of term?" asked Chris.

"No, he doesn't," said Sam with a sigh. "He has said that the chen do of tai chi is 'the realization that all the chen do are the same,' but I'm not sure what that's supposed to mean."

"It seems like dim mak is that way, too," said Chris.

"What do you mean?" asked Sam.

"Well, the chen do isn't just one thing. They can cause pain, and paralyze people... or stop your heart."

"But those skills are not chen do," said Sam. "When you use dim mak to cause paralysis, for example, you're disrupting the person's chi flow. But your chi isn't coming into contact with theirs. That's what makes the chen do different. When you do a chen do, your chi interacts directly with someone else's, or with the chi around you. As far as I know, dim mak has only one chen do: taking chi. Jaaku can use that skill to do the death touch, or to take someone's prenatal chi.

"But I have to be honest, we don't have a complete picture of how dim mak works."

"Why don't we ask Sebastian!" suggested Sara sarcastically. "Seems pretty certain he's an Arashi by now, so I'm sure he knows all about it!"

***

"Hey Jelly, are you going to the dance Friday?" asked Sara. It was Sunday night. Everyone was in the lounge, doing their homework.

Katana was at the next table, helping Chris with geometry. They'd gone beyond what he'd done back in Croton the previous year, so he was struggling almost as much with math now as he was with French. Katana was glad that Dana, at least, was having a much easier time with geometry than she'd had with algebra. Katana had spent many an evening the previous year dividing her time between Chris *and* Dana.

"There's no dance Friday," said Jelly, looking confused.

"Yeah there is—oh, wait, it's only for the high school kids," said Sara.

"Yeah, I can't go to that, fatty!" said Jelly. "You guys are so lucky that your dances are way better than ours."

"Well... you can if you go with me," she said.

"You mean like as a date?"

"Yeah... Why not? You wanna go, don't you?"

So that Friday night, Jelly went with Katana, Sara and Jason back to Lincoln for the high school dance. As much as Katana had enjoyed the Fall Ball, she thought it was nice to go to a dance without dressing up.

The high schoolers were also a lot less shy about dancing, Katana thought, than the kids at the middle school had been the previous year. Sara didn't have to drag everyone out by brute force.

They danced for a while, and finally the DJ played a slow song. Katana danced with Jason. "They make a cute couple," he said, pointing over her shoulder.

Katana turned to look. She realized he was talking about Sara and Jelly. "Yeah," she said, "except that she's so much taller!"

"Do you think they're gonna go out?" he asked.

"I don't know," said Katana. She'd never given it much thought.

But watching them now, she realized that it did seem as if they liked each other sometimes.

They took a break after the song was done, and went over to the refreshments. "I wanna trick," said Jelly.

"You always want to trick!" replied Sara.

But Jelly was already walking away. "Come on!" he said.

Jelly moved away to an empty spot on the floor. He started doing backflips and aerials, and linking different tricks together. Within a minute, a crowd had gathered around him. "He's *such* a show-off!" Sara complained.

"Yeah he is," said Katana. "So why are we letting him have all the fun?" She grabbed Sara by the hand and tried to pull her into the middle of Jelly's tricking circle.

"Save me!" Sara said pleadingly to Jason.

"Hey, don't look at me!" he said. "I can't even do a cartwheel!"

Katana let go of Sara's hand. She ran forward and did a huge gainer flash.

"Come on Sara!" she yelled. "Do something!"

The crowd that had gathered around them started cheering for Sara to jump in. "Oh, fine!" she yelled, running into the middle of the circle. She spun a round-off into an exceptionally high flash kick.

Katana had a better time in the trick circle than she'd had dancing. Jelly showed her and Sara how to link some of their tricks together. Katana almost forgot they had an audience.

They tired themselves out finally, and went to find Jason. He wasn't by the refreshments where they'd left him.

"I give up," said Katana. "I don't know where he is. Let's go outside though; it's sweltering in here." They walked outside and sat down on one of the benches in front of the school.

"I can't believe Chris and Jimmy wouldn't go tonight," said Jelly. Katana looked at Sara and shook her head.

"What?" asked Jelly.

"Those two are getting kinda antisocial these days," said Sara. "All they do is sit around and play video games."

"Well, they don't like dancing very much either," said Katana.

"Me neither," said Jelly. "I just like tricking."

"We know," mumbled Sara.

They went back inside a few minutes later and found Jason. He was quiet, and said he didn't feel like dancing anymore. They took the next bus back to the Hall. Jason said goodnight before heading into the lounge.

"What's up with him?" asked Sara as they walked up to Chris and Jimmy's room. "He's not in such a good mood all of a sudden."

"No idea," said Katana.

"Surprise, surprise," said Sara when they walked into the room. "You two are playing video games." But Chris and Jimmy didn't seem to hear her.

"It's hot," said Katana. "I'm going out on the balcony."

She went outside and sat on one of the deck chairs. Jelly and Sara followed. They talked for a few minutes, until Jelly fell asleep with his eyes open.

"That's so *freaky*!" said Sara. Just then, they heard the sound of the front doors opening below. Sara looked at Katana in surprise.

"Now who's sneaking out for midnight lessons?" Sara asked sarcastically. They stood up and looked over the railing. It was foggy; Katana found it difficult to see very far.

"It's Nash... and Sam!" whispered Sara. "And Hua's there, too!"

Sam and Master Hua walked with Nash out to the middle of the courtyard. Nash said, "This should do—give it a try." Katana thought that Nash sounded much closer than he was; she supposed it was a trick of the fog.

"Right," said Sam, and stood there for a moment. Then she started to take a step forward, and disappeared. For a moment Katana thought she might've just been hidden by the fog.

"That didn't work so well." It was Sam who'd spoken—Katana could hear her, but couldn't see where she'd gone.

"Over there," whispered Sara, pointing down. Sam had apparently faded to the front doors, but was now walking back toward Nash.

"You have to visualize your dojo, Samantha," said Nash. "Don't look at the front doors. Close your eyes if you have to, but you need to see your dojo in your mind's eye for this to work."

"Let's try it again," she replied. She stood still for a moment, then once again looked like she was taking a step forward. She disappeared.

Katana looked down at the front doors. When a patch of fog rolled by, she could tell that Sam wasn't there this time. It seemed that she'd made it to her dojo.

After a minute, the doors opened and Sam came outside again. She walked over to Master Nash. "I did it. All the way to the dojo."

"Good. Now do it again."

"I knew you were going to say that." Sam did it half a dozen more times before Nash was satisfied.

"Now you need to try to take Master Hua with you."

"Right..."

"You were able to do it inside the dojo, Samantha," Nash reassured her. "You know it's not any more difficult than going by yourself. As long as you extend your shen around him before you go, it will work."

Sam grabbed Master Hua around the waist, made like she was going to take a step forward, and then the two of them disappeared.

"That's cool," Sara whispered.

The two masters walked back out the front doors a minute later. Master Nash had Sam repeat the exercise a half dozen more times, taking Hua along with her each time.

"That's good for tonight," he said when they returned the last time. "This weekend we'll try it from downtown Eureka."

"Are you kidding?" asked Sam. Nash walked to the front doors without another word.

"I'll take that as a no," she muttered, following him into the Hall.

Katana walked inside. "You guys missed it. Sam faded from the courtyard all the way to her dojo!"

"Cool," said Chris, but kept playing the video game.

Katana shook her head.

"Hey! There's an army of Arashi out in the courtyard!"

"That's good," Jimmy said absently.

"Boys," said Katana, and walked back outside.

"I'm gonna go to bed," she said to Sara.

"Yeah, me too," said Sara. "I'm beat."

"Are we gonna wake up Jelly?"

"Nah, leave him here. He'll wake up eventually."

***

"Sam," said Katana when they sat down for sushi in her suite the next evening, "can you *please* tell us about this mission you're going on? We promise we won't tell anyone."

"Yeah," said Chris, looking hopeful. "We promise!"

For a moment, Katana thought Sam was going to crack. But she only laughed and said, "You get an A for effort—but I absolutely cannot discuss this."

"Did you fade from Eureka yet?" asked Sara with a mischievous grin.

"How do you know about that?"

"We were out on the balcony after the dance last night," said Sara.

"You're too much. And yes, for your information, I faded from downtown Eureka to my dojo this morning. That much I *can* tell you."

"Whenever I saw the Arashi fade last year, there was always a flash of light," Katana observed. "But that didn't happen when you did it. Why not?"

"It has something to do with the disturbance you create in

the surrounding field of energy," Sam explained. "The farther you fade, the stronger the disturbance. When someone moves across a great distance, the effect becomes strong enough to create a flash of light. But fading locally, like from the courtyard to my dojo, doesn't do that."

"What's the threshold?" asked Sara. "What's the shortest distance that will cause a flash?"

"I'm not sure," Sam replied. "Daniels knows more about this than I do."

"How far are you going to have to fade on your mission?" asked Katana.

"A whole lot farther than Eureka," she said with a sigh. "But I can't say where, so don't ask."

"How is it possible to fade long distances?" asked Sara, looking bewildered. "I guess it *kind of* makes sense going across a room or something... but not somewhere miles away."

"Well, what I realized today is that fading is exactly the same no matter how far you're trying to go. I always assumed it would be much more difficult to fade somewhere far away than it would be locally. But it's not. As long as you can clearly visualize the place you're trying to go, you can get there just as easily regardless of the distance.

"We get attached to ideas about what we can and cannot do," she continued, "like the notion that our bodies are solid physical objects. But to learn how to fade, you have to stop thinking so logically."

"So it's kinda like a koan," suggested Sara.

"Yes, exactly," said Sam.

"What's a koan?" asked Chris.

"It's a riddle," said Sam, "that doesn't have a logical answer."

"Like 'Imagine the sound of one hand clapping,'" added Sara.

Chris held up one hand, looked at it and said, "But you can't clap with one hand."

"Exactly!" said Sam. "You *can't* clap with one hand. But a 'clap' is just an idea. So by trying to think about what one hand clapping sounds like, you eventually realize that it doesn't sound like anything."

"I don't get it," said Chris.

"I think I do..." said Katana tentatively. "If you're attached to the *idea* of fading, and how impossible it seems, you'll never do it. But if you stop *thinking* about it, and let go of that idea, you can get it."

"Right," said Sam with a smile.

"Oh, I get it!" said Chris.

"Really?" asked Sara.

"No," said Chris. "Not at all."

"Eat your sandwich, Chris," said Sam, shaking her head.

***

A few hours later, Sam lay in bed, unable to fall asleep. She couldn't stop thinking about her breakthrough with fading. It felt so natural now, after all the difficulty she'd had with it. And it gave her greater confidence in the mission she would undertake with Hua.

But when was that mission going to start? Jaaku's attacks against the other temples had become more frequent. Yet Nash still lacked the key piece of information they required to achieve their objective.

He'd told Sam and Hua that the Shaolin Temple was working to solve the problem, but how much longer would it take? The delays had become frustrating. Sam wanted to get it over with already.

Sleep continued to elude her; she decided to get out of bed. It was almost two in the morning. She changed into a pair of karate pants and a tank top and ran down to her dojo. After stretching for a few minutes, she ran through several kata, trying to get her mind to stop racing. She felt her chi flowing as she moved from one stance to the next, throwing punches and kicks at imaginary opponents.

When she was done she sat down against the wall in full lotus position, her hands palm-up on her knees. Focusing on her breathing, inhaling through her nose and exhaling out her mouth, Sam allowed her anxiety to melt away. After several minutes of meditation, she rose to her feet to head back to her apartment. Hopefully now she'd be able to get some sleep.

But she stopped halfway across the atrium, gazing at the front doors. For some reason an old memory struck her at that moment, a time from her own days as a student here at the Hall. Adrian had broken up with one of his many girlfriends at a school dance. He'd run up to the girls' dorm to talk to Sam but her nosy roommate refused to give them any privacy. So instead, Sam and Adrian had gone down to the atrium, out the front doors and across Highway 101 to the beach.

On a whim, Sam closed her eyes and imagined the ocean. Releasing her chi, she faded to the beach—to the very spot she'd gone with Adrian that night so many years ago.

It was cool out, but Sam's chi was still flowing strong; she felt warm. She sat down in the sand, gazing out at the water, listening to the crashing of the waves. It seemed like only yesterday she'd sat here with Adrian. She could almost sense him sitting next to her now.

It was hard to believe he was gone. Despite the intervening years, she still felt his absence inside of her. She'd managed to suppress this feeling of loss for a long time, but lately it had resurfaced more powerfully than ever.

"Stupid," she muttered to herself, wiping tears from her eyes. Wallowing in memories wouldn't bring Adrian back. Nothing would.

She got to her feet and brushed the sand off her rear end. Closing her eyes, she faded back to her apartment.

The next morning, Sam and Hua met Nash in the tai chi dojo to continue working on fading. But Nash's expression was grim when they arrived. Sam knew something was up.

"I've had word from Shaolin," he told them. "They've finally acquired their spy. Someone deep within Jaaku's inner circle."

Hua grunted. "No fun job, eh? Dangerous."

"Does the spy have the information we need?" asked Sam.

"Not yet," said Nash. "But it's only a matter of time. Plan on leaving here right after the holidays. We'll have to make arrangements to cover your classes for the second term."

Sam had known this time would come eventually. But thus far, it had been an indefinite point in the future, looming somewhere over the horizon. Now it was real, imminent.

She trained harder than ever this morning.

Chapter Ten: Christmas in Croton

Sometime later, Katana and Chris decided they should invite Sara to spend Christmas in Vermont with them. Sara loved the idea. "Thank you guys *so* much—I hate going to Japan for Christmas!"

Chris called his mom to make sure it was okay with her, which they had no doubt it would be. Sara called her father in Japan. It took quite a bit more convincing than it had with Mrs. Boyd, but he finally agreed. They had Sara's dad call Chris's mom to make the arrangements.

Katana and Sara went down to Sam's dojo the next Saturday with Jelly and Scott. "So... are you gonna work on levitating today?" asked Jelly.

"Yeah, why not," said Katana with a sigh. "I don't know if I'm ever gonna get it though."

"You'll get it," said Jelly.

Katana stretched for a few minutes first, then she and Scott practiced the wall flip a few times. "Those are good," said Jelly. "You're getting a lot higher now—you're pushing off harder with your second foot, too."

"Jelly, you're a genius!" said Katana.

"Huh?"

"That's what I've gotta do to make the gainer flash work in sparring!" Katana had tried it a few more times on Jason since that first day, but kept ending up in a back handspring. She couldn't generate enough momentum to get over without touching her hands to the mat.

"I don't get it," said Jelly.

"I've gotta do it like a wall flip!" said Katana excitedly. "I've been throwing my leg up and going over right away. But that's wrong. I have to lean into it and push off harder."

"You're gonna pretend Jason's the wall," said Jelly with a grin. "I think you're right—that should work way better!"

"I hope he gets here soon. I wanna try this now."

"Did he stop being moody yet?" asked Sara.

"Yeah. I think he felt a little left out at the dance because we went to do tricks without him," said Katana. "Having a boyfriend is a lot more work than I thought it would be."

"Yeah," said Jelly, "boys are stupid. All right, come on! Try to levitate!" Sara gave him a funny look.

Katana and Scott tried running around the corner on the walls again. They could both get two steps on each wall, but couldn't get any higher than usual. "I don't know how I'm ever going to get this," said Katana.

"Just *do* it!" said Jelly.

"Okay," said Katana, "just do it." But she couldn't. "This isn't happening."

Jason and Chris came in a minute later. "Exactly the person I wanted to see!" said Katana.

"Yeah, I love you too, Kat," said Chris.

"No, not you!" she said. "Jason—I figured it out finally. I have to pretend I'm doing a wall flip and push off of you harder!"

"Oh, the gainer flash," said Jason. "Kat, you're pushing me back as it is; if you do it any harder you're gonna knock me right on my butt."

"I think it'll work," said Jelly, sizing Jason up. "But Kat, you're gonna go too high if you keep taking two steps. Unless you wanna kick him in the face..."

"Um, no," Jason said with a scowl.

"Right, so lunge in with one foot and jump, then push off him with the other foot and flip!" said Jelly, walking through the move right in front of Jason.

Jason smacked him in the head.

"Hey!"

"That's going to be a problem, though," Katana said thoughtfully. "They're not gonna stand there and *let* me do this."

"No," said Jason, walking through the move himself now. "But look, if you cock your fist back as you lunge, like you're gonna punch them in the head..."

"They'll keep their guard up to block, and I can stick my foot in their ribs," Katana finished for him.

They put on their gear, and she gave it a try. She lunged in with her hand pulled back for a punch, leaping into the air. She kicked her other foot out hard, and pushed herself over backwards. It worked—she over-rotated this time. She and Jason both fell down, landing on their rear ends.

"Ow," said Jason, rubbing his chest, and coughing to catch his breath. "You knocked the wind right outta me that time."

"That definitely worked though," said Katana. "I can only do this on someone bigger than me—I won't be able to push hard enough on anyone smaller than you."

She practiced the move several more times. She was able to fine-tune it enough that she could land her kick and push over without putting her hands down, but do it without hurting Jason.

"You owe me for this, Kat," said Jason when she was done.

"Now that you've had your fun," said Sara, "it's my turn. I am getting a chen do *today*. I promised myself I'd get one before the end of term."

"Hey, I had an idea about this," said Chris.

"Whoa!" said Jelly.

"What?" asked Chris.

"Oh, nothing," Jelly replied with a mischievous grin. "I just didn't know you had ideas."

Chris reached to smack him in the head, but Jelly backed up and stuck his tongue out at him. Chris started to chase after him, but Sara said, "Leave it alone—what's your idea already?"

Chris gave Jelly one more dirty look. "Well, when Kat deflected intent the first time, it was during a dragon circle..."

"And I got overwhelmed because Osaka called so many people at once," Katana added. "This is a great idea, Chris."

"Uh-oh," said Sara. "I don't know if I like the sound of this..."

"You said you wanted to get it," Katana reminded her. She had everyone make a circle around Sara. "We won't call out names—just attack her when you feel like it."

Sara prepared herself. Jason lunged in first; he tried to tackle her. Sara backed up and pushed down on the back of his head, knocking him to the floor.

Jelly attacked next, and tried to grab her in a bear hug. Sara simply picked him up and threw him to the mat.

"Hey!" he yelled. "That wasn't nice!"

"Shut up, shorty," said Sara.

Katana jumped in and threw a punch at her head. Sara blocked her punch, wrapped her arm, and swept her leg out, knocking her to the ground.

Scott attacked next. As Sara defended, Katana caught Chris's eye. She pointed at him, then at herself, and Chris nodded. When Sara was done with Scott, Chris lunged in with a punch. But as Sara blocked that, Katana jumped in and grabbed her from behind, throwing her arm around Sara's throat.

Sara squealed in surprise, but dropped down to a low stance and grabbed Katana's arm to flip her over. But as she grabbed Katana, Chris stepped in to try to punch her in the head again. Sara saw this and panicked. She closed her eyes and screamed, but threw her left hand out in front of her at the same time.

Chris fell over to the side.

"You got it!" he said, getting back to his feet.

Sara opened her eyes and asked timidly, "I did?"

"Sure looked like it," said Katana, letting her out of the stranglehold.

"Definitely," said Chris. "It felt exactly like it does when Jason does it."

"Yes!" said Sara.

She tried the chen do several more times but she only managed it twice more.

Katana and Jason could already deflect intent, so Chris, Jelly and Scott each took a turn. They set it up the same way they had for Sara. But none of them were able to match Sara's success. Jelly took a punch in the face for his trouble—Scott had grabbed him from behind, and Sara moved in to punch him. Jelly held out his hand the way Sara had done, but it didn't work. Sara's fist connected with his face.

"Oh Jelly—I'm so sorry!" she said.

"Ow! That hurt, fatty!"

***

It was the last week of classes at Lincoln Academy. The teachers spent all of their class time reviewing for exams, which were taking place the following week. Katana remembered everything in all of her classes, so she found that she was bored out of her mind.

On Friday at the team sparring practice—the last one of the term—Katana and Jason showed Sam the progress she'd made with the gainer flash.

"Wow, Kat," said Sam, looking quite impressed. "That definitely works. Keep working on it. You can use that as your secret weapon if you end up going against someone a lot bigger at Golden Gate."

"Hey, you going to dinner?" asked Jason at the end of practice.

"No, I'm sorry," said Katana. "I promised Jelly I'd come and watch tonight." She'd skipped the wushu team practice the past couple of Friday nights to have dinner with Jason and his friends.

"Oh, okay. I'll catch up with you later," said Jason, looking somewhat dejected.

Katana ran up to the wushu dojo with Sara and Chris. "Now he's gonna start pouting again," Sara observed.

"Hmm," said Katana. "Maybe. Oh well, I *did* promise Jelly."

Master Hua was running the team through tricks when they arrived, and he had the three of them join in. Chris had spent the entire term trying to clean up his backflip, and he was finally able to land it consistently. "Good, Chris. Try flash kick now?"

Chris thought about it for a minute. "No, I don't think so. I don't wanna screw up my backflip now that I finally have it."

When they were done with tricks, Master Hua said, "Katana, you have chains. Whole form now?"

"Yes..." said Katana.

"Show me," he said with a smile.

Katana always felt nervous performing for Hua. He was one of those people she never wanted to disappoint. Katana fetched a set of chains from the weapon rack, and walked to the corner of the floor. She'd only had the whole form for a couple of weeks. She'd still been feeling a little shaky with the butterfly kicks near the end—but she was determined not to screw it up in front of Master Hua.

She opened the form with a flash kick, then threw the chains out the moment her feet hit the floor. She whipped the chains around as fast as she could during the flowers in the beginning, and reminded herself to keep breathing. She got up to the butterfly kicks, and paused for a moment to focus. But she nailed them this time. She dropped down for the full body jumps—which had been consistent recently—and finished the form.

"Very good, very good," said Hua. The rest of the team cheered for her. "Now do again, with Dana, please."

Katana looked at Dana and sighed. "I was afraid this was going to happen," she said.

"Don't worry, Kat," Dana reassured her. "You can do it."

"Just don't go as fast as you went in Eureka!"

The girls went through the form together. Hua came over and patted Katana on the back when they were done. "Sasha graduating this year," he said. "Maybe next year Donnie do broadsword, you two girls do chains."

Dana and Katana looked at each other. "That would be really cool," said Katana.

At the end of practice, Paul asked, "Hey, do you three wanna come up to Hua's again? We're doing another movie night. Some team from Georgia has *two* kids doing double backflips together in their demo. Hua got the video from a buddy of his who coaches a team in that region."

"Yeah, definitely," said Katana. Sara and Chris both nodded.

Everyone went upstairs to shower and change, and met in Master Hua's suite. He'd ordered pizza again. They spread out around the sitting room and got comfortable while he started the video.

The quality of the footage wasn't very good but Katana could still make out what the team was doing. She didn't think they were very good; it sounded like the others agreed with her assessment. But then two of the performers moved to the back corners of the stage. They ran diagonally past each other, and did round-offs into perfect double backflips.

"That's not fair!" yelled Jelly.

"It was only a matter of time," said Paul. "But you don't think they'll make nationals, do you?" he asked Master Hua.

"Maybe," said Hua with a frown. "But first, have to beat Supernova—not so easy, eh?"

On their way back up to their rooms that night, Katana ran into Jason on his way out of the student lounge.

"Hi!" she said.

"Where were you?" said Jason. He didn't look happy.

"Uh-oh," said Sara quietly. She grabbed Chris. "Let's go," she said, dragging him up the stairs.

Katana watched them go, then turned to Jason. "We went to a movie night in Hua's room with the wushu team," she said. "Why?"

"Why? I thought we were going to hang out tonight, that's why."

"Oh… I'm sorry," said Katana, trying to pull him into a hug. Jason stepped away. "I didn't realize we had definite plans."

"Katana, sometimes you seem like you'd rather be with Chris."

"Chris? Jason, we're just friends," Katana replied as delicately as possible.

"If you say so," said Jason. He started up the stairs.

"Jason!" said Katana, but he kept going. Katana felt like she didn't know the first thing about having a boyfriend.

"Is he being moody again?" asked Sara when Katana got back to their room.

"Yeah," she replied with a sigh as she plopped down on the couch. "I guess we were supposed to hang out tonight."

"He seems like he's a little possessive," said Sara. "You hung out with him a *lot* the last two weekends."

"I know," said Katana. "I think he's jealous of Chris."

"Hmm," said Sara. "Well, maybe you just need a break—you have a whole month away from each other. You can both see how you feel when you get back."

For the rest of the weekend Katana spent most of her time in the student lounge with her friends, who were up to their eyeballs with textbooks and notes, studying for their upcoming exams. She quizzed Sara and Chris on the material they needed for French, but when the other two switched to geometry, Katana kept going through her French book instead.

"What are you doing?" asked Chris after watching Katana rifle through the appendices at the back of the book.

"Huh?" she said, looking up at him. "Oh—they have all the other tenses back here. I'm learning the past, past imperfect and future tenses for all the regular verbs."

"Are you kidding me?" asked Sara. "We don't need any of that for the exam!"

"I know," said Katana, burying her nose in the book. "But it's interesting. It's so logical. It's almost like math, in a way."

"Aren't you going to study for geometry?" asked Chris incredulously.

"Nah," said Katana. "I'm done studying."

"Done!" said Sara. "Kat, you haven't even started!"

But by the time they went to bed, Katana had taught herself everything else in the rest of their French text. Sara and Chris both thought she was crazy, but she breezed through their exams that week without so much as touching her notes.

"I don't know how you get straight A's every term without studying," said Sara as they went down to dinner Friday evening. "I don't have to work as hard as Chris, but you didn't study at all!"

"I don't know," said Katana. "I was a little nervous about it after what Sam said at the beginning of term—remember, she said high school would be harder? But it wasn't."

Chris and Sara looked at each other in disbelief.

The three of them were leaving first thing the following morning to go back to Croton. Katana and Sara decided to sit at the sushi bar since they'd be missing their weekly meal with Sam for a whole month.

"Hi, Terry-san," said Sara as they sat down on the stools.

"Konichiwa," said Terry-san.

Sara ordered, and Terry-san began preparing the sushi for them. "Make sure you girls say goodbye to Master Samantha before you go," he said. "She may not be back for a long time."

"What?!" asked Katana.

"What are you talking about?" asked Sara.

"Oh... You don't know about the mission?" asked Terry-san.

"No!" said Sara. "We know there is one, but no one will tell us what it is!"

"But you do!" said Katana. "Terry-san, what's it all about? We know she's going with Master Hua, but no one will tell us where they're going!"

"I should not have said anything," he said regretfully. "I assumed she would have told you two about it."

"Can you at least tell us *when* they're leaving?" asked Katana.

"No, I'm sorry girls. If Master Samantha has not told you, it is not my place to do so."

"How do you know about the mission?" asked Sara. "I thought it was supposed to be a big secret?"

"Ah," said Terry-san. "It is. But headmasters tell their sushi chefs *everything*."

***

Katana and Sara got up early the next morning. There was a knock on the door as Sara came out of the bathroom.

"Hi," said Katana when Jason walked in.

"Well, I'm outta here," he said. He gave her a kiss, and Sara turned away.

"Don't mind me," she said. "It's not like I'm standing here or anything!"

Katana gave Jason a hug. "Well, have a good holiday."

Once Katana had closed the door behind him Sara asked, "So you two patched everything up?"

"Yeah, for now," said Katana. "We talked last night. I guess he felt like I was spending more time with you and Chris and everyone than I was with him. I don't know."

"Boys," said Sara, and finished getting ready.

Once they had everything together, they dragged their suitcases downstairs and met Chris and Sam in the atrium. She was driving them to the airport in one of the big SUVs. She helped them load their luggage into the back, and they climbed in.

"Sam," said Katana as they pulled onto Highway 101, "Terry-san said you're leaving soon and not coming back for a long time. How long is a long time, exactly?"

"Terry-san needs to learn to keep his mouth shut," said Sam, shaking her head.

"Well, he thought you'd already told us," said Katana. "He didn't say anything else once he realized that you hadn't. But you *are* leaving soon, aren't you?"

"Yes, Kat. Probably right after the first of the year," said Sam with a grim smile. "Listen, all three of you—Nash is going to tell everyone that Master Hua and I are taking a leave of absence to go train at the Shaolin Temple. I need you to go along with that story, and pretend that you don't know anything else. Promise?"

"We promise," they agreed reluctantly.

"Do you know how long you're going to be away?" asked Sara from the back seat.

"No, I don't," said Sam.

The three of them kept asking questions about the mission the rest of the way to the airport, but Sam wouldn't give up any more information. She walked them to their gate, and gave them each a big hug. Katana thought she could see tears welling up in her eyes. "Sam... you *are* coming back, aren't you?"

"Yes, I'm coming back," she said. "I promise."

"I'm worried," said Sara when they got to their seats on the plane. "Sam seemed really upset."

"Yeah, she did," Katana agreed.

The three of them slept for most of the trip. They went outside to find Mrs. Boyd's Jeep once they had collected their luggage at the airport.

"Hi, Mom," said Chris as he got in the front seat.

Mrs. Boyd reached over and gave him a kiss. "Hi Sara, I'm Nancy Boyd," she called over to the back seat. "I'm sorry my son's manners are so poor that he didn't bother to introduce us."

"Oh, don't worry about it," said Sara.

"Well Chris, you told me she was pretty, but I think she's absolutely gorgeous!" said Mrs. Boyd.

"Mom!" said Chris. Katana stifled a giggle. She wondered if Sara was going to turn a deeper shade of red than Chris.

***

During the next few days, Katana and Chris showed Sara around Croton. It hadn't snowed yet, but it was bitterly cold. They had to bundle up before they went out. The three of them also spent a lot of time training at Sensei Mike's dojo.

"Wow," said Sara. "So this is where Osaka used to teach."

"Yeah," said Chris. "It's a *lot* smaller than any of the dojo at the Hall."

"It's the same size as my school in Japan," said Sara.

They spent Christmas Eve at Chris's house, and the Boyds made an enormous amount of food. Katana's aunt Leanna came over when she got out of work, and they went into the living room to open presents after dinner. The Boyds always seemed to get at least as many presents for Katana as they did for Chris. This year they'd done the same for Sara. But the highlight of the evening was the new computer Leanna had bought for Katana.

"Cool," said Sara. "Now I can talk to you more over the summer."

They sat up late around the fireplace. Katana and Sara both stayed at the Boyd's house that night, in the room that Katana always used. Katana woke up early Christmas morning when Sara got out of bed. By the delicious aromas drifting into the room, she could tell that Mr. and Mrs. Boyd were already hard at work preparing Christmas dinner.

She followed Sara into the living room. Looking out the window, she discovered it was snowing. "I love snow on Christmas."

"Hey, Kat," said Mrs. Boyd, poking her head in from the kitchen.

"Good morning," said Katana with a smile.

"Can you two go wake up Chris for me, please?" she asked. "He'll sleep right through dinner if we don't drag him out of bed."

Katana looked at Sara with a mischievous smile and said, "Yeah, sure!" Then she said to Sara, "Follow me."

She led Sara outside, through the snow to the barn the Boyds used as a garage.

"Kat, what on earth are we doing out here?"

Katana was rummaging through a big box on one of the shelves. Finally she held up two water guns and said, "We're getting ready to wake up Chris!"

"Yes!" said Sara.

They filled the guns with frigid water at the spigot on the side of the house, then went up to Chris's room. "Wake up, Chris!" Katana yelled as they both opened fire.

Chris woke up faster than Katana had ever seen him wake up in her entire life. "ARGH!" he yelled. "That's FREEZING!" He grabbed his pillow and began battering them with it.

Finally Chris grabbed Sara's water gun. Katana and Sara ran downstairs, Chris in hot pursuit. He opened fire as Sara got to the bottom of the stairs. But she ducked and he missed—hitting his dad in the face instead.

"Morning," said Chris, trying to hide the water gun behind his back. Mr. Boyd gave him a stern look, which Katana didn't think looked very serious for all the water dripping down his face. He held out his hand and Chris turned over the water gun.

Sara went to shower and Katana and Chris returned to his room. Katana sat down in the beanbag chair in the corner as Chris flopped down in his bed. "So," she said with a bemused expression, "you told your mom Sara's pretty?"

Chris turned a bright shade of red. "Well, she is, isn't she?"

"You don't have a crush on her, do you?"

"Not on Sara, I don't," Chris said evasively.

"Not on Sara... but you like someone. Who is it?" asked Katana. Chris did his best to change the subject, but Katana was relentless.

"Fine!" he said finally. "Olivia Gomez."

"Really?"

"Yeah—what's wrong with that?" asked Chris, misinterpreting the look on Katana's face.

"Nothing! She's really pretty. I don't know how you can tell her apart from Sierra—they're identical twins. I can't tell them apart to save my life."

"Yeah..." said Chris, looking even more embarrassed now. "I'm actually not sure Olivia's the one I like... But Jimmy likes the other one."

The three of them hung out by the fireplace for the rest of the morning, and talked to some of their friends from the Hall on the computer. Leanna came over a little later, and everyone sat down for dinner.

The Boyds were known for preparing a ridiculous amount of food for the holidays, and they'd outdone themselves this year. Katana assumed this was for Sara's benefit.

"I'm stuffed," said Sara, leaning back from the table partway through the meal. "That was really good."

"Full already?" said Mrs. Boyd, sounding disappointed.

"That was only the appetizer," said Chris with a sigh.

"Are you kidding me?" asked Sara in alarm.

It was no joke. They'd already had a full round of appetizers, and lots of shrimp, and lasagna, but the Boyds were just getting started.

Ham and turkey and a dish with rice and more shrimp came out next, and Mrs. Boyd insisted that Sara keep eating.

"Okay..." she said, digging in.

By the end of dinner Katana was so full that she was afraid she'd be sick if she tried to move. Everyone else seemed to feel the same way, so they sat around the dinner table and talked for another hour or so. Sara told them all about living in Japan.

Finally Sara excused herself from the table, and Katana felt a twinge of worry. She hadn't caught Sara forcing herself to vomit for several weeks now, but she felt suspicious nonetheless. She excused herself a minute later to follow her.

And sure enough, when she got upstairs, she heard Sara retching in the bathroom. Katana knew she needed to do something. The idea of ratting out her friend wasn't too attractive—she'd been through something like this the previous year. But being labeled a "rat" was a small price to pay; Sara needed help. Katana decided to talk to Mrs. Boyd as soon as she had an opportunity to do so without Chris or Sara overhearing. Hopefully she'd know what to do.

On Monday, Katana and Chris dragged Sara to the karate school to work out for a while. Sensei Mike was walking around the dojo, talking on the phone when they arrived. They went to change into their uniforms.

After stretching for a while, Chris told Sensei Mike about the way Katana was using the gainer flash in sparring. Mike asked to see it. Katana performed it on him, and realized that it worked even better on someone taller and heavier than it had on Jason. She had no problem getting over without touching the ground, and Mike didn't fall back as far as Jason always did.

"That's incredible," said Mike, clearly impressed with the move. "I don't imagine anyone's going to be expecting *that* in a tournament!"

They goofed around sparring for a while, then Mike asked Chris if he could deflect intent yet.

Chris merely scowled, but Sara said, "No, but I can!"

Katana attacked for her, and she did the chen do several times. "I was worried I wouldn't be able to do it again."

"Yeah, I was too, after I did it the first time," said Katana. "Sam made me show it to the whole class when I first got to the Hall, remember? And that was only the second time I'd ever done it."

Mrs. Boyd came to pick them up later that afternoon. When they returned to the house, Katana stalled as Chris and Sara got out off the Jeep. "Mrs. Boyd, can I talk to you in private?"

"Sure, Kat." She rolled down the window and called out to Chris. "Katana and I are going for a ride. We'll be back in a little while."

Chris looked confused, but shrugged and walked into the house. Sara stood inside the door, looking at them as they pulled away. Katana wondered if Sara knew what she was up to.

Mrs. Boyd drove to Turtle Beach.

"What's going on, Kat?"

She worried that Sara would be angry with her for doing this, but she had to do *something*. Even if it meant sacrificing her friendship, she knew Sara needed help.

"I'm worried about Sara," Katana began. "I followed her

upstairs after Christmas dinner, and I heard her throwing up in the bathroom. That happened a few times at the Hall, and it seemed like she was doing it on purpose. But then she didn't do it for a long time."

"It's possible she was still doing it, but hiding it better," said Mrs. Boyd, looking quite concerned.

"Do you think she's making herself throw up to try and lose weight or something?"

"Yes, Katana, that's exactly what I think. A friend of mine at work went through this with her daughter. It turned out she had bulimia."

"What's that?" asked Katana.

"It's an eating disorder," said Mrs. Boyd. "I guess people with bulimia often don't feel good about their bodies, and think they're too fat, even if they're not. They eat a lot of food when they're feeling bad, but throw it up because they don't want to gain weight."

"What can we do?"

"I'll call my friend and get the number of her doctor—they were very happy with him. And I'll call Sara's dad in Japan. He needs to know about this, obviously. But one of us should sit down and talk with her about it."

Mrs. Boyd offered to approach Sara, but Katana felt like this was something she needed to do herself. They returned to the house and Mrs. Boyd found an excuse to drag Chris and his dad out of the house.

Katana went into the spare bedroom. Sara was lying in bed. "Where'd you go?"

"I had to talk to Mrs. Boyd," Katana replied. She felt anxious—she had no idea how to start this conversation.

"What about?" asked Sara.

Katana paused. "You." Sara rolled onto her side, turning her back to Katana. They sat in silence for a minute; Katana tried several times to start talking again, but couldn't get the words out. Sara got out of bed and stormed past her, running out of the room.

"Sara!" Katana followed her. Sara was in the living room, staring out the window. She had her arms folded across her chest, as if she were trying to hug herself. Katana walked up to her, placing one hand on her shoulder. Sara shrugged her off.

"Sara... Mrs. Boyd says she knows a doctor you can talk to..."

"About what?!"

Katana sighed. "You're making yourself throw up all the time." Sara didn't answer. "I know you're doing it to try to lose weight, but Sara, you're not fat. You look great. All the boys at school think you're hot..."

"Whatever, Kat."

"It's true! Look, throwing up like that isn't healthy. You could get really sick. Mrs. Boyd has a friend at work, and their daughter did this. She had an eating disorder, Sara. You should go to the doctor. They can help..."

"I DON'T NEED HELP!" Sara screamed, turning to face Katana. Tears were streaming down her face.

"Sara, you don't have to do this anymore." Sara turned to look out the window again. "The doctor can help you and you'll feel better..."

"I can't believe you told Chris's mom," said Sara, shaking her head.

"I had to. I didn't know what else to do."

"It wasn't enough that you're better than me at *everything*—you had to rat me out, too. Now she must think I'm crazy..."

"She doesn't think that! She wants to *help* you!"

"How is a doctor going to help? I'm ugly, Kat. Doctors can't fix *that*."

"You're *not* ugly."

"Next to you I am!" Sara faced her again. "You're freakin' gorgeous. Why do you think *you* got asked to the Fall Ball and *I* didn't? I can't compete with you—you'll *always* be prettier than I am." Katana was stunned. "I figured if I could just lose some weight it'd be better. But it won't. You're still prettier, and smarter, and better at karate..."

"Sara! None of that is true."

"Who made the sparring team, Kat?!" Sara shouted. "Who can do all the chen do? Who always aces her classes without studying? Not me—that's for sure!"

Katana didn't know what she'd expected from this conversation, but this certainly wasn't it. "What are you talking about? Your grades are just as good..."

"STOP!" Sara screamed. "Just *leave me alone!*" She ran back into the bedroom and slammed the door behind her.

Katana couldn't believe what she'd just heard. She'd never known that *she* was playing any role in making Sara feel so bad about herself.

Mrs. Boyd talked to Sara's father, and set up a meeting for

Sara with her friend's doctor. Sara reluctantly agreed to go. The doctor called the guidance department at Lincoln Academy. One of the counselors specialized in eating disorders, so they set up an appointment for Sara to see her at the beginning of the next term.

Katana told Chris what was going on, but warned him not to say anything unless Sara brought it up first. But Sara didn't bring it up—with Chris *or* Katana. They enjoyed the remainder of the vacation as if nothing had happened. Katana didn't understand what Sara was going through, but she was relieved that she was getting help.

Chapter Eleven: The Mission Begins

Sam walked into the atrium with a huge duffel bag over her shoulder. Gerald, Nash and Master Hua were there already. "I'm not late, am I?" she asked with a lightheartedness that she didn't feel.

"I'll be waiting in the car," said Gerald quietly before walking out the giant oak doors.

"This is it," said Master Nash, giving them each a hug, and slapping them on the back. "Fu is waiting for you in Hawaii. Stick to the plan. I want you both to train there for a couple of weeks, and Sam..."

"I know," she said. "We've been over it a hundred times. We'll do it, don't worry."

But Sam didn't feel so confident. A powerful sense of dread had overcome her the previous evening. Looking around the Hall, she wondered if she'd ever see the place again.

She walked out to the limousine with Master Hua. Gerald drove them down Highway 101 to Eureka Airport, over to a hangar at the end of one of the runways. Sam and Master Hua retrieved their bags from the trunk.

"Well, Gerald, if everything goes according to plan, we'll see you again in a couple of weeks," said Sam.

"I'll be ready," said Gerald, giving them both a hug. "Good luck."

Sam and Hua walked into the hangar and boarded the Hall's private jet. They sat in silence for the entire trip.

When the plane landed, Master Hua followed Sam across the tarmac to a man sitting on the hood of a Jeep. "Nelson!" said Sam, running the last several feet. The man jumped off the front of the Jeep, and walked over to pick up Sam in a big bear hug.

"Samantha, how are you?" he asked. "It's been ages. This is your first time back in Hawaii?"

"Yes, that's right. This is Nelson Fu," Sam said to Master Hua. "Nelson, this is..."

"Master Hua Xiang, I know," he said shaking his hand. "I attended the seminar you gave in Baltimore at the big wushu tournament last year. It's a pleasure."

"Ah, yes," said Master Hua.

They climbed into the Jeep, and Nelson drove them across the island, up the coast. They followed an isolated road that hugged the coastline along the top of a cliff. They arrived at a clearing in the woods, and Nelson parked the Jeep in front of a one-story building at the end of the parking lot. A driveway extended behind the first building up to a little house right at the edge of the cliff.

"This sure brings back memories," said Sam as she got out of the Jeep.

"So how's Osaka doing these days?" asked Nelson. "I haven't seen him in... well, since he sold me this place, actually."

"Sold it to you for a song," said Sam.

"That he did," agreed Nelson. "The land, and the dojo. I was able to save enough money to build my house and pay for it in cash. I owe that man quite a lot."

"Don't we all. He's doing well. He's back at the Hall now. Something's different about him lately, though." said Sam.

"How do you mean?" asked Nelson.

"I don't know—I can't put my finger on it. He keeps things to himself a lot more these days. He's not as open as he used to be when we were at UH.

"Hey, is that the memorial over there?" she asked, walking to a large stone sticking out of the ground at the edge of the cliff.

"That's right, you haven't seen that yet," said Nelson. He and Master Hua followed her over to the stone.

"Immortal in our memories," Sam read. "Adrian and Kristine Kahanu."

She couldn't believe it had been so long since she first heard the terrible news. She'd never forget the profound sadness in Osaka's voice as he told her. He'd barely been able to choke out the words: "Adrian and Kristine... are dead."

"Katana's parents?" asked Master Hua quietly.

"Yes," said Sam, fighting back tears. "I guess their car went off the cliff, right here."

"So... can Katana really do two of the chen do already?" asked Nelson.

"She's almost got a third," said Sam with a sniffle. "One of her friends is trying to teach her levitation."

"Really?" asked Nelson.

"Yes," said Master Hua. "She get levitation soon—very close now."

"Isn't she only like thirteen?" asked Nelson.

"Fourteen," said Sam. "She just turned fourteen. You should see her, Nelson. She reminds me so much of Adrian. She moves like him when she does kata. And her eyes—they're this vivid green—I don't know where that comes from. But when she looks at you, you feel like she's looking right through you—just like Adrian."

"Yeah," said Nelson. "That made it scary to spar with him. It looked like he was going to kill you! Come to think of it, you always had that look too..."

"You train at Hall of Dragon as well?" asked Master Hua.

"Oh, no—not me. I met Sam and Adrian at the University of Hawaii," said Nelson.

Sam gazed over the cliff, imagining the fiery wreck of Adrian's car on the rocks below. It was too much to bear.

"Well, let's get started," she said, turning to walk back to the dojo. "Reliving the past isn't going to get this mission done."

"You wanna go up to the house first and drop your stuff off?" asked Nelson.

"No," said Sam. "We have work to do. The sooner we do it, the sooner we can get out of here. No offense, Nelson."

"None taken," he said. "So, Master Hua, I began my training in wushu, and it'll always be my first love, of course. But I started kempo in college, with Master Osaka, and I've been getting pretty heavily into the sport karate scene the last few years.

"All the demo teams out there now are either straight wushu, or straight sport karate—none of the teams put the two styles together. So I've been thinking, what if someone assembled a team that used the best of both worlds? Imagine having a samurai sword set, a wushu staff set, then nunchucks and double whip chain?"

Master Hua raised his eyebrows. "Interesting—use the best weapons."

"Right, exactly," said Nelson, becoming more excited as he talked. "And I think you could do some intense choreography with that... Well, we have other things to worry about right now, obviously, but I'd like to talk to you about this more sometime. I'd love to come to the Hall of the Dragon and work with you on this. Do you think Master Nash would consider taking on an extra staff member?"

Master Hua shrugged. "Maybe—we can talk to him."

"He's always saying the arts have to evolve," said Sam. "I bet he'd be interested in the idea."

They arrived at the dojo. Nelson unlocked it and opened the door for them, following them inside.

"Wow," said Sam. "It looks exactly like it did the last time I was here."

Sam and Master Hua put down their bags and went into the dojo to stretch. "So Nash tells me you're supposed to work on fading, and train here for a couple of weeks. Then he wants you to fade back to the Hall of the Dragon?" asked Nelson.

"Yeah, that's the plan," said Sam with a sigh. "I'd rather do it now and get it over with, though."

"I guess he wants you to fade here a bunch first. He says doing it in unfamiliar territory is useful to..."

"To build the skill," said Sam. "I know."

They finished stretching and Sam said, "Nash wants us to go two on one, using whatever chen do we can. I guess I'll go first!"

"Okay," said Nelson. "I can do a chi hit, deflect intent and levitate."

"Same with Hua," said Sam, and Master Hua nodded. "I can't levitate, but I can fade, obviously. Let's do it!"

Sam and Master Hua took turns for the next couple of hours fighting one against two. Nelson was not accompanying them any further on their mission, so he didn't need the extra training.

They used external techniques as well as chen do. Sam had no trouble fading. Every time the other two ganged up on her, she simply faded behind one man, threw him to the floor, and fought the other.

Master Hua used levitation the same way. If they both attacked him at once, he would flip over them, and attack one of them from behind.

Sam showed Nelson how to use a ball of energy to catch someone else's fireball, like Katana had done to Jason. "She came up with this on her own, huh?" he asked. "Are you sure she's only fourteen?"

Once the three of them were thoroughly exhausted, they took a break. "So what exactly is this mission about, anyway?" asked Nelson as he sat down on the mat.

"Sorry Nelson, Nash won't let us discuss it with anyone," said Sam. "He says the key to our success lies in secrecy. I guess he figures if nobody knows what we're doing, nobody can let anything slip."

"Good call," said Nelson. "That's probably enough for today. Right?"

"Yes," said Sam. "That's enough. I'm beat. So are you gonna feed us?"

"No, I thought I'd let the two of you starve for two weeks," said Nelson sarcastically. "Of course I'm going to feed you. Get your stuff—I'll take you up to the house."

***

Katana returned to the Hall of the Dragon near the end of January. She went with Sara and Chris down to the student lounge as soon as they arrived.

"Hey!" yelled Jelly from the other end of the room. "Fatty's back!"

Katana glared at him. She marched straight across the lounge, grabbed him by one arm, and dragged him into the cafeteria. The room was only dimly lit, as it had been empty since dinner. "Look, you can't call her that anymore," she said sternly.

"Why?" asked Jelly, looking confused. "I'm just teasing her, she knows that..."

"You have to swear you won't tell her I told you this," said Katana, and continued when he agreed. "Sara's got an eating disorder. She stuffs her face when she's feeling bad, and pukes everything back up on purpose. She thinks she's fat and ugly."

"Are you kidding me?" asked Jelly, looking utterly dumbfounded. "She's the hottest girl in the whole grade! Everyone thinks so!"

"Well try telling her that instead of calling her 'fatty'!" said Katana.

"I will," said Jelly. "I was gonna ask her out when we got back from break."

"Aw, really?" asked Katana.

"Yeah... I've wanted to ask her out since last year. But I didn't think she'd say yes."

"Why not?" asked Katana.

"Well, she's older than me, and a lot taller and... I don't know, usually the hot girls have boyfriends already. But when she asked me to the dance at the end of last term, I thought I might have a shot," he said with a smile.

"That's so cool. You two make a cute couple," said Katana.

"Thanks," said Jelly. Suddenly he looked stern and pointed a finger in Katana's face. "I'll stop calling her 'fatty,' but you gotta get her to stop calling me short!"

"But Jelly... you *are* short!" said Katana. She squealed as he tried to smack her on the head.

They returned to the lounge. Sara asked, "What was that about?" when Katana sat down next to her on the couch.

"Oh, nothing," said Katana. "I wanted to yell at him for being so short."

"Oh," Sara replied.

A few minutes later, Katana smiled to herself when Jelly came over and said, "Hey, Sara—I gotta talk to you for a minute."

When Katana walked into the wushu dojo for class the next afternoon, she was surprised to see Nash there. She knew Master Hua was gone, but somehow seeing Nash start the class made it seem more real. When she heard the chatter break out all over the dojo, she remembered that nobody besides her, Chris and Sara, had known this was coming.

"Everyone please kneel," said Master Nash. "Master Hua and Master Malloy have gone on a leave of absence for the second term. They will be training at the Shaolin Temple in China and a couple of the other temples in the network. For the duration of the term, I will be running the wushu classes for Master Hua, and coaching the demo team. Bobby Wellington will be taking over the tae kwon do classes for Master Malloy, and coaching the sparring team. I apologize for the short notice, but we do expect them both to return to us by the end of the term."

Master Nash took them through the same warm-up exercises and stretches that Master Hua always did, then lined them up in four lines on the springboard floor to work on tricks. Once everyone had had a few turns through the line, he said, "Master Hua planned to have you start linking tricks together this term. We'll be sticking to that plan.

"First, we will be doing a front aerial to an aerial into a split," he said. "Please pay attention." He took two steps into a front aerial, and launched from that into a regular aerial without any steps in between. At the end of the aerial, instead of landing on his feet, his left foot continued forward and he landed in a perfect front split.

Several of the students gasped, and someone at the other end of the floor yelled, "I didn't know Nash could trick!"

Everyone laughed. Master Nash said, "Yes, I can trick. I am

slowing down a little in my old age, however. I used to be able to do aerials both ways—now I can only do them on my left side."

"And he calls that slowing down?" whispered Chris. "I still can't do a split on either leg!"

Master Nash had them try the aerial into the front split first. Then they worked on going from the front aerial right into the regular aerial without any steps in between. Eventually, Katana and Dana were able to link all three elements together.

"Very good, girls," said Master Nash when he came over to watch them. "Master Hua wrote in his notes that he was considering adding this combination to the demo. We'll have to try it on Friday."

Katana was surprised to see Dana scowl at him when he walked away. "What's wrong? Don't you like Nash?" she asked.

"Nash is fine, I guess—but this is Hua's team! He shouldn't be messing with the demo. And I can't believe Hua would go away like this without telling us!"

Katana suddenly felt very guilty for withholding information from Dana. But she'd promised Sam she wouldn't say a word about the mission to anyone.

"Well, he did say he was following Hua's notes," Katana pointed out.

"Yeah, I guess," said Dana.

Katana arrived at Sam's dojo the next afternoon, and had half-forgotten until she walked in the door that Sam wouldn't be there. Bobby Wellington lined up the class. He'd been assisting Sam during the first term, and had been one of Van Heldon's assistants the year before.

Everyone knelt down. Bobby gave them a speech that was virtually identical to the one Nash had given the wushu class the day before.

"Is she really training at Shaolin?" asked Jimmy. "Or is that what they're telling us because she left and isn't coming back?" Katana was surprised at first that Jimmy was taking this so hard. Tears were welling up in his eyes. But then she remembered how Sam had helped him out the previous year when Van Heldon was nasty to him.

"No, Jimmy, she's definitely coming back," Bobby assured him. "I stayed here over break and worked with her the whole time. She just left a week ago. She went over her lesson plans with me for the entire term—several times," he said, rolling his eyes. "She's really going to Shaolin, and at least one other temple. And she's definitely coming back."

Bobby started the class like Sam always did, and split them into four groups to work on sparring. "Golden Gate isn't that far away, people," he said.

After he'd gone around to all four groups and run several matches, Bobby called Katana into the ring. "You and me," he said. "Sam wants you to keep working your gainer flash. So you get to do it on me!"

"Oh great," she said sarcastically, but was actually happy for the opportunity.

"We won't go for points or anything—throw in your move whenever you want," he said.

They circled around each other, then Bobby launched a series of kicks at her head. Katana was able to block these, then moved in with one of the feinting combinations they'd practiced during the first term. "You're too tall," she complained. "I can't *reach* your head with a kick!"

They kept going, and finally Katana decided to try the gainer flash. She lunged in and cocked her hand back to fake a punch, then jumped up and pushed off with one foot, just like in the wall flip. It worked just as well on Bobby as it had on Sensei Mike.

"Whoa!" said Bobby. "Well, that definitely works. I didn't see it coming—I thought you were jumping for a punch! Nice job, Kat."

By the end of class, Katana decided that Bobby was an excellent teacher. He'd always done a good job helping Sam with the class. But Katana thought he'd done equally well leading the class. Katana hoped she could teach like that herself one day.

For the rest of the week all the buzz around the school was about Sam and Master Hua's seemingly sudden departure. A lot of people were suspicious about the story Nash and Bobby had given them. They started inventing a variety of alternative explanations. Katana heard one boy say that they'd left to start their own temple together.

But Dana seemed deeply hurt that Hua hadn't told her he'd be leaving. Jimmy seemed to feel the same way about Sam. Katana talked to Sara about the situation Tuesday night as they were getting ready for bed. But Sara agreed that they couldn't tell them anything because they'd promised Sam that they wouldn't.

Sara also asked Katana if she'd go with her to her first counseling session, which was scheduled for the following afternoon. It was the first time she'd raised the subject. Neither had spoken a single word about Sara's outburst at the Boyd's house.

"Sure! Do they allow that?" asked Katana.

"Yeah," said Sara. "They said I can bring a friend if I want."

Katana didn't feel entirely comfortable with this, but she went to support Sara. The discussion was illuminating. Katana had never realized how insecure Sara truly was. And Katana had to confess— she didn't understand where this came from. Sara was smart, incredibly talented at martial arts, and the envy of most girls for her physical beauty. But Katana also learned that Sara didn't view herself that way.

The counselor knew that Katana and Sara were best friends and roommates. She asked Katana if she'd be willing to help out. She wanted her to keep an eye on Sara, and be there to talk when she was feeling bad about herself. She also asked Katana to remind Sara of what they'd discussed during the counseling session if Sara seemed like she was going to go on a binge.

"I can do that," said Katana. "I'd do anything for this girl."

Katana asked Osaka about the mission during their private lesson that Thursday. He refused to tell them anything more than they already knew. "Sam seemed worried about it when she dropped us off at the airport for winter recess," said Sara.

"I can tell you that it's quite dangerous," said Osaka. "But that is the reason for the secrecy. If the wrong people were to find out what they are attempting... it would go very badly for both of them. However, if they are successful, we will all be safer in the long run."

Katana was excited to go to Sam's dojo that Saturday. She was eager to work on linking tricks the way Nash had shown them.

"I can't get it," said Jelly. "I can do a split, but I can't stop myself from putting my foot down at the end of the aerial!"

"You mean for once *I* get to help *you* with a trick?" teased Katana.

With Katana's help, and a few hours of hard work, Sara and Jelly were both finally able to get the combination. Chris couldn't do a split in the first place, but was at least able to link the front aerial with the regular aerial. Scott was having the same problem as Jelly, though, and despite Katana's help, couldn't get himself to stop putting his foot down at the end of the aerial.

Eventually they tired themselves out, and sat on the mats to talk.

"So I wonder what's really up with Sam and Hua disappearing," said Jelly. Katana and Sara looked at each other. "You two know something, don't you?"

"No," said Sara, averting eye contact.

"Hey, we're going out now. Doesn't that mean you're not supposed to keep anything from me?" Jelly said accusingly.

"No, dummy, that's when you get *married*!" said Sara.

"Whatever, same thing!"

"It is *not* the same thing!" said Sara.

"Fine," said Jelly. "But tell me anyway!"

"No!" said Sara.

"You two sure *sound* like a married couple!" said Katana. "But we promised Sam, Jelly. We can't say anything. We don't know that much to begin with."

Right at that moment there was a flash of light at the front of the dojo, next to the altar. Sam and Master Hua materialized there. Sam said "Whoa!"

"SAM!" they shouted.

"*And* Master Hua!" yelled Jelly.

"You're back already?" said Katana. "I thought you were gonna be gone *way* longer than this!"

Sam looked around for a minute, like she couldn't believe she was actually here. "No, Kat, we're not back yet. Well—I am back, right now—you know what I mean. We have to leave again. We're only here long enough to find Gerald and get back to the airport."

"Where did you fade from?" asked Sara.

"I can't tell you that, Sara," she said evasively. "Gerald!"

"Hello, Samantha," said Gerald from the doorway. "It worked, I gather."

"Yes, Nelson. They're here," he said into a cell phone.

"Yeah! That was... incredible!" said Sam. "We'd better get going." She and Master Hua walked across the room.

But then Sam stopped, and turned to look at the kids. They were standing there, mouths wide open, still in shock at her sudden appearance. "I'm sorry, you guys. I can't talk about it. And I have to go..."

Master Nash walked in the door next to Gerald. "I told you it was no harder than fading across the room."

"Wow," said Katana as Sam and Hua swept out of the room with Gerald and Master Nash.

Chapter Twelve: Shaka-In

Sam and Master Hua had just landed in Kumamoto City, Japan, and were on the way to collect their bags. "Now where's Mitch?" said Sam, looking around the baggage claim area. "There he is—MITCH!"

Across the room, Mitchell Brown looked around, then walked over to them. "Samantha, it's good to see you again," he said, shaking her hand.

"You too," said Sam. "This is Master Hua Xiang."

They shook hands as well. "Sara very strong at wushu," said Hua. "Learning staff this year, maybe her and Katana be in team demo next year."

"Hey!" said Sam, suddenly surprised. "You're not taking Katana away from me are you?"

"Eh, maybe do both team?" said Hua with a wide grin.

"Sara speaks very highly of the both of you," said Mitch, as they walked to the car that was waiting for them outside. "She seems to be doing better now, after her ordeal over the winter recess."

"Ordeal? What ordeal?" asked Sam.

Mitch told them what had happened. "So I guess she has bulimia," he said, sounding very emotional. "I wanted to fly out as soon as I talked to Mrs. Boyd, of course, but you know

Sara—she's very independent. She insisted that I stay here. She's started counseling, though. I guess Katana is going with her to the sessions."

"They watch out for each other, Mitch. Don't worry. Kat'll take good care of her."

The car took them outside of the city and dropped them off at the Brown residence. Mitch escorted them inside to the guestrooms.

"Patty's making dinner. You'll probably both want to get right to bed after that. Tanaka's expecting us at first light tomorrow."

Before dawn the next morning, another car came to drive them into the mountains of Kumamoto Prefecture. "Here we are," said Mitch when they stopped in the center of a tiny village. They got out of the car, and followed Mitch up a path that led through the trees.

"How far up the mountain is it?" asked Sam.

"Quite a ways," said Mitch.

After hiking for over an hour, they finally came to the temple, nestled in the forest between two peaks. A large torii gate marked the entrance to the grounds. A monk wearing gray robes came to meet them. He spoke to Mitch in Japanese for a moment, then guided them across the complex.

They came to the main temple building, which looked similar to the main building of the Hall of the Dragon, if somewhat smaller. A fierce-looking man with short, dark hair and a goatee trotted down the stairs to greet them. "Thank you for escorting our guests, Mitchell," he said.

"Master Tanaka, this is Master Samantha Malloy, and Master

Hua Xiang," said Mitch. They shook hands. Master Tanaka led them up the stairs, into the temple.

Once inside the main doors, he turned to the left, and guided them into a room with a long conference table in the middle. "Please, have a seat," said Master Tanaka, sitting down himself at the head of the table. "So how are you enjoying Terry-san's services?"

"Oh…" said Sam, surprised at the question. "We enjoy his services very much," she said with a smile. "He's an excellent sushi chef."

"No, he is the *best* sushi chef," said Mater Tanaka with a frown. "Master Nash is going to pay for taking him from Shaka-In. Maybe I will hire you two when this mission is complete, and we see how Master Nash likes that?"

"Um…" said Sam, suddenly uncomfortable.

"I'm joking," said Master Tanaka. "Jordan and I are very good friends. And I deserved it—I took his favorite chef from the Hall of the Dragon, many years ago when I came to visit. I guess he finally has his revenge."

"Oh," said Sam with a nervous laugh, feeling relieved.

"Let us get down to business," said Master Tanaka. "Jaaku continues his attacks, here and at Shaolin. He has been sending his Arashi on raids to steal anything they can find from our archives."

"But I thought they couldn't get into the temple?" said Sam.

"At Shaolin, only Lu can enter. The archives are in the same building as one of the training halls, so they are protected from unwanted invasion. Unfortunately, at Shaka-In the archive building is not connected to the temple. So it has no such protection."

"Not good," said Master Hua. "They steal anything important?"

"No," said Master Tanaka. "Fortunately, they took only some of the scrolls that document the history of the Shaka-In. They are valuable to us, and we would like to retrieve them, but they will be of no help to Jaaku. Since the first attack, we have posted guards in the archive building. The Arashi still make regular raids, but we have been able to keep them out."

"What about the spy?" asked Sam. "Nash told us that Chan's got someone embedded in Jaaku's inner circle—has he been helpful?"

"Chan claims his spy has special knowledge of Jaaku's plans," said Tanaka. "But he's been useless thus far. He never seems to know about the attacks until after they happen. I question his true loyalty."

"Then I assume he hasn't found the information we need for our mission yet, either?" Sam said with a frown.

"No, he has not. I want to capture one of the Arashi myself. If we can do so, we may be able to learn something useful," Tanaka replied. "But so far that effort has been unsuccessful. The Arashi are too strong."

"It may be futile," said Sam. "Jaaku may not share his plans with *any* of his servants. But we'll certainly help, should the opportunity arise," she added, looking at Master Hua. He nodded in agreement.

"Master Nash tells me you will be here for several weeks," said Master Tanaka. "Not a week goes by without at least one Arashi attack, so I am sure the opportunity *will* arise."

They finished their meeting, and Sam and Master Hua bade farewell to Mitchell Brown. "I'll be back every week to check up on you," he said, and started out back down the mountain.

Master Tanaka showed Sam and Master Hua to their quarters in the dormitory building, and then escorted them to the temple to train with the monks.

***

January slipped into February. The masters at the Hall of the Dragon began gearing up for the Golden Gate Classic, scheduled for the second weekend of March.

Dana joined Katana and her friends every weekend to work on her whip chain form. She knew that Becca Stratton tended to get stronger as the season progressed, and wanted to train as much as possible before she had to face her again. Katana practiced the form with Dana, and could almost keep up with her now.

"You know," said Dana, "you should think about competing in weapons. You're getting really good at this."

"Nah," said Katana. "I wanna focus on the sparring division. Maybe next year, though."

Master Nash worked with the wushu team to polish the choreography in their demo. Jelly had perfected the combination Nash had taught them, so he and Dana started practicing it together right before the broadsword set. Dana still expressed misgivings, however, about Nash's "tampering" with the demo. Katana liked working with Nash, but realized that Dana had drawn strength from Master Hua. She clearly had a very special relationship with him, and was unable or unwilling to draw strength from Master Nash the same way.

Bobby Wellington was turning out to be every bit as demanding as Sam herself had always been. Katana found that she was exhausted by the end of the sparring team practice every Friday.

She continued to work on the gainer flash, and was getting good enough that she could count on it for earning her two points in a match. She'd tried using it on Jimmy once, though, and that hadn't worked out so well. Jimmy wasn't much bigger than Katana, and she wasn't able to generate enough momentum to flip properly. She sent him sprawling on the mat, and had to put her hands down to avoid crashing. "Definitely save that move for the bigger kids," Bobby reminded her.

Katana did her best to pay more attention to Jason, and things improved between them. There was another dance at the end of February, and Katana, Jason, Sara and Jelly decided to go again. "We gotta get Chris and Jimmy to go," said Sara. "They hardly ever leave their room anymore."

"I know," said Katana. "I think they've wired their brains directly into that video game."

Katana and Sara put together an elaborate scheme to convince them to go. Katana told Sara about the boys' crushes on the Gomez twins, Sierra and Olivia. Sara talked to Sierra and Olivia at dinner one night. She told them that Chris and Jimmy wanted to ask them to the dance, but were too shy. She pretended that the boys had asked her to act as a go-between, and ask the twins to the dance for them.

The twins agreed to go, so Katana used the same ploy with Chris and Jimmy. Of course, the boys were thrilled when they learned that the twins wanted to go to the dance with them.

After their plan proved successful, Katana and Sara gave each other a high-five and congratulated themselves for their genius. And that Friday night, everyone loaded onto the buses to head over to Lincoln.

Katana made sure to spend the whole night with Jason. When Jelly and Sara showed off, tricking for a large audience again, Katana made a point of staying with Jason instead.

Chris joined in though, apparently motivated by a desire to show off for Olivia. Katana had to admit, his backflip was looking much sharper these days. After Katana and Jason had watched their friends show off for a few minutes she excused herself to use the bathroom.

She walked out of the auditorium, and made her way down the hall. When she went around the corner, she stopped at the sight of Ed Golia and Tommy Cosgrove at the other end of the hall, walking toward her.

Actually, Katana noticed, they were stumbling rather than walking. She tried to turn back around the corner to avoid them, but it was too late.

"Hey Kanahicky," said Ed loudly. Tommy sniggered.

"It's Kahanu, you idiot," said Tommy.

"That's what I said," Ed replied, giving Tommy a push, "Kanahu."

They both stood there and giggled for a moment. Katana tried to walk away again.

"Hey Hanaku, they got anything in those archives up at that

freak school to help you grow some boobs?" Ed called after her.

Katana froze. How did Ed Golia know about the archives at the Hall of the Dragon? She turned around and walked toward them. "What did you say?"

Ed and Tommy stumbled up to her. "Or maybe," said Tommy, "you can find something to teach you how to defend against mim dak..."

He grabbed her by the hair and jammed his other hand against her chest, to the left of her sternum. But Katana was ready—she grabbed his arm, turned around and flipped him onto the hard floor.

"Hey!" Ed yelled. He took a step toward her, but Katana threw her hands out and hit him with a fireball. Ed slammed into the lockers and landed in a heap on the floor.

Katana ran back to the auditorium.

"What's wrong?" asked Jason, looking worried as she hurried over to him.

"Nothing," said Katana. "I ran into Ed and Tommy in the hall." She told him what had happened, but avoided mentioning their knowledge of the archives.

"Those sons of..." said Jason, and made to walk out of the auditorium. But Katana grabbed him by the arm.

"Leave it alone. I took care of them. I think they're drunk anyway."

Jason looked at her hard for a moment, but finally gave in. "Fine. But if they touch you again..."

They returned to the Hall, and Katana gave Jason a kiss goodnight before he went to the lounge to catch up with Matt and

Bobby. She followed Sara and Jelly up to Chris and Jimmy's room.

"So Chris," said Sara, flopping down on the couch, "did you ask Olivia out?"

"Yeah," said Chris, as he sat down at his computer.

"Except the idiot asked Sierra out first before he realized he had the wrong twin!" said Jimmy.

"I bet that was awkward!" said Katana.

"Yeah, it was," Chris agreed, turning a bright shade of red.

"We're gonna have to figure out a way to tell them apart," said Jimmy.

"Yeah, they really are *identical* twins," said Sara.

"Hey!" said Chris. "Katana, come here and look at this!"

"What is it?" She walked over and squatted down next to him.

"There's an article about you on U.S. Sport Karate's website. Wow—this is from back in December. It's about how you're competing in the boys' division this year."

"Are you joking?" asked Katana.

"What does it say?" asked Sara.

"Not a lot," said Chris, reading the rest of the article. "It talks about how you're sparring on the boys' team for the Hall. It says that Sam's hoping more girls will compete in sparring if they see you do well on the team this year."

"Hey, it talks about how you did at the Eureka Challenge," said Sara, pointing at the bottom of the screen.

"Yeah," said Chris. "But it just says you were injured in the semi-finals and unable to continue. It doesn't say anything about what

Golia did." Katana looked at him sharply. She hadn't had a chance yet to tell him or Sara what had happened at the dance.

"Well, it wouldn't," said Jimmy. "The chen do are supposed to be a secret. I'm sure dim mak's not exactly common knowledge, either."

"That's true," said Sara. "And anyway, we wouldn't know about dim mak if we hadn't seen Van Heldon learning it last year, or if the Arashi hadn't attacked the school."

Jimmy and Jelly sat down to play video games, so Katana motioned Chris and Sara out to the balcony. She told them what had happened with Ed and Tommy at the dance.

"How on earth do they know about the archives?" asked Sara.

"Well, I'm betting Sebastian told them," said Katana. "I'm sure he heard about it from Sato. You remember back at Halloween when we played hide-and-seek in the tunnels? Well, I think I saw an Arashi down in that storage room. I thought it was you at first, Chris. Do you remember that?"

"That's right, I was wearing the samurai costume."

"But since it wasn't you, it must have been an Arashi. And I bet it was Sato."

"Kat, we need to tell someone about this," said Sara, looking worried.

"Yeah," said Katana. "Normally I'd talk to Sam about it, but obviously that's not going to happen. I'll talk to Nash after tai chi on Monday morning."

They went to Sam's dojo the next afternoon, and Sara asked, "Hey, Kat, I forgot to ask you last night—how'd everything go with Jason this time?"

"Pretty good," said Katana. "He was very happy that I stayed with him instead of going to trick with you and Jelly. He seems to think I'm too much of a show-off..."

"Can't imagine what gave him that idea," muttered Chris.

They tricked for a little while, then decided to work on the chen do. Sara was still very excited about her newfound ability. She'd started working on the chi hit as well.

Katana had Chris and Sara try the tai chi form holding a ball of energy. Chris was able to make it almost a third of the way into the form that way, but Sara couldn't sustain it beyond the first few moves. Jelly and Scott were still unable to form the ball in the first place. "Stupid ball," Jelly complained. "I can still levitate though!"

They also tried doing the dragon circle several times to help Chris, Jelly and Scott learn to deflect intent. But as well as this had worked for Sara, the boys weren't making much progress.

"I miss Sam," said Sara, plopping down on the mat once they'd given up for the day.

"I know," said Katana. "We don't even know where she is now. Osaka refuses to talk about it, and I don't feel comfortable asking Nash."

"We could try Terry-san," Sara suggested. "He did say that the headmasters tell their sushi chefs everything."

"Yeah, but last time he refused to tell us anything," said Katana.

"Can't hurt to try," said Sara. "Come on!"

Katana and Sara went to sit at the sushi bar for dinner that night.

"Konichiwa," said Sara as they sat down on the stools.

"Konichiwa!" said Terry-san with a smile. "The usual tonight, girls?"

"Yeah," said Sara.

"Terry-san, do you know where Sam is now?" Katana asked with the sweetest smile she could manage.

"I do."

"Can you tell us?" asked Sara.

Terry-san stopped what he was doing, and looked at her for a moment. "You two are very close to Master Samantha, aren't you?" They nodded, and he continued. "I will share this with you, but you must not tell anyone I told you. Master Samantha is in Japan right now, at the Shaka-In temple. She and Master Hua are working with the headmaster there."

"So they really are training at some of the other temples," said Katana.

"Shaka-In," said Sara. "Isn't that where you used to work?"

"Yes," he said.

"So she's okay?" asked Katana.

"Yes, she's fine," said Terry-san, "for now anyway."

"What do you mean, 'for now'?" asked Sara.

"Things are very dangerous at the other temples. Jaaku is desperate to learn the secret of the Scroll of the Five Masters. His Arashi attack regularly, trying to gain access to the archives. Part of Master Samantha's mission is to help fight the Arashi."

"I don't get it," said Katana. "Why can't the other temples fight the Arashi on their own? Why do they need Sam and Hua?"

"It is not that they *need* them," said Terry-san. "But Master Nash believes that it is the Hall's duty to help. He feels responsible for the attacks."

"Why?" asked Sara.

"If Jaaku had failed to take the scroll from the Hall of the Dragon, he would not be attacking the other temples now."

"So he sent Sam and Hua," said Katana.

"Master Hua and Master Samantha are very brave," said Terry-san. "Master Nash did not require them to participate in this mission. They volunteered."

***

Sam woke with a start. It was the middle of the night. She heard the sound of bells ringing frantically somewhere outside. It was an attack.

She jumped out of bed and ran down the hall, out to the grounds. About a dozen Arashi were in the heat of battle with the warrior monks of Shaka-In. They'd already torched one building, and were trying to get inside the archives.

One of the Arashi nearest Sam drew his sword, using it to throw a line of fire at an approaching monk. The fire slashed the monk across the throat. He fell over backwards, and did not move again.

"Hey!" yelled Sam, rushing toward the Arashi. He turned to face her; she threw a fireball at him. The Arashi caught her chi and threw it back at Sam, then ran toward her.

Sam deflected the fireball, and engaged the Arashi in hand-to-hand combat. She realized very quickly that she couldn't do much to hurt him through his armor, so after a minute she backed off. They circled each other, looking for an opening. Suddenly Sam jumped forward, leaped into the air and kicked the Arashi in the chest with both feet. The Arashi fell back, and Sam dropped to the ground. She got up on one knee and formed an enormous ball of energy between her hands. And precisely as she'd anticipated, the Arashi threw a fireball at her. Sam caught the fireball in her own energy, and hurled the whole flaming mass back at him.

The fireball launched the Arashi into the trunk of a nearby tree. He fell to the ground. Sam ran over to make sure she'd accomplished her objective. She had: the Arashi was unconscious.

Sam heard someone shout her name; she turned to see who it was. Master Hua was at the main door to the archive building, single-handedly battling two Arashi who were attempting to gain entrance. Sam faded over, directly behind one of the Arashi. She grabbed him from behind in a chokehold and pulled him to the ground. The Arashi struggled ferociously. He regained his feet, but Sam didn't release her grip. He thrashed about, trying to shake her off. But she didn't let go. Finally the Arashi drove an elbow into Sam's rib cage. She winced in pain and the Arashi squirmed out of her hold. He dropped to one knee and faded away.

She looked up in time to see the Arashi Hua had been fighting fade away too. From the flashes of light around the grounds, she guessed that the other Arashi were fleeing as well.

Sam headed toward the main temple with Hua. Several monks were busy dousing the flames that still engulfed the far building. Smoke rolled across the grounds.

They ran into Tanaka heading the other way. "That was the fiercest attack yet," he said. "They nearly overwhelmed us."

"Well, I got you your prize," said Sam. "There's one live Arashi lying unconscious against that tree over there."

Tanaka turned to see where Sam was pointing. He looked at her in surprise for a moment before trotting away. Sam and Hua followed.

Tanaka bent down and removed the Arashi's helmet.

"Who is he?" asked Mater Hua.

"Master Yamazoto," said Tanaka, shaking his head. "He is a judo master from Tokyo. There were rumors that he'd trained in dim mak when he traveled to China a few years ago. I am not surprised that he is an Arashi now."

"I hope he proves useful," said Sam.

"We shall see," replied Master Tanaka. He called over a young monk and instructed him to fetch someone from the infirmary. "We'll keep him unconscious until I have a chance to question him—we wouldn't want him fading away."

Sam and Hua followed Tanaka toward the main temple.

"Tell me, Master Samantha, how was it that you were able to render the Arashi unconscious? We've tried to capture one for weeks without success."

"Well..." said Sam. "I used a technique I learned from one of the students at the Hall of the Dragon."

"From one of the students?" said Master Tanaka in total surprise, but then a look of comprehension washed over his face. "From the girl who can do two of the chen do, I am guessing?"

"Yes," said Sam, surprised that Tanaka knew about that. "Her name is Katana."

"Ah yes," said Master Tanaka. "Master Nash has told me about this one. An interesting name. According to legend, the katana carries the soul of the samurai who wields it. I wonder whose soul this girl might contain? Perhaps she is the reincarnation of one of the samurai warriors of legend? Perhaps Musashi himself?"

"Um..." said Sam. Master Hua looked at her and shrugged.

"Ah, perhaps not," said Master Tanaka. "I do not believe in reincarnation myself. Very unusual for a child to grow so powerful, but not entirely unheard of. Master Kosho, the founder of Shaka-In, was said to have mastered all five of the chen do at a very young age. No doubt this girl is destined for greatness herself.

"I would very much like to meet this Katana someday. Perhaps I will take her from Nash, eh, in exchange for Terry-san?"

Before Sam could reply, there was a deafening crash across the grounds. The earth shook. Sam turned in time to see a dozen Arashi appear behind a blinding flash of light. Their leader wore white armor.

"Jaaku..." Sam whispered.

Several nearby monks ran to the archive building, blocking the entrance. Suddenly, the grounds began to glow red. Sam could feel the electricity in the air. A bolt of lightning struck the dirt directly in front of the archives, knocking a monk through the air. Barbs from the main bolt hit three others and they fell to the ground, motionless.

Tanaka shouted in alarm. The Arashi rushed into the archive building unimpeded.

"NO!" Tanaka yelled. He ran toward Jaaku. Sam sensed the grounds beginning to glow red once more.

"Tanaka—stop!" There was no time. She faded to his side, enveloped him in her shen, and faded away again, reappearing next to the captured Arashi. A bolt of lightning struck the spot where Tanaka had been standing only a moment before. A monk from the infirmary was kneeling next to the Arashi hostage; he started in surprise, jumping to his feet.

"I don't understand..." said Tanaka, staring at Jaaku.

But a moment later, Jaaku vanished behind a flash of light. Tanaka ran into the archive building. Sam followed. The place looked ransacked.

"They've taken dozens of priceless volumes..." Tanaka whispered, running his hand along one of the shelves. "Historical texts, treatises on internal energy..." Other books and scrolls were strewn across the floor.

A monk ran into the room. "Master Tanaka, you need to see this."

He led Sam and Tanaka out of the archives. Thirty feet from the entrance, a charred corpse smoldered on the ground. The monk from the infirmary was kneeling next to the body; Hua was with him too. The monk looked up at Tanaka, tears running down his cheeks, and spoke to him in Japanese.

Tanaka listened quietly.

"What did he say?" Sam asked when he was done.

Tanaka only shook his head at first and gazed around at the other monks who lay still on the ground outside the archive building.

"They're all dead. The lightning..."

"What was that?" asked Sam. "I saw the air glowing... I've never seen anything like it."

"Neither have I," said Tanaka. "Jaaku extended his shen into the field of energy... he controlled the chi around him as if it were his own."

"Nash told me about this... that's how Jaaku throws the jet of fire..."

"Yes, but this was far more powerful. He hit those monks with the chi of the very planet. They died instantly."

She looked around at the bodies, hardly able to believe her own eyes. A chill ran down her spine, and she felt profound fear—almost panic. She took a deep breath, forcing herself to stay calm.

"How are we supposed to fight *that*?" she asked.

"I do not know," Tanaka replied.

At that moment, someone began screaming. Sam turned to find the source of the noise. It was the Arashi hostage. He was writhing on the ground. Steam was issuing from his body. Seconds later, he vaporized completely.

"What on earth?" Sam asked. "The death touch from a distance..."

"Jaaku didn't want him talking," said Tanaka. "He must have taken his prenatal chi at some earlier time."

"But why?" asked Sam. "He was just another Arashi, wasn't he?"

Tanaka shook his head. "This nightmare only worsens."

Chapter Thirteen: The Golden Gate Classic

Katana spoke to Master Nash on Monday morning. She told him about the Arashi she'd seen in the archive room. Master Nash seemed neither surprised nor worried and said simply, "Thank you, Katana." She decided that if Nash wasn't concerned, there was no sense in her worrying, either.

By the time Golden Gate arrived, Katana could pull out a win against every other member of the sparring team—except Bobby— every time they sparred. This seemed to irritate Jason a little. He could accept being beaten by his girlfriend once in a while, but losing to her *every* time did nothing to improve his mood.

But Katana still couldn't beat Bobby Wellington more than once or twice. His height advantage was overwhelming. The one technique Katana could count on to score against him was the gainer flash. Bobby hadn't found a way to block or counter that move, but he'd become quite adept at denying her an opportunity to use it in the first place.

Katana ran up to the wushu dojo with Chris and Sara the week before the tournament to watch the team practice. Usually as they got closer to a tournament, the team seemed to pull itself together, becoming sharper and more focused. But Master Hua's absence was taking a toll. Everyone liked Master Nash, but they had an established chemistry with Master Hua. It was tough to change that chemistry midstream.

The situation was affecting nobody as badly as it was Dana. She seemed like she'd lost her confidence. Katana had never seen her so scattered before. She wanted desperately to tell Dana that Master Hua was still okay. But she'd promised both Sam and Terry-san that she would reveal nothing, and she couldn't break her word.

The weekend of the tournament finally arrived and everyone loaded onto the buses right after school on Friday. San Francisco was a little over five hours away from the Hall of the Dragon.

Katana and Sara got settled in their hotel room, then went downstairs to find something to eat. They decided to try the restaurant in the lobby, and joined the line to wait for a table.

"Where's Chris?" asked Sara.

"Oh, he went with Jimmy and the twins to some restaurant up the street," Katana replied.

"Katana!" said the girl in front of them.

"Hey, Becca!" said Katana. "Hi, Bobby."

"You two wanna join us?" asked Bobby.

Katana nodded, and Sara said, "Yeah, sure."

The hostess sat them at the far end of the restaurant, right next to a little waterfall.

"So Katana," said Becca once they had ordered their meals. "I read that article about you on U.S. Sport Karate's website. Did you get stuck talking to Harvey at the last tournament?"

"No, who's Harvey?" asked Katana.

"Harvey Ryder," said Bobby, rolling his eyes. "He's the sole reporter for that site. He goes around to all the tournaments on the circuit and harasses the top competitors until they give him an interview."

"He probably didn't get a chance to bother you because of what happened in your last match," said Sara.

"That's true," said Bobby.

"Bobby told me about that," said Becca. "I'm glad they disqualified that kid. Anyway, try to stay away from Harvey or he'll talk your ear off. He's hard to miss—he's got these glasses that make his eyes look huge."

"Seriously, Kat. Stay away from him," Bobby agreed. "At least until you're done sparring. I've seen him hound people so bad that they miss their events."

Katana and Sara went to bed early that night. They ran downstairs first thing Saturday morning. After a light breakfast, they went into the convention hall. Katana was excited. They'd been disqualified from this event the previous year, so this was a whole new experience.

On their way to find the weapons ring, Katana heard a nasal voice behind her call out, "Katana! Katana Kahanu? Katana, please wait." She turned around to see who it was. A very large man was waddling over to her. He wore glasses that made his eyes look enormous.

"Oh no," said Sara quietly. "This must be Harvey."

"Katana," said Harvey, reaching out to shake her hand. "Do you have a moment? I'd like to ask you a few questions for the U.S. Sport Karate website."

"No," said Katana, shaking his hand very briefly. "I don't—I have to be in ring two right now. Sorry!"

The girls ran off before Harvey could detain them any further. They found the weapon rings, and sat down next to Dana. "Hey," said Katana. "You ready?"

"Yeah, I guess," said Dana. But she'd never seen Dana look less confident. Becca sat down across the ring, and gave them a little wave. Katana was worried. Dana usually thrived under pressure, but Katana knew she was feeling a whole different kind of stress this time. The pressure of competition was what Dana loved, not the anxiety of losing a mentor.

The center judge called the competitors up for roll call. Katana and Sara wished Dana luck. "She doesn't look so good," said Sara.

Once the officials had organized everything, the center judge called up the first competitor. "Dana Arlington," he yelled.

"Oh no," said Sara. "She *hates* going first. She always gets pumped when she sees everyone else go before her."

Katana could tell that Dana was in trouble right from the start. She'd been opening with a flash kick since the previous year's Golden Gate Classic, but this time didn't get enough height. She had to put her hands down, and ended up doing a back handspring instead.

"That's not good," said Katana.

Dana seemed to recover her composure a bit once she started moving, and went as fast as always through the flowers. When she got to the butterfly kicks, however, she started falling apart. One of the chains wrapped around her leg on the last kick; she had to untangle it before she could continue. She got to the full body jumps, and missed her third jump—she landed on the bottom chain, and wasn't able to continue the move. And then the worst thing imaginable happened. As she kicked to her feet, one chain flew out of her hand, landing limply at the side of the ring.

Dana stopped and stared at the chain for a moment. Then she turned and bowed to the judges, walked out of the ring, and left the convention hall.

"Oh no," said Sara.

"She's disqualified, isn't she?" asked Katana.

"Yeah," said Sara. "Dropping your weapon automatically disqualifies you."

Katana picked up Dana's chain. They walked out to the lobby to look for her, but Dana was nowhere to be seen. They went back inside to find Master Nash and let him know what had happened. He was watching one of the older kids from the team.

"Don't worry girls, I'll find her." He walked out of the convention hall. Katana and Sara went back to watch Becca.

They returned to the ring just in time—the judges called Becca up next. And as Katana had anticipated, Becca was even stronger here than she'd been at the Eureka Challenge. Katana tried to watch the form more carefully to figure out how she was able to spin the nunchucks around her fingers, but it still looked impossible. And Becca's tricks were higher than ever.

Becca finished her form and the crowd went wild. It was obvious that Becca had made nationals—over Dana.

Katana and Sara didn't bother sticking around to watch the end of the division. They already knew who'd won. They were able to get over to the younger boys' ring in time to see Jelly compete.

Jelly was doing the exact same staff form he'd competed with the previous year. And unlike Dana, he didn't seem fazed by Master Hua's absence.

"Nothing ever gets to that kid," observed Katana.

"Nope," agreed Sara. "As long as he can trick, eat and sleep, he's fine."

Jelly was totally focused for his entire form. He moved his staff around faster than ever. He did his release skill with ease—landing a perfect gainer flash while the staff soared over his head. And he nailed his double backflip, to the shrill pleasure of the crowd that had gathered to watch.

"First place, ya think?" asked Sara when he was done.

"No doubt," said Katana.

Katana and Sara went to find their kata ring next. Becca came over to them when they got there. "What happened to Dana?" she asked quietly.

"She's been off since Master Hua left," explained Sara. "She's taking it really hard."

"Yeah, Bobby told me about that," said Becca. "I can imagine how she feels. I know if my instructor disappeared, I'd be lost. It's too bad, though. Dana's one of the best competitors on the circuit. I've never seen her lose her composure like that. Well, good luck, you two."

The judges called everyone up for roll call. Katana tried to get herself in the right frame of mind and focus on the task at hand. There was nothing she could do for Dana. And if she could take first in kata this time, she'd be going to nationals.

The ring started. Katana gathered her energy as she watched the first few competitors. Although there were many more people at Golden Gate than there'd been at the Eureka Challenge, she felt pretty sure that her main competition would still come from Sara and Becca.

The judges called Becca next. As always, she was exceptional. Her details were perfect, but her intensity was her strongest attribute at every event. Becca finished her form, and Katana gave her a high-five as she came back to sit down.

The judges called Sara next. "Go Sara!" yelled Katana as Sara walked up to the judges.

"Representing the Hall of the Dragon," she yelled, "My name is Sara Brown."

"GO SARA!" yelled Becca.

Sara began her form, and Katana couldn't believe how strong she looked. Katana was certain she'd never seen her so intense. And like Becca, her details were flawless.

"What got into you up there?" asked Katana when Sara was done.

"Becca did," Sara said. "Going right after her was the best thing that could've happened to me!"

"I guess," said Katana.

Several more girls went, and Katana ended up going last. "GO KAT!" Sara and Becca both yelled as she went up to the judges. She gave her introduction, and backed up to the center of the ring.

As she started, everyone else in the giant room ceased to exist. Katana was in her own world. She hit every stance and slammed every strike. She ended her last move with a loud kiai, then bowed to the judges and turned to take her seat.

Becca and Sara both screamed for her, each giving her a high-five as she returned to the side of the ring. "Well, it's up to the judges now," said Sara.

And the judges took their time conferring with the scorekeeper. But at last they finished. They called up the competitors.

"In fourth place, Jasmine Hedalgo!" yelled the center judge. Jasmine came up and shook his hand.

"We have a tie for second and third place," he yelled out. "Sara Brown and Katana Kahanu, please come up."

Katana and Sara walked up to the center judge.

"Call!" He pointed to Katana along with one other judge. The other three judges pointed to Sara.

"Kahanu, third place! Brown, second place!" yelled the center judge. Sara and Katana gave each other a hug, and took their places in line. "And in first place for girls' black belt kata, ages fourteen and fifteen... Becca Stratton!"

Becca walked up and shook the center judge's hand.

Then Katana heard that nasal voice again. "Girls, can we get a picture, please?" Harvey Ryder had come over with his photographer this time.

"Oh, why not," said Becca. "One picture won't hurt." The photographer had them line up together, with Becca in the center, and snapped several shots. Becca bolted the moment he was done.

"Katana, can I have a moment of your time now?" wheezed Harvey.

"No, definitely not—I have sparring next!" said Katana. She grabbed Sara by the arm and dragged her away.

"Wow," said Sara. "That guy sure is persistent."

Katana found Chris, Jason and Jimmy. "Hey guys," she said, and gave Jason a peck on the cheek. "You ready?"

"Yeah," said Jason. Katana thought he looked nervous.

"I'm ready," said Jimmy, punching his fists together. He was already wearing his gear. "I just wish Golia was here!"

"Yeah, me too," said Chris. "How'd your forms ring go?"

"Good," said Katana. "Becca got first. Sara and I tied, and Sara won the tiebreaker."

"So you didn't make nationals," said Chris. "I thought for sure you would this time."

"Nah, you shoulda seen Becca," said Katana. "She gets stronger every time she competes. She definitely deserved the win. And anyway, *this* is the event I really care about this time."

Katana and Jason both put on their gear, and the center judge called everyone up for roll call. Katana looked around at the other competitors. She saw several who looked big enough to use the gainer flash against. She couldn't wait.

The judges called Katana first, with a boy who definitely wasn't big enough for her secret weapon. Just as well, she thought. She wanted to save it for the end anyway.

The judges bowed them in, and the match began. Katana circled around the other boy for a minute then tested the waters with a front kick to roundhouse kick combination. She landed both kicks.

"UP!" yelled the center judge. They awarded her two points—only the first kick in a combination could score.

The match continued and Katana wondered if the boy was afraid to hit a girl as Ed Golia had claimed at the last tournament. He didn't throw a single kick or punch for the entire match. Katana scored with two more kicks, winning 6-0.

"I hope my first match is that easy," said Chris when Katana came back to sit down.

Chris had no such luck. The judges paired him with one of the tallest people in the ring. Unlike the boy Katana had just faced, Chris threw countless kicks and punches. But he lost 6-0.

"That was rough," said Katana. "He was huge."

Jason and Jimmy both won their first matches, so they advanced into the next round with Katana.

Katana's next match was against a boy with unusually long legs. Katana doubted he had enough mass for the gainer flash. She would have to wait again.

The judges bowed them in, and the boy did the strangest thing Katana had ever seen in a sparring match: he held one foot over his head, and hopped toward her on the other. She thought she knew exactly what he was up to; as soon as she tried to move in, he'd drop an axe kick right on her head. Katana wasn't going to give him the chance.

She edged toward him, faked a punch, but instead dropped down and swept out his base leg. Duped by her feint, he'd dropped his raised leg. He crashed to the floor when Katana swept his other leg. Katana immediately rolled over and snapped a kick to his head. She'd gained an early lead, 4-0. The boy didn't try that tactic again.

He was, however, very good at feinting combinations. He threw a roundhouse kick at Katana's head next. When she blocked it, he snapped his leg around the other way, and dropped an axe kick across the back of her head. Katana fell to the floor. It was 4-2.

The match began again. Katana started with the front kick to roundhouse kick combination—the boy blocked the first, and dodged the second. He apparently thought she was done, and lunged in to throw a punch. Katana caught him across the jaw with a hook kick. She won the match 6-2 and advanced to the third round.

Jimmy lost his next match 5-4, but Jason won his 6-4, so he advanced as well. "Me and you," said Katana when he came back to the side of the ring.

They were down to eight competitors. Katana had only to win her next match and she'd be in the finals.

She had a harder time in that next match. The boy was big enough that she probably could've used the gainer flash. But he was so aggressive that she never had a chance. Every time the judge started the match, he plowed right through her with a volley of kicks and punches. She was able to get out of the way, but after he'd driven her out of the ring twice, the judge warned her they'd award the boy two points if it happened again.

Katana realized this must have been his strategy. She kept her weight on her back foot, ready to snap a roundhouse kick the moment the judge started the match again. It worked. The boy charged right into her foot, and she earned two points.

She tried the same tactic again, this time throwing an axe kick. This also worked. Katana was up 4-0.

The boy had finally figured out that his strategy would no longer work against Katana. So instead he circled around and waited for her to make the first move. But he was no match for Katana's kicking combinations. She did her triple, and landed all three—the front kick, the roundhouse kick and the axe kick. She won the match 6-0 and advanced to finals.

Jason's next match was tough. He went up against one of the taller boys, and the two were evenly matched. It played out like a chess match, each of them out-thinking the other's strategy. Finally it was 4-4, and they both circled around, looking for an opening. Jason threw a side kick. The other boy sidestepped, trying to lunge behind Jason and hit him in the head. But Jason had practiced the leg scissors takedown to perfection. He jumped up, grabbed the boy with both legs, and twisted over hard. The boy rolled away too quickly for Jason to follow up with a kick but it didn't matter—Jason had won 6-4.

Jason had also advanced to finals, along with Katana, the boy who'd beaten Chris in the first round, and another tall, skinny boy.

Jason began by sparring against Chris's first opponent. It was an excellent fight. Katana was disappointed though, as this boy would have been perfect for the gainer flash. The boy she was going to fight didn't look heavy enough.

Jason managed to pull out a win, 5-4.

Katana was next. She discovered very quickly that this opponent was her equal with feinting combinations. He started with a front kick to roundhouse combination—Katana blocked the front kick, then dodged the roundhouse. But as she lunged in for a punch, she realized she'd fallen for the trick she'd used so many times herself. The boy caught her in the face with his foot as he raised it for an axe kick.

The boy was ahead 2-0. Katana's lip started bleeding profusely. She tried to ignore it and focus on the match. She managed to win the next round using the same combination the boy had used against her. It was 2-2.

They both fought more cautiously after that. Back and forth they struggled, trading kicking combinations, but neither could land a single kick.

Finally the boy tried a different tactic. He faked with a kick but lunged in with a punch instead. Katana had lifted her foot for a side kick at the same moment. When he punched, she jumped in the air and grabbed him with both legs. She twisted over hard, dropped him to the floor, and turned over to land a kick to his head. She won the match 6-2.

A second later, she realized she had to fight her final match against her boyfriend.

"Not again," he said with a smile as she sat down next to him.

"Yeah, but this time we actually get to fight," she said. "No dim mak to stop me today."

The two boys who'd lost to Katana and Jason sparred with each other for third and fourth place. The judges called Katana and Jason next. They hugged each other, and the match began.

They had sparred so many times they knew how to read each other, and were able to anticipate each other perfectly. They traded kicking combinations back and forth, but neither could earn a point. Finally Jason took her down with the leg scissors, but Katana rolled away before he could land a kick. He was ahead, 2-0.

Katana did her triple kick combination next, but Jason blocked the first kick and dodged the other two. But the moment Katana's foot hit the floor, she jumped in—without even bothering to fake with a side kick—and performed the leg scissors takedown. Jason was so surprised that she had time to land a kick before he could roll away.

Katana was ahead, 4-2.

She realized that if she was going to use the gainer flash, now was the time. As soon as the judge started the match, she launched her secret weapon. She lunged in with her fist raised, and Jason lifted his guard to block. The next moment she was airborne, kicking Jason's chest with one foot. Katana kicked over and landed a perfect gainer flash.

The crowd went wild. Katana noticed for the first time that a huge audience had gathered around their ring to watch the girl who was fighting in the boys' division. When the girl won the whole ring, with a gainer flash kick no less, they went absolutely berserk.

Katana heard Sara scream. She and Becca ran into the ring and hoisted Katana up on their shoulders. Katana heard a nasal voice yell, "KATANA!" and she looked down to see Harvey Ryder. "Could I have a few moments now, please?" he asked.

"NO!" yelled Sara and Becca.

They put her down as the center judge calmed the commotion to award trophies. Once that was done, they steered Katana out of the crowd—and away from Harvey—and they went to find seats for team demo. They sat with Chris, Jimmy, Scott and Bobby.

"Where's Jason?" asked Katana.

"I don't know," said Bobby. "I thought he was with you three."

Katana stood on her chair and looked around, but couldn't find him anywhere. The demos were starting, so she sat down again.

There were five teams present: the same five who had competed at Golden Gate the year before. Katana knew that Strike Force and the Hall of the Dragon were the teams to beat. They had both blown away the competition the previous year. And the same would hold true this time as well, Katana thought as she watched the first three teams.

Finally Strike Force took the stage. Katana thought they'd improved significantly. They performed with sport karate weapons— bo staves, nunchucks and samurai swords. Their choreography was excellent, and they used many of the same tricks as the students from the Hall, minus the double backflip. They nailed their demo.

Katana was worried for her team now. She wondered if Nash had been able to calm Dana down enough to compete.

But when the Hall of the Dragon took the stage, Dana was with them. Katana thought she looked totally focused. As the demo began, it seemed that Master Nash had found a way to snap them out of their funk. They looked as sharp and strong as ever.

Jelly and Dana nailed the trick combination, and Paul, Scott and Sasha flew through their new broadsword set. Staff came out, and they executed the set perfectly—the crowd still couldn't get over Jelly's double backflip, and roared approval.

Katana felt herself fidget when Dana and Donnie jumped out to start chains. But Dana was on point—as was Donnie. The set itself wasn't as good as what Dana had done with Kelly the previous year, but they nailed it and the whole team finished strong.

It turned out that Strike Force had edged them out in the scores—winning by the narrowest of margins. But they'd been close at the first event as well, so they were virtually tied going into nationals.

The team demo was the last event of the day. Katana went with Sara and Chris to look for Jason again. But nobody had seen him, so they went outside. Katana was about to board one of the buses back to the Hall, when she heard a nasal voice behind her say, "Katana, may I *please* have a few moments of your time?"

Katana looked at Sara and sighed. "Sure," she said. She was beginning to feel bad for avoiding the man all day.

"So how does it feel to be the only girl in the history of U.S. sport karate to compete in the boys' division?" asked Harvey. At that moment, Jason emerged from the hotel. He stopped to watch her.

"Um... Well, it was a little weird at first," said Katana, "but I always sparred with my friend Chris and my instructor back home. I always practiced with guys, so I realized it wasn't that big of a deal."

Jason looked away and boarded one of the other buses. "I beg to differ," wheezed Harvey, "and so do many fans of the sport. No girl has *ever* competed in the boys' division before, much less won a major tournament." The other buses pulled away. The last one was waiting for Katana to finish with Harvey. She answered his next couple of questions very tersely, then excused herself and boarded the bus with Chris and Sara.

Katana fell asleep on the way back to the Hall. It was a little after ten by the time they arrived. The girls said goodnight to Chris and went up to the third floor. When they opened the door to their hall, Katana saw Jason sitting outside their door.

"Hey," said Katana.

"Hi," he said. "Can we talk?"

"Sure." She gave Sara her bags to bring inside. Katana sat down next to him on the floor. "What's up? We lost you after sparring."

"I'm surprised you noticed," said Jason.

"What's that supposed to mean?"

"Kat, sometimes it seems like you don't care about me. You only care about your friends and showing off all the time."

"I tried to look for you as soon as the ring was over," said Katana.

"You mean once your friends put you down?" asked Jason.

"Well... yeah," said Katana. "They were happy for me, is there something wrong with that?"

"It's always about *you*, Katana. Why'd you use the gainer flash in our match?"

"What? You know how hard I've been working on that move. Why wouldn't I use it?"

"It was the *final match*, Kat. No matter which of us won, our team was going to get maximum points. You hadn't used it yet, and you could have saved it for nationals. That way nobody would have seen it before. You've beaten me plenty of times without it. But you had to show off. That was the only reason to use that move in that match. If anyone was taking video, it's gonna be all over the internet. Now when you try to use it at nationals, someone's gonna be ready for it. And that's going to cost the *team*."

Katana stared down at her hands. She couldn't refute anything he was saying.

"But you didn't think about any of that. You only thought about showing off your new move. That's all you ever think about, Kat. Either you're showing off your gainer flash, or how many chen do you can do... or double whip chain, it's always something. And it's always about you."

Katana felt terrible. She had to admit that on some level, he was right. She did enjoy showing off. And she'd never considered saving the gainer flash for nationals. "Jason... I'm sorry. I don't know what to say. You're right. I... I do show off too much. I'm sorry."

"I'm sorry too, Kat. But this is it. I don't think I want to go out with you anymore." He got up and walked away.

Katana went inside. She felt hot tears streaming down her cheeks.

"Oh, Kat..." said Sara. Katana realized that Sara was crying, too.

"You were listening through the door, weren't you?"

"Yeah..."

Katana half-snorted and half-laughed. She pulled Sara into a hug. The two of them went to sit on the balcony. "He's wrong, you know," said Sara.

"What do you mean?" asked Katana.

"Well, you're definitely a show-off. But it's never just about you. You're one of the most giving people I've ever met. I don't know where I'd be without you after everything that happened over Christmas break. And you're *always* helping people with their homework, or with the chen do—hell, that ungrateful jerk wouldn't be able to deflect intent if it weren't for you!"

Katana felt extremely grateful to have Sara as a friend at that moment. "He was right about the match, though," said Katana. "I should have saved the gainer for nationals once I got to finals."

"Live and learn, Kat."

They sat in silence for a few minutes, then Katana laughed. "Well, I finally found something I suck at."

"What's that?" asked Sara.

"Having a boyfriend."

The girls went to bed a few minutes later, but Katana was unable to sleep. She couldn't stop thinking about how everything had gone with Jason. Despite what Sara said, she was worried that Jason might have been right about everything.

She was feeling quite depressed about losing Jason as a boyfriend. She liked him a lot. What had she done to make him think she didn't care about him? Well, she had to admit, Chris and Sara *were* more important to her. But was that so wrong? They were her best friends. If Jason couldn't understand that...

Katana finally gave up trying to sleep. She jumped down from the top bunk. It was two in the morning already. She slid the door open and went to sit on the balcony again. As she sat there staring through the fog, some movement at the end of the south wing caught her eye. It was hard to tell what it was through the fog, but there was definitely something moving. Katana stood up and leaned out over the railing to get a better look. Her heart skipped a beat—there was someone out there. She couldn't tell who it was, but a shadowy figure walked up to the main doors, pulled one open and slipped inside.

Katana thought her heart might pound a hole right through her chest. An intruder had entered the Hall! She had a suspicion she knew exactly who it was. Her mind raced back to Halloween. She was certain she'd seen an Arashi down in that storage room.

She walked through her room, ran down the corridor and hurtled down the stairs. She emerged from the hallway into the atrium, but it was empty and silent. Katana knew there was only one place Sato would go: the archives in the storage room.

She ran back through the doors to the north wing, across the short hallway and down the stairs to the tunnels. Where was that storage room again?

Katana made her way through the maze of passages for a minute, then located the hallway where she'd found the storage room the first time. Sure enough, one of the shoji screen doors was open. She crept along as quietly as she could. Just as she was about to enter the room an Arashi walked out the door and froze on the spot, staring directly at her.

In the split second it took Katana to see his shen, she formed an enormous ball of energy in her hands. When the Arashi threw his chi at her, she was ready—she caught his fireball in her own, and spun around to hurl the glowing mass back at him. But he disappeared in a flash of light before it hit him.

"Katana!" someone yelled behind her.

Katana spun around and saw Osaka standing there, Master Nash running up behind him.

"Osaka! There was an Arashi—he was in the storage room! I saw him coming in..."

"Katana, are you all right?" asked Nash, looking concerned.

"Yeah, I'm fine, but what about the Arashi? I think it must have been Sato again!"

Osaka and Nash looked at each other. Katana thought she could see Nash give the slightest nod.

"It's no cause for alarm," said Osaka. "We've been expecting Sato."

"You've been *expecting...*?"

"Jaaku has sent his Arashi to search the archives at several of the temples," said Nash. "He is desperate to figure out the scroll. It stands to reason that he would send someone here as well. But don't worry. We have nothing that will help Jaaku."

"But Sato walked in the front door—why didn't he fade inside?"

"Master Nash can sense when someone fades here," Osaka explained. "As the caretaker of this facility, his chi is imprinted quite heavily on the building."

"It's not every day that someone fades into the Hall," Nash added. "Sato knows that with all the traffic through the front doors, however, I am unlikely to notice that type of entry. Undoubtedly, this wasn't his first visit to our archives."

"But Sato doesn't belong here anymore," said Katana. "Why is he able to get in?"

"He hasn't been gone that long," Osaka replied. "His own chi is still imprinted here. It will take a few years for that to wear off."

"Sato is only interested in the archives," Nash told her. "I don't believe he'll venture anywhere else in the Hall. But I think it's a good idea if you and your friends refrain from coming down here for the time being."

Katana couldn't agree more.

Chapter Fourteen: The Shaolin Temple

Katana slept late the following morning. When she got up, she found Sara had already gone to breakfast. She went down to the cafeteria without bothering to change out of her pajamas.

Everyone was talking about the tournament when she sat down at the table.

"Hey Paul, how'd you do yesterday?" she asked.

"Second place," he said with a shrug.

"So you didn't make nationals?" asked Sara.

"No, but I was so close," he said. "The kid who won took second at his first event, so he only just beat me."

"How about you, Scott?" asked Katana.

"I got third this time," said Scott.

"So Kat's the only one who made nationals?" asked Sara.

"Hey!" said Jelly, glaring at Sara. "I made nationals, too!"

"You don't count," said Sara. "You're too small."

He swung out of his chair and walked over to her. "I'm gonna kill you!"

Sara squealed and ran out of the cafeteria, Jelly on her heels.

"They're so cute," said Dana with a sigh.

Chris and Katana walked up to her room after breakfast. Sara and Jelly were already there. Sara was lying in bed and Jelly was using her computer.

"Hey, Kat. Check this out!" said Jelly.

"What is it?" asked Katana. She walked over to the computer and sat down next to him.

"Watch; it's your gainer flash from the tournament yesterday. It's on U.S. Sport Karate's website. It's so sweet!"

"Jason was right," said Sara from her bed.

At the end of the video, Chris chuckled and said, "Check out the look on Beecher's face!"

"That was perfect, Katana!" said Jelly excitedly.

"Yeah, perfect," she said. She flopped down on the couch.

"What's wrong?" asked Chris. "You've been working on that move for months. I thought you'd be psyched."

"I shouldn't have used it," said Katana. "I was already in the final match. Jason was right. I should have saved it for nationals at that point. Now it's on the internet, and everyone at nationals is gonna be ready for it."

"I don't see why it matters," said Chris. "No one's gonna be able to counter it." But Katana wasn't so sure about that point.

She waited until Jelly went back to his room to shower, then she told Chris and Sara what had happened the night before.

"So they didn't seem surprised by an Arashi breaking into the Hall of the Dragon?" asked Sara incredulously.

"No, they sure didn't," said Katana.

"How can they be so sure there's nothing in the archives that'll help Jaaku?" asked Chris.

"I have no idea," Katana replied.

Katana woke up Sara the next morning since she was still waking up without the alarm clock every morning, and they walked to the tai chi dojo. Since Sam and Master Hua left, they hadn't seen anyone doing lessons with Master Nash in the mornings. "Daniels only does aikido," said Sara, "and maybe Osaka trains with Nash later in the day." The students went into the dojo to stretch every morning since it was empty when they arrived.

Master Nash came in and walked over to Katana. "Congratulations," he said. "I just found out about your victory in the sparring division—most impressive. I'm sure Samantha will be very proud." Katana wondered if she was the only one who felt bad about her performance that weekend.

The kids' routine returned to normal in the coming weeks. Only the students on the competition teams had to prepare for nationals. For the rest of the students at the Hall, tournament season was over.

Bobby Wellington kept up the same demanding pace after Golden Gate, so Katana still found herself thoroughly exhausted by the end of practice every Friday night. She was worried it would be awkward to be around Jason now, but this turned out not to be the case. He was perfectly pleasant around her, and seemed to have shut off his feelings like a switch. Katana wished she could do the same. But she couldn't help feeling sad about the breakup for the next few weeks.

The teachers at Lincoln were already doubling their workload.

Katana had no problem with French, as she'd already learned the rest of the textbook during exams the previous term. But even she had to spend extra time in the lounge every night doing her homework—especially in geometry.

Everyone was very happy to get a whole week off from both Lincoln and the Hall at the end of April. Katana had been hoping to sleep late that week, but on Saturday morning, found herself awake as usual at five in the morning. She'd decided to jump ahead in world history the way she had in French, so she lay in bed for a while reading their textbook.

Finally at eight, there was a knock at the door. Sara stirred in the bottom bunk and yelled "Go away!" But Katana jumped down to answer the door.

It was Jelly. "Get up, you two. We're going to play Frisbee!"

"Ugh," said Sara. "Why do you *always* have so much energy when I want to sleep?"

They had breakfast first, then went out to the field behind the rock garden.

"You should try levitating," suggested Jelly.

"I thought we were playing Frisbee," Katana asked, feeling confused.

"Yeah, dummy, but we'll throw it really high so you have to jump to catch it. If you wanna catch it badly enough, you'll levitate!"

Katana thought this plan was ridiculous, but tried it anyway. Every time one of them threw her the disc, they aimed far above her head. She jumped with all her might, but couldn't go any higher than usual. As a result she ended up having to traipse through the woods behind the field to find the disc.

As she went to retrieve it one time, she realized there was a path that led deeper into the woods. Curious as always, she walked farther along it. "Where are you going?" Chris yelled to her. When she didn't answer, he ran after her.

"Where are you going?" he asked again.

"I don't know," said Katana, handing him the Frisbee. It felt like something along this path was beckoning to her.

They walked for several minutes, until Chris began to protest. "Kat, this is stupid. Where do you think we're going?"

Katana saw something off to the side of the path. "Right there," she said, pointing. They walked closer and realized it was an old foundation, in the middle of a clearing in the trees.

"What is this?" asked Chris.

"It looks like there used to be a building here," said Katana. "I wonder what was ever out here in the middle of the forest. It looks like it was pretty big."

They rummaged around for a few minutes, but could find no indication of what kind of structure might once have stood upon the foundation. It seemed like it was glowing with energy.

Finally they walked back to the field. Their friends were gone. "Where'd they go?" asked Katana.

"Well they couldn't very well play Frisbee since *we* had the disc!" he said, handing it back to her.

They went to Sam's dojo that afternoon, and Sara was very insistent about working on the chen do. "I can deflect intent now," she said, "but I wanna get the chi hit, too." Katana did the tai chi form with her, and helped her hold the energy ball further into the form.

"You have to stay relaxed," Katana told her. "If your shoulders tense up, you're going to lose it."

As it was vacation, Chris, Jelly and Scott didn't feel like working hard on anything. Jelly and Chris swung their staffs at each other in mock battle, and Scott lay on the mat laughing at them.

"Down with the mighty midget!" yelled Chris, swinging his staff at Jelly.

"Hey!" Jelly yelled as he ducked. He slammed Chris's staff down on the mat with his own, and in his surprise Chris dropped it.

"Uh-oh," said Chris. He ran as Jelly chased him with his staff.

"Watch where you're going!" yelled Katana. Chris was running directly toward her and Sara. Chris stopped in his tracks. He turned around and threw a fireball at Jelly, knocking him off his feet.

"Hey!" yelled Sara. She was in the middle of the form with Katana, still holding the ball of energy. Chris turned to look at her, and Sara glared at him. She looked down at the ball of energy in her hands, then back at Chris. She hurled the fireball at him.

For an instant, Chris stared in total surprise. Then he yelled, tried to duck and threw his hands out in front of him. The fireball dissipated into the air around him.

For a second, everyone gaped in stunned silence.

"No way!" said Katana. "I don't believe it! You both got another chen do!"

Sara and Chris looked at each other in shock for a moment. Finally Chris said, "I wanna do that again!"

For the next half hour, Katana helped Sara form the ball of energy and throw a chi hit at Chris. Sara's fireball was relatively weak, but she could throw it almost every time.

Then Sara, Jelly and Scott attacked for Chris, and he practiced deflecting intent. He discovered he could do it as easily against external techniques as he could against Sara's chi hit.

"It isn't that hard," he said. "You were right, Kat. You just have to visualize the person falling away."

"I wanna try this!" said Jelly after Chris had had several turns. Jelly and Scott each took a turn, but failed to execute the chen do.

Jelly stomped his feet in sheer frustration. "This is *so unfair*!" he complained. "I really wanna get this!"

They went to dinner a few minutes later. Katana and Sara went to sit at the sushi bar.

"Konichiwa," said Terry-san.

"Hi, Terry-san," said Katana. "Hey, Sara got a chi hit!"

"Did you?" asked Terry-san, raising his eyebrows. "So now you can *both* do two of the chen do?"

"Yeah, and our friend, Chris, too—he just learned how to deflect intent," said Sara.

"This is most remarkable," said Terry-san. "I had never heard of anyone your age doing two of the chen do before. But now three of you can do exactly that."

"Four of us, actually," said Katana. "My ex-boyfriend has been able to do two of them since last term."

Terry-san finished preparing their sushi and Sara asked, "Terry-san, do you know where Sam is now?"

"Yes," said Terry-san. "She and Master Hua have been at Shaolin for the past two weeks. They will leave from there on the final leg of their mission."

But Terry-san refused to say what that final leg might entail.

Much to her despair, Katana woke up a little before five again on Monday morning. She tried to get back to sleep for a few minutes, but something was gnawing at the edge of her consciousness. She finally realized what it was: the old foundation in the forest.

She jumped down from the top bunk, careful not to wake Sara. She put on a pair of sweatpants and a sweatshirt, laced up her sneakers, and crept quietly out of their room.

She moved out to the rock garden and walked across the field. It was still dark out as she made her way through the forest, but the path was wide enough that she could see it in the moonlight.

As she approached the foundation, she was shocked to see that someone else was already there. She wondered who else would be crazy enough to be out in the woods at this hour. She crept up to the edge of the clearing and saw that it was Osaka doing tai chi. He held an incredibly strong ball of energy as he moved through the postures. Katana also saw the brightest glow around him she'd ever seen. His aura seemed to pulsate with energy.

Without warning, Osaka stopped mid-form and turned to see who was there. "Katana!" he said with surprise. She walked over to the edge of the foundation. "What are you doing here?"

Katana suddenly felt embarrassed. "I found this place when we were playing Frisbee the other day. What used to be here?"

Osaka sat down on the edge of the stone. "This was a dojo many decades ago. When Master Chow came to California, he built this place first. He used it to practice during the years it took to complete the Hall of the Dragon."

"Wow," said Katana, sitting down next to him. "I could feel the energy coming from it. I thought it would be a neat place to practice tai chi."

"That it is," said Osaka. "I come here myself every morning to do precisely that. Chow chose this place to build the dojo because it is one of the oldest parts of the forest." Osaka gestured around them with one hand. "Some of these trees have been here for over two thousand years. As you become more adept at tai chi, you'll be able to feel the energy of every living thing around you. And the energy in this place is the strongest I've ever felt.

"Come, Katana," he said, rising to his feet. They walked to the center of the foundation. "You know the 24-posture form?"

"Yes," she replied. Katana followed Osaka through the form, both of them holding a fireball the entire time. Katana thought she almost *could* feel the energy of the forest as she moved slowly from one posture to the next.

Katana kept her practice session with Osaka to herself. She felt like she had been initiated into something very special, and didn't share it with anyone—not even Sara and Chris. But every morning that week, she rose a little before five and went out to the woods to practice with Osaka.

They hardly spoke during these sessions. Osaka would simply smile as Katana joined him on the stone and they began the form. Osaka started teaching her the longer 108-posture form, which he told her was called simply "the long form." By the end of the week, Katana knew all 108 postures although even she found it difficult to memorize so much movement in such a short amount of time.

Katana and her friends spent the rest of the week playing Frisbee and soccer out on the school grounds, swimming in the pool and practicing in Sam's dojo. At night they would either play video games or watch movies, or just hang out and enjoy their time off.

Once the week was over, they went back to their normal routine, and the competition teams trained hot and heavy to get ready for nationals.

***

Sam and Master Hua followed a monk into one of the chambers in the main hall of the Shaolin Temple. The monk wore the orange robes of Shaolin and his head was shaved bald.

Sam was furious. This man owed her an explanation.

"All right, Liang," she said, "what the hell is going on?"

"You are referring to the attack?" The Arashi had raided the temple in the dead of night, only a few hours earlier.

"Yes, the attack," said Sam. "How did they get in? And why did you order the monks to *let* them in?"

"The Arashi commander was Master Lu," Liang explained.

Master Hua whistled through his teeth. "Lu's chi still imprinted," he observed.

"Yes," Liang confirmed. "Lu can still enter the temple."

"We could have stopped him. The Arashi were badly outnumbered. But you *ordered* the monks to let them pass!" Sam accused.

Liang sighed. "Master Samantha, Lu is our spy."

"What?"

"Lu has been passing information to the headmaster for months," Liang explained. "He is one of Jaaku's top lieutenants. But we must be very careful. If Jaaku realizes Lu is a traitor, he will kill him instantly. We must arrange his meetings with the headmaster in a way that escapes Jaaku's notice."

This was too much for Sam to take in all at once. "But... but how can Lu defy Jaaku like that? Jaaku took his prenatal chi. Doesn't he control him completely?"

"You must understand, Lu was the first Arashi, that we know of, who was taken against his will," said Liang. "Lu was extremely loyal to Shaolin for decades. He was the headmaster at the temple in Shanxi before it was abandoned. Before Jaaku took it for his headquarters."

"Then Lu deputy headmaster here, in Henan, many years," Master Hua added.

"Yes," Liang agreed. "After you turned down the post, Master Hua, and the headmaster appointed Lu instead, Lu became his most trusted adviser."

"Wait," said Sam. "Hua was going to be the deputy headmaster at Shaolin?"

Liang and Hua looked at each other for a moment.

"Yes, but Master Hua chose to leave Shaolin to accompany Master Nash to California instead. Master Nash is one of the most powerful masters who has ever trained at Shaolin. Some believe he may be a match for the headmaster. I cannot blame Hua for going with him. But I think I will let Master Hua tell you the rest of that story some other time.

"In any event, because of his strong loyalty to Shaolin, to the headmaster, Lu is able to assert his own will in certain situations. He cannot defy Jaaku's direct commands, or withhold information that Jaaku is specifically seeking. But of course, Jaaku's attention isn't always focused on him. Lu can act independently so long as his actions are congruous with Jaaku's desires. When Jaaku commands Lu to infiltrate Shaolin, he is able to meet with the headmaster, albeit briefly."

"So it's the same thing that happened to Sato," said Sam. "He's able to function autonomously to some degree. But if Lu were to come here against Jaaku's wishes..."

"Jaaku would sense it, and take his chi immediately," Liang finished for her. "But the connection sometimes works the other way. For example, Lu can *feel* Jaaku's obsession with the Scroll of the Five Masters. It's as if *he* wants to know its secret as desperately as Jaaku does. And he can see the scroll in his mind, as Jaaku sees it with his own eyes. That is how we hope to ascertain its location."

"So that's what Tanaka was talking about," said Sam. "He told us the spy had 'special knowledge.'"

"Indeed," Liang replied. "But Jaaku has relocated the scroll with some regularity—undoubtedly he is paranoid that we will attempt to reclaim it. He moved it again in the past few days, but Lu cannot yet determine the location."

"Yet?" asked Master Hua.

"This time, Lu feels he recognizes the vision in his head, the spot where Jaaku has hidden the scroll. But he cannot place it."

"I hope he figures it out soon," said Sam. "We can't very well take the scroll back if we don't know where it is."

"Agreed," said Liang. "Do not lose hope. As soon as Lu knows, he will tell the headmaster."

"On a different topic," Liang continued, "the headmaster has requested that I ask you about the child prodigy currently training at the Hall of the Dragon. Is it true that she is close to mastering a *third* chen do?"

"You mean Katana?" asked Sam, surprised at the question. "Yes, she can deflect intent and do a chi hit, and she is apparently close to getting levitation. Why does the headmaster want to know about her?"

"He is concerned about this child. Master Nash is not helping—he is careful not to mention the girl's progress. His silence on this matter only serves to heighten the headmaster's concerns." Liang didn't seem entirely comfortable with the subject.

"Why should Katana be a cause for concern?" asked Sam. "I

know it's unusual for someone so young to be so powerful, but it's not totally unheard of. I trained at the Hall with Katana's father, and he was able to do three of the chen do by the time we graduated. As far as I know, the headmaster was never concerned about *him*."

"No, it is not unheard of," said Master Liang. "We have a boy here, about the same age, who we believe is also on the verge of learning a third chen do. But we have only one. There are now *four* students at the Hall of the Dragon who can do two of the chen do."

"Four..." said Sam, trying to figure out who the other three might be. "I know there's Beecher. So there are two now..."

"There are four," said Master Liang. "The headmaster learned of this from Master Tanaka, whom you met at Shaka-In. Tanaka heard about it from his old sushi chef. He says the other three are very close to this Katana girl."

"It must be Chris and Sara," Sam said to Master Hua. "They must have learned another chen do since we left. But what difference does it make that they're close to Katana?"

"Have you noticed that every member of the Arashi is able to fade?" asked Liang. "Does that not seem a little unusual? We know of three masters who were unable to fade before they became Arashi. Yet as soon as they joined Jaaku, they attained this ability seemingly overnight. I understand it took you many months to learn this skill?"

"Yes, it did," said Sam. "That is... interesting. But I don't see what this has to do with Katana."

"According to Lu, Jaaku has taken the prenatal chi of *every* Arashi..."

"*Every?*" asked Hua in amazement.

"That explains how he was able to kill the Arashi I captured at Shaka-In," Sam observed.

"Yes," Liang agreed. "Jaaku can control every one of his servants, or take their chi if they disobey. But he is also able to use that connection to share power with them. That's why they can all fade. And now we have heard that three other students—who are very close to the prodigy— are also growing unusually powerful. The headmaster is worried that perhaps this girl has somehow mastered dim mak and is able to share power with her peers the same way that Jaaku does with his Arashi."

"Now that's ridiculous," said Sam. "Katana is the sweetest, most good-natured... if you met her, you would know there's no way she's covertly doing dim mak."

"You say so, and yet Master Nash is unwilling to discuss the girl with the headmaster, much less allow him to meet her," said Master Liang.

"But..." said Sam. She couldn't explain this situation.

"You begin to see the dilemma," said Master Liang. "You must understand, the very existence of dim mak is the shame of Shaolin."

"The shame of Shaolin? Why? Jaaku didn't learn dim mak *here*—did he?"

"He learn from Master Tong," said Master Hua. "Tong was tai chi master at Shaolin, and first master of dim mak. He left Shaolin and establish dim mak temple in desert in Xinjiang Province over two hundred years ago."

"I had no idea the first dim mak master trained at Shaolin..." said Sam.

"Yes," said Master Liang. "And the headmaster at the time failed to stop him. Tong established the original dim mak monastery. It was there that Jaaku learned the art. Ultimately, Jaaku killed Tong, and we believe he stole the dim mak manuscript—a text that contains all the secrets of that dark art. The monks of Shaolin raided the temple in Xinjiang after Jaaku killed Tong, but were unable to find the manuscript. And ever since, we have endeavored to defeat Jaaku to pay our debt for allowing dim mak to spread into the world."

"And now the headmaster is worried that even if he defeats Jaaku, Katana will grow up to be a dim mak master herself. I think I'm beginning to understand," said Sam. "I wonder why Nash won't let the headmaster meet her," she said to Master Hua. "I'm sure if he did, it would allay the headmaster's concerns immediately."

"Yes," said Master Hua. "But I no think Nash and headmaster get along so well. My fault, maybe."

"Not entirely," said Master Liang, looking apologetic. "Ever since the days of Master Chow, the Hall of the Dragon has remained somewhat independent from the other temples. There has always been some friction between the two. But when you left to join Master Nash... well, that did widen the gap between Master Nash and the headmaster."

"We can try to talk to Nash when we get back," suggested Sam. "If he understood the headmaster's concerns, he might allow him to meet Katana. Then he could see for himself that he has nothing to worry about."

"Excellent," said Master Liang. "I was hoping that you would say that."

Chapter Fifteen: The U.S. Nationals

Katana, Chris and Sara spent an enormous amount of time over the next few weekends working in Sam's dojo. Sara's newfound ability to do a chi hit had ignited her interest in sparring. The same could be said for Chris. And now that they could both perform a chi hit and deflect intent, they discovered that sparring with the chen do could be great fun.

"I wonder if we still can't do them on each other," said Chris one Saturday afternoon, the weekend before nationals.

"One way to find out," said Katana. She threw a fireball at him. Chris was totally unprepared; he merely stood there and grimaced. But he was in no danger—the fireball completely fizzled out long before it reached him.

"Now we know," he said.

Since Sara could do the chen do against both Chris and Katana, she got the most practice. "This is so cool!" she said after throwing a fireball at Chris and launching him into the wall.

"Yeah... so cool," Chris muttered as he walked back to continue the match.

"You guys should try to catch each other's fireballs and throw them back," suggested Katana.

"No thank you. I don't wanna do what you did to Jason that day!" said Chris, misunderstanding her.

"No, I didn't mean to catch it with a ball of energy," said Katana. "You're definitely not doing that. But you can start to deflect it, the normal way, then gather the rest of it to you and throw it back."

Sara threw a fireball at her, and she captured it and held it between her hands. "Just like that," she said, "only then you throw it back at them."

"Oh, just like that," said Chris. "Well, let's give it a shot."

He and Sara tried the skill for the next half hour, but succeeded only in knocking each other down repeatedly. Neither of them could do it. Finally they called it a day and headed down to dinner.

Katana and Sara went to sit at the sushi bar. Terry-san seemed flustered. "This is it, girls," he said quietly.

"I know," said Sara. "U.S. nationals, right in our backyard. Are you helping with the preparations, too?"

"No, no... The tournament is but a trivial concern. I am talking about Master Samantha and Master Hua," he said conspiratorially.

"What are they doing now?" asked Katana. She felt her heart leap into her throat.

"They will leave Shaolin very soon to complete their mission," whispered Terry-san. "We will have no further contact with them until they return to the Hall of the Dragon."

"And how long is that going to take?" asked Sara.

"Nobody knows," said Terry-san ominously. "Maybe a few days, maybe weeks... we will see."

Katana lost her appetite worrying about Sam and Hua.

Master Nash had made arrangements with Lincoln Academy for the students from the Hall to have that Friday off from school. He had been organizing the volunteer schedule along with Master Daniels, who was running a great deal of the event much to his own dismay. They were asking the students from the Hall who weren't competing to sign up for a few hours over the course of the weekend. Chris and Sara had volunteered to help set up the event on Friday so they'd be free during the actual tournament. Although she wasn't required to do so, Katana decided to volunteer as well so she could spend the day with her two best friends. They went to the Pacific Hotel in Eureka first thing Friday morning with Master Daniels and a dozen other students.

Katana almost didn't recognize the place. The U.S. nationals was a much bigger event than the Eureka Challenge. The hotel was forced to allocate not only their main convention hall, but their smaller conference rooms as well.

As they walked into the convention hall to check on preparations Katana saw that the stage was already set up, although it wasn't in its usual location in the center of the room—it was against the back wall instead. Workers were setting up scaffolding along the front wall, with spotlights and big television cameras.

"Is this going to be on TV?" Katana asked.

"Yes," muttered Master Daniels. "ESPN or some such thing, as though anyone in their right mind would want to watch this nonsense. They should take their cameras and go home—they're only making things more complicated than they already were."

Just then Harvey Ryder waddled over, wiping his sweaty hands on his pants. "I couldn't agree more," he said to Master Daniels. "They *should* go home. I've been covering the circuit for twenty years, and they never bothered before. But in the past couple of years they've discovered there might be an interest in martial arts competition. They only want their ratings to go up. So instead of covering it for the love of the sport, like I always have, they're doing it for the money!"

Katana noticed that Sara had stepped back a little, and was looking back and forth between Master Daniels and Harvey Ryder. "Sara, what are you *doing*?" she whispered.

"I'm trying to decide who's wider," said Sara. They broke into a fit of giggles. Chris snorted.

Master Daniels scowled at them. "Well then I imagine you have nothing to worry about. Their ratings could only possibly go *down* after covering an event like this. Maybe they won't come back once they realize that this isn't real martial arts."

"What do you mean, not 'real martial arts'?" said Harvey, looking highly offended. "It takes amazing skill to whip those weapons around like that!"

"Show me someone who can 'whip around' a live blade—a *real* samurai sword mind you, not one of these aluminum decoys, and *then* I'll be impressed. Of course if they tried that, they'd cut off their own arm..."

Katana began to feel like this conversation might go on for hours.

But a moment later Becca Stratton poked her head in the door. She saw Katana, smiled, and started to walk over to them. But when she saw Harvey Ryder she turned to walk right back out of the room.

Harvey had spotted her. "Excuse me, Master Daniels—Oh, Becca! Becca Stratton, I wonder if I might be able to have a few moments of your time…"

Master Daniels watched Harvey waddle away and shook his head. "I need you three to help move tables to each of the rings."

Katana spent the next few hours with Chris and Sara setting up everything for the event. Once their hours were done, they hung out in Katana and Sara's hotel room for a couple of hours.

Later, they headed back downstairs to grab a bite to eat—the competition was starting at three—and met Becca in the hotel restaurant.

"So we found out today that everything we're learning isn't real," said Sara rolling her eyes.

"What does that mean?" asked Becca.

"Don't mind her," said Chris. "Master Daniels was shooting off his mouth about how only traditional martial arts are legitimate."

"Oh, yeah, Bobby's told me about him. He's the aikido guy, right?"

"That's him," said Katana.

"A lot of people feel that way," said Becca. "But my instructor says that if the martial arts don't evolve, they'll die. And he loves traditional karate—that's his main thing. But he recognizes that sport karate has a lot to offer, too."

They finished eating and moved into the convention hall. They wished Becca luck in her weapon event as she went off to stretch and warm up.

The center judge started the ring a few minutes later. He lined the competitors up and called off their names one at a time. Katana gave Becca a thumbs-up when she went back to take her seat, but Becca was so focused that she didn't see her.

"Where's Dana?" asked Chris.

"I don't think she wanted to watch," said Sara. "She's still upset about Golden Gate."

The competition started. Katana watched some of the best weapon forms she'd ever seen. Most of the competitors were armed with sport karate weapons—she saw a lot of bo staff, samurai sword and nunchuck forms. Only a few people had wushu weapons—one girl did broadsword and two did staff. Nobody did whip chain—single or double. Katana asked Sara about this. "Northern California has a big concentration of wushu schools, but most of the circuit does sport karate," she explained.

Becca went up right after that, and Katana was once again very impressed. Everyone in the ring had been excellent, but most seemed to emphasize either tricks or weapon control. Becca alone dominated in both respects. Her tricks were some of the best in the ring, and no one had matched her dexterity with the nunchucks.

The judges apparently agreed with Katana. Becca took first place.

"So what happens now?" asked Katana as they followed Becca to her kata ring.

"Well, Becca will go into grands tomorrow night with the winner from the boys' ring," said Sara. "They'll compete against the girl and boy who win the sixteen- and seventeen-year-old divisions. Whoever wins that is the national champion."

Becca's kata event started, and Katana was blown away. Every single person in the ring seemed to be as sharp and intense as Becca. Katana was glad *she* didn't have to judge—she would've been hard-pressed to decide who was the best. But the judges seemed to think that Becca had something special in this competition as well, and she advanced to grands in her second event.

"Your turn," Becca said to Katana as they walked over to the sparring ring. "Good luck, Kat."

Katana put her gear on, and sat down next to Jimmy and Jason. She looked around the ring, sizing up her competition. There were more boys she could use the gainer flash against than there had been at Golden Gate. Katana started feeling nervous. She wondered how many of them had seen her move on the internet, and if any of them had devised a countermove. She'd know soon enough.

"Katana?" she heard to her left. A short man in a fancy suit was squatting down next to her.

"Yes?"

"My name is Walter Knox," he said. "I'm a reporter for Black Belt magazine."

"Oh. Hi," said Katana, shaking his hand.

"I was wondering if I could get an interview with you after the competition tonight?"

"Yeah, sure."

"Thanks," he said, and patted her on the back. He seemed a lot better at this than Harvey. "Good luck up there."

The center judge came over and lined them up for roll call. "We will be eliminating down to the final four tonight," he said when he was done. "The winners will compete on stage tomorrow night in grands."

"Good luck, guys," said Katana, giving Jimmy and Jason high-fives.

"Good luck, Kat—really," said Jason. He looked like he genuinely wanted her to do well.

"Thanks," she said. They sat down again to wait for their first matches.

Jimmy was called up first. He had to go against a very tall boy, and didn't do very well. The boy was able to keep Jimmy away with his long legs, and beat him 6-0. Jimmy had been eliminated.

Jason went next, and fared much better than Jimmy. Jason's opponent was also quite tall, but Jason sparred with Bobby Wellington all the time, so he was ready for it. The match went to 2-2 very quickly. Then Jason used the leg scissors takedown, and rolled over to score a kick as his opponent hit the floor. Jason won 6-2.

Katana went next, and also had to fight a taller boy. But she discovered very quickly that he didn't want to hit her. Katana won easily with her kicking combinations. The final score was 6-0.

"He didn't throw a single kick," said Jimmy when she sat down.

"It seems like a lot of boys refuse to hit a girl," replied Katana with a shrug.

"That's dumb," said Jimmy with a look of disgust.

Jason won his next match as well, although it was much tougher. He and the other boy both earned four points early in the match, but after that neither could score for several rounds.

Finally the other boy tried the leg scissors takedown, but missed—he slid down Jason's body instead. Jason reached over and punched him in the head. He won 5-4.

The next boy Katana sparred with had no problem hitting a girl. He opened up very aggressively, nailing Katana in the face with a roundhouse kick after she'd blocked his front kick.

Katana was able to win the next round with a kicking combination of her own; her axe kick across the back of the boy's head earned her two points.

They traded kicking combinations back and forth for a minute, then Katana dropped to sweep the boy's leg when he threw a side kick at her. He fell face-down on the floor. When he landed, she turned over and kicked him in the back of the head. She won the match 6-2.

"One more win and we go to grands," she said to Jason when she returned to the edge of the ring.

"Hey, I'm sorry about what I said after Golden Gate," Jason told her. "Don't *not* use the gainer flash just because I said you're a show-off. If you have an opportunity, take it, okay?"

"Don't worry," said Katana. "I will."

And she had that opportunity in her next match. The boy she had to spar with was as tall as Jason and a little heavier. He was the perfect candidate for her secret weapon.

The match started, and the boy tried to jam Katana's legs to stop her from using her kicks. He rushed in with a punch, but Katana was able to deflect it before he drove her out of the ring.

They started again, and Katana was ready. She snapped a roundhouse kick to his head as soon as the judge said "Go!" She was up 2-0.

The boy learned his lesson very quickly, and didn't rush her again. They circled each other for several seconds, until the boy faked with a front kick. Katana anticipated a roundhouse kick next, and dodged. But he turned for a hook kick instead, catching her in the back of the head. They were tied 2-2.

The boy tried to charge with a punch next, but Katana jumped in the air, caught him with both legs and twisted over hard—she took him down with the leg scissors takedown. The boy scuttled out of the way before she could land a kick. She was up 4-2.

She decided it was time. When the judge started them again, Katana faked with a punch as she lunged forward for the gainer flash. But as she leaped into the air, the boy backed off and dropped. It was too late for her to stop; she'd already committed her body weight. But there was nobody there to push against.

That's when it happened. Katana was fighting hard to land the gainer, but didn't have nearly enough momentum to get around. But just as she should have crashed, she arced up instead, landing on her feet.

She had levitated.

The entire convention hall seemed to fall silent. The center judge stared at her for a moment before he yelled "UP!" Katana had a bad feeling she knew what was about to happen. He told her and the boy to kneel down while he went to confer with the other judges.

He came back a minute later. "Kahanu is disqualified for using an illegal technique," he announced. "Fisher advances to the final four."

After another moment of stunned silence, the crowd broke into applause for Fisher.

Katana felt terrible. As she'd feared, someone had figured out a way to counter her gainer flash. By using it unnecessarily against Jason at Golden Gate, she'd ended up hurting her team at nationals. Jason had been right.

"Katana!" yelled Chris as he ran over to her. "You did it! You got levitation!"

"That was awesome, Kat!" said Sara.

"Oh yeah, it was great," said Katana sarcastically. "I couldn't have picked a *better* time to get it, either, could I?"

She sat down with them to watch the next match, which Jason won easily. "At least *he* didn't let the team down," Katana thought as she cheered for him along with the rest of the crowd.

When the ring was over, Katana wanted to get out of there as soon as possible. A lot of people were giving her really strange looks and whispering to each other as they went by. But Sara reminded her that they still had to watch the team demos.

Katana was perfectly happy to see that Walter Knox from Black Belt magazine had decided to interview Jason instead of her. Jason looked at her apologetically and shrugged as she walked by to find a seat in front of the stage.

The first team took the stage and Sara said, "Hey, I think this is the team with the two double backflips."

Sara was right. The team did the exact same demo Master Hua had shown them at the movie night. Katana didn't care much for the rest of the demo. But she had to admit, the two competitors doing double backs at the same time was the coolest thing she'd ever seen.

"Wait," said Katana when the team was finished. "I thought Master Hua said they'd have to beat Supernova to make it to nationals?"

"They did," said an older woman sitting next to her. "I don't know what those judges were thinking. But Supernova advanced anyway because they're one of the top teams."

Strike Force and two other teams went next; Katana thought they were quite good. The other two teams did pure sport karate, and had excellent choreography and tricking skills. But the next team that came up was unlike anything Katana had ever seen.

They took the stage and the first thing she realized was that they were wearing military fatigues. "What the hell?" asked Chris. Then the music started—it was a loud, belligerent rap song and if Katana wasn't mistaken, the lyrics, which were heavily bleeped, advocated taking over the government.

The team began their routine. They used wushu weapons— broadswords, straight swords and staves—but they were hacking the air with them like machetes. This was unlike any wushu Katana had ever seen.

For their finale, one of the team members brought a large drum to the center of the stage. He pounded on it while the rest of the team ran back and forth doing a variety of tricks.

"Well, that was... different," said Sara when the team was done.

"That's a word for it," said Katana.

The Hall of the Dragon took the stage next.

"Dana looks stressed out," Katana observed.

"After that performance, wouldn't you be?" asked Sara.

Dana was on point, however, along with the rest of the team. But Katana thought the demo might be getting a little stale. It was good, but it hadn't changed much in two years. It wasn't as exciting anymore. The crowd seemed to agree, and didn't cheer as wildly as it usually did when Jelly landed his double backflip. Apparently, after seeing two people do that trick simultaneously, it wasn't very impressive as a solo.

Supernova came up next; they were the last team to go. Katana was immediately impressed with their stage presence and the level of choreography. Their demo opened with an absolutely explosive tricking sequence—the most impressive of the night despite the absence of a double backflip. Several of the kids had linked three or four difficult tricks together, along the lines of what Nash had taught them earlier that term.

By the end of their performance, Katana had no doubt who would be winning grands the next night. The Hall of the Dragon had beaten Supernova the previous year, when Supernova had been reigning champions. But they seemed perfectly poised for a big comeback.

The under-black belt events took place on Saturday. Katana spent the day with Sara and Chris in the hotel's swimming pool, avoiding people as much as possible.

"Don't let it get to you so much, Kat," said Sara, when they sat down for dinner late that afternoon.

"Sara, the fact is that if I had made grands with Jason, our team could have won. But now..."

"We could still win," said Sara. "I did the math. If Jason wins first, and that kid with the military fatigues takes second, the military team wins. But if Jason is first and the military kid is third or fourth, we win. So you might not have cost the team anything."

"Yeah but if I hadn't been such a show-off at Golden Gate, I would've made grands. We would've been guaranteed a win no matter what," said Katana.

"Who cares, Kat?" said Chris. "You still got levitation! Now you can chase Jelly for me when he runs up the wall."

After dinner, they went to find their seats for grands. As they walked into the convention hall, Katana thought it looked more like a rock concert than a karate tournament. The room was dark; the only source of light on the stage came from ESPN's spotlights. There was also an enormous video screen mounted behind the stage, so people sitting farther back could see the action up close.

Katana started to feel better—the energy in the room seemed to be contagious. Finally, the emcee began the event.

"Ladies and Gentleman," he said, "welcome to the Grand Championships of the United States National Karate Tournament.

We'll be getting underway with the youth weapon grands. First up from the Hall of the Dragon right here in Northern California will be Stephen Gallo, our winner from the boys' weapon division, ages twelve and thirteen."

Jelly took the stage. "You know," said Sara, "I forgot his real name was Stephen! I think I'm going to call him that from now on."

"Oh, he'll love that," said Katana.

Jelly performed his staff form stronger than ever. Like Dana, he seemed to draw energy from a large audience. But unlike Dana, Master Hua's absence hadn't had any noticeable effect on his exuberance.

The audience cheered loudly for Jelly, and the emcee announced the next competitor. It was a small nine-year-old girl who'd won the girls' eleven and under division.

"Hah," said Chris as she took the stage. "She's only nine and she's the same height as Jelly!"

The girl did a sport karate bo staff form. Her weapon control was excellent, as was her intensity. Katana thought she'd give Jelly a run for his money. But she was disqualified when she dropped her staff near the end of her form.

"Aw, that's too bad," said Sara. "I thought she might have beaten Jelly and put that midget in his place for once. It would drive him nuts to lose to a nine-year-old girl!"

"Nah," said Chris. "Jelly woulda beaten her even if she hadn't dropped it. Don't forget his double backflip—that's hard to beat."

A boy and a girl both came up and did traditional Japanese

bo staff forms next, but they couldn't touch Jelly. He won grands for weapons.

The older group went next. Becca swept the division, winning weapons and kata.

"She's amazing," said Katana.

Finally the event Katana most wanted to see took the stage: the sparring grands.

Jason was called first. He was sparring Fisher, the boy who'd beaten Katana when she got disqualified. "GET HIM!" yelled Katana at the top of her lungs.

Jason trounced Fisher. He won the match 6-2.

"YES!" yelled Katana.

The boy with the military fatigues went next, and had to spar with the boy who had eliminated Jimmy in his first round. But the boy with the fatigues failed to get through the other boy's long legs—just as Jimmy had—and lost the match 6-0. Katana, Chris and Sara got up and screamed. This meant that the Hall of the Dragon would win the team sparring division as long as Jason could win his next match.

And once again, Jason's practice time with Bobby seemed to pay off. He coped with the other boy's long legs much better than anyone else had. It was a close match, but Jason used the leg scissors takedown to win the match 6-5.

Katana went wild along with everyone else from the Hall of the Dragon. Jason had won his division individually for the second year in a row, and won for the team as well.

Only the team demos remained. The Hall of the Dragon was called to the stage first. They performed well, but Katana was left feeling that Master Hua would need to revamp their demo if they wanted to be competitive against Supernova the following year.

The belligerent team with the military fatigues went next, and Supernova went last. Both performed as well as they had the night before, but it was much more exciting to watch under the spotlights.

The judges deliberated, and then stunned the audience. Supernova had won, but the team with the fatigues had taken second place over the Hall of the Dragon.

"That's weird," said Chris. "I didn't think they were that good."

"Maybe the judges are trying to send a message that they appreciate originality," suggested Sara.

"Well they were definitely original," Katana said as they joined the throng trying to get out of the convention hall.

The tournament was officially over, so they boarded the buses back to the Hall. Katana was exhausted, and went straight to bed when she got to her room. As she drifted off to sleep, she thought of Sam and Master Hua, and wondered where they were that night.

Chapter Sixteen: Mission Accomplished

Master Liang unrolled an enormous map on the stone table.

"You've got it?" Sam asked anxiously. "You know where the scroll is?"

Liang nodded. "Lu was here last night. He was supposed to be sneaking into the archives for Jaaku. Lu finally recalled the place he was seeing." Liang pointed to a spot on the map. "Rebel's Cave."

"In Shanxi?" asked Master Hua.

"Yes," Liang confirmed. "It's the ideal hiding place. The location makes it impossible to access unless you can levitate or fade. A small group of monks fled there when the government burned down the temple in the 1600s. They stayed there until the political climate changed and they could rebuild. Lu went to visit the cave right after he became headmaster in Shanxi."

"Close to temple," said Master Hua, examining the map.

"Too close," Liang agreed. "If anyone fades to the cave, Jaaku will be able to sense it. You will have to go on foot. But be careful—if anyone sees you and alerts Jaaku to your presence, the mission will fail."

"That's not likely, is it?" asked Sam. "The temple is in the middle of nowhere."

"There are always Arashi coming and going," Liang replied. "That is the danger. And you must leave as soon as possible. We are afraid that Jaaku will learn of Lu's betrayal. If that should happen, he will surely move the scroll again. We will lose this opportunity."

Liang bent over the map and pointed to a spot near the temple in Shanxi. "You will approach from here. You must be careful to keep your distance from the monastery. You will travel around the valley to this ridge, just north of the temple. The entrance to the cave is halfway up the cliff face. Master Hua, you will have to levitate up to the opening."

"Well, once we get there, this should be easy," Sam observed, sounding more optimistic than she felt. "Hua jumps up, grabs the scroll, and we leave."

"Let's hope it's that simple," said Liang. He rolled up the map and handed it to Hua. "I must confess, I wish I were still accompanying you on this final leg of your mission."

"You were going to go with us?" asked Sam.

"If you hadn't learned to fade in time," said Liang. "I would have joined you, and faded you back to the Hall of the Dragon once you'd retrieved the scroll."

Sam and Master Hua left the Shaolin Temple in Henan Province the next morning. They set out due north for Shanxi. They were able to travel on tourist buses for the first few days, going from one village to the next. But when they reached a village on the edge of the forest where the temple was located, they set out on foot.

They hiked through the woods as long as the daylight lasted, then set up camp for the night. They lit a small fire in a clearing next to a large outcropping of rock, and dug into the provisions the headmaster had sent with them.

"Hua," said Sam after they had sat in silence for some time, "would you really have been the deputy headmaster if you'd stayed at Shaolin?"

"Yes," said Master Hua quietly.

"Why did you leave?"

Hua stared into the fire for a moment. "I am teacher, Samantha. I love practice martial arts, I love teach martial arts. The headmaster no teach. He only administrate. All politics at Shaolin. Bad for the soul.

"I knew with Master Nash, I teach. So with Master Nash I go."

"Then why did you agree to go on this crazy mission?" she asked.

"Because I love teach."

"I don't follow..."

Hua looked back at the fire. "Jaaku very, very bad. Evil. He attack Shaolin, monks cannot teach, monks cannot learn—they fight. Some die. He attack Shaka-In. Same there: monks cannot teach. If he attack Hall of Dragon, same for us, eh? We cannot teach, kids cannot learn. Dana, Jelly, Paul—they in danger.

"I go on mission for kids, Samantha. We take back scroll, Nash hide it somewhere far away, Jaaku have no reason to attack. Monks at Shaolin and Shaka-In can learn again. And our kids not in danger. Dana keep learning. I keep teaching."

Sam felt tears welling up in her eyes. She thought of Katana. "I know exactly how you feel."

They got what little sleep they could and broke camp at first light. For the next two days they traveled through the forest, until finally as dusk began to settle on the second day, they reached the temple.

"What happened here?" asked Sam. They had come up to the top of a hill. The monastery was located in the valley below. But the trees around the temple were burned out, as if from a fire. Only blackened trunks remained.

"Don't know," said Master Hua.

Sam examined the building more closely. A faint red glow emanated from the structure. She spotted two Arashi milling about in front of the entrance. Beyond them, along the front wall, was a pen. At least two dozen people were inside, huddled together in small groups. Sam didn't know what they were doing there. But the sight sent a chill down her spine.

They continued through the forest, around the perimeter of dead trees. Finally they came to a trail. The trees grew much sparser farther ahead. They were close to the ridge where Sam knew they would find Rebel's Cave.

"We stop here, wait until night time," said Master Hua. "Nobody see us in the dark." He set down his gear beside a tree.

"Good idea," said Sam.

They sat down, each leaning against a different tree, and waited. Nighttime settled around them. It was quiet, except for the crickets. There didn't appear to be any activity at the monastery, visible through the trees only in silhouette. But they were taking no chances. They waited a few more hours for the moon to set so Master

Hua could approach the cave in total darkness.

But suddenly there was a noise. Sam listened closely—she heard voices. Someone was coming down the path. She grabbed her pack, dashed a few yards into the woods and hid behind a large tree. She could see Hua attempting to take cover on the other side of the trail but the trees were too sparse. He was exposed.

Sam wanted to yell to him, to warn him, but it was too late. Someone walked into view around a bend in the path. It was an Arashi. Another followed, shouting commands behind him.

Sam's heart hammered in her chest. She watched a group of peasants follow the Arashi along the trail. There were at least twenty of them—men, women and children. They looked terrified.

Three more Arashi brought up the rear, one of them shouting at the captives in Chinese. Sam held her breath.

A moment later the entire group came to a stop. One of the Arashi ran into the trees on the other side of the path.

He'd found Hua.

The Arashi shoved him into the group of peasants, hollering at him; Hua stumbled a few steps before recovering his balance. The entire group began moving again. It appeared as though the Arashi had mistaken Hua for one of the peasants attempting an escape.

Sam felt the adrenaline coursing through her veins—her instinct was to run out and fade away with Hua. But if she did that, they'd lose their shot at retaking the scroll. She waited until the group had moved out of view before following as stealthily as possible.

Her only hope was to sneak into the group undetected and remove Hua to safety—or perhaps Hua would have an opportunity to slip away unnoticed. But one of them would have to act before they reached the temple. If they brought Hua inside, Sam would have no choice. She would have to fade him away, and that would be the end of their mission.

Sam stopped when she caught sight of the group again. They'd left the trail to move through the dead trees. She waited until they'd emerged into the clearing beyond, then followed, careful not to make any noise.

The Arashi led the peasants across the open field. Sam waited at the edge of the blackened trunks, becoming increasingly desperate. Without the cover of the trees, there would be no hope of rescuing Hua unseen. They'd reach the temple any minute now. Sam moved into the clearing, prepared to fade to his side. She understood the ramifications of what she was about to do. She knew they may never have another opportunity to retake the scroll. But she'd made her decision. She couldn't sacrifice Hua.

But the Arashi weren't headed to the temple entrance. It looked like they were bringing their captives to the pen. Sam stopped and retreated to the tree line, ready to fade if she was wrong. But she'd guessed correctly. The Arashi met two others at the pen. One of those opened a gate and ushered the peasants inside.

Sam knew what she had to do. She moved around the edge of the clearing and approached the pen from the side, out of view of the guarding Arashi. The enclosure was constructed from wood and chicken wire. A woman inside caught sight of her; she eyed Sam suspiciously, but didn't say anything.

Sam spotted Hua halfway across the pen, gazing out at the forest. "Hua," she hissed.

Hua saw her. He walked slowly across the enclosure, careful not to attract attention.

"Not good," he whispered, shaking his head. "But lucky Arashi not know me. Think I am peasant."

"Let's get out of here," said Sam. "The wire won't prevent me from fading you—"

"No!" he replied. "If you fade, Jaaku will know we're here."

"Hua—it's over. We failed. I'm fading us back to the Hall."

"No, Samantha. You must complete mission. Go back to cave— fade to entrance. *Get scroll*!"

"I'm not leaving you here," she insisted.

At that moment, there was a brilliant flash of light across the pen. Two Arashi had faded outside the entrance to the temple. They conferred with the others for a moment before walking inside the building.

"Samantha. Go," Hua whispered. "Now!"

"No," Sam replied flatly. "I won't leave you behind."

"I will escape," Hua told her. "Find way back to Shaolin."

"You're crazy!" Sam hissed. "This place is crawling with Arashi. How the hell are you going to get away?"

Before Hua could respond, there was a commotion on the other side of the pen. Sam crept away, around the corner of the temple. She peered out from behind the brick wall as one of the Arashi opened the enclosure. He walked inside, shouting at the captives in Chinese. He grabbed a teenage girl, yanking her from her father's grasp. The girl screamed as the Arashi pulled her out of the pen. Another Arashi closed the barrier behind them.

The girl's father cried out to her, banging his fists against the wooden frame until one of the Arashi shot a fireball at him. It knocked him halfway across the pen. He landed in the dirt and curled up in pain. Sam could hear him sobbing.

The other Arashi faded away with the girl. A moment later, Sam could hear her screams echoing from somewhere deep inside the temple. They intensified, then abruptly stopped.

Sam crept back to Hua.

"They must be bringing these people to Jaaku so he can take their chi," she said with a shudder.

"Yes," Hua agreed. "But no matter. You must go."

"I've got an idea," she said. "I can fade us to the tree line, and we can complete our mission together."

Hua shook his head. "Never work. Jaaku sense you."

"True, but with the Arashi fading in and out of here, he'll never know it was me. Nash told me he can tell when someone fades nearby, but he has no way of knowing *who* it is. If we faded to the cave, we'd be in trouble. Nobody's supposed to be out there. But right next to the temple? Jaaku won't know the difference."

"But what about flash?" asked Hua. "You fade, Arashi see light—they know we here."

"No," said Sam, "that's not far enough to create a flash. They won't see a thing. Trust me."

Hua looked skeptical. "I don't know…"

"It's either that, or I fade us back to the Hall," Sam told him. "At least this way, we've still got a shot."

Hua seemed to consider this for a moment, then he nodded.

Sam turned to look across the clearing. She focused on a point at the edge of the trees, adjacent to the temple and hopefully out of the Arashi's line of sight. In the next instant, she enveloped Hua in her shen and faded them away.

They crouched low and stayed still for a minute, watching the pen. But their departure seemed to have gone unmarked. They moved through the dead trees into the forest, and made their way back up the path to where they'd left their gear.

They waited for several minutes in the cover of the trees, not daring to move any closer to the cave for fear of being seen. They kept an eye on the temple; Hua wanted to make sure they hadn't alerted Jaaku to their presence. But the monastery was quiet.

"I jump in, take scroll, jump out," Hua said. "You see me hit ground, we fade back to Hall."

"I understand," said Sam. "Good luck."

Hua scurried away. Sam lost sight of him immediately—he blended into the darkness. She worried for a minute that she wouldn't be able to see him jump down from the cave, and wouldn't know when to join him. But then she spotted him against the cliff face, a shadow moving among shadows.

Hua jumped. Sam could see him rise against the rock wall, to a point halfway up the cliff. Then he disappeared inside the cave.

Sam felt as if time had stopped. It seemed like an eternity before she saw Master Hua again. He ran out of the cave, jumping immediately over the edge. He floated down to the ground, his arms pumping the whole time as if he were trying to fly.

But as he hit the ground, Sam heard a ghastly screech. It seemed to come from the monastery. And she sensed something terrifying. The glow of the temple itself began to grow and reach out to the surrounding forest. Sam panicked.

Hua seemed to sense it, too, because suddenly he jumped again, toward the trees. But as he leaped into the air, there was a deafening crack of thunder. An enormous bolt of lightning struck the spot where Hua had been standing only a moment before. "NO!" Sam screamed. A branch from the main bolt struck Master Hua and knocked him to the ground mid-jump.

Sam began to take a step forward, then disappeared. She faded right next to Hua—he was unconscious. She squatted down and grabbed the scroll out of his limp hand. She reached underneath him with her other arm, pulling him into her. Then she pictured her dojo back at the Hall.

As Sam started to fade, Jaaku emerged from the cave above, gathering his energy for another strike.

***

"YOU GOT LEVITATION?!" yelled Jelly. They were at breakfast, the morning after the tournament. The entire cafeteria stopped talking to see who was making all the noise.

"Yeah," said Katana with a sigh. "But it was right in the middle of a sparring match, so I got disqualified." She explained in detail what had happened when she'd tried the gainer flash.

"Who cares about the stupid sparring match?" said Jelly. "You can levitate!"

That afternoon, Katana went down to Sam's dojo with Sara and Chris to work on the chen do. Chris and Sara goofed around, sparring and throwing fireballs at each other, but Katana wanted to levitate again. She wasn't sure how to go about it. She tried Jelly's trick of running up the wall a few times, but wasn't able to get any higher than usual.

Nothing she did seemed to work. Frustrated, she went to referee for Sara and Chris. Once those two had tired themselves out, they sat down on the mat and talked more about everything that had happened at nationals.

"I can't believe you can do *three* chen do now," said Chris.

"Well, I can't today," Katana replied. "But I sure could the other night!"

At that moment there was a brilliant flash of light at the front of the dojo. Katana looked over in time to see Sam and Master Hua appear there. Katana, Sara and Chris ran over to them.

Sam was on her knees next to Hua. He was lying on the mat, unconscious.

"Go get Master Nash!"

But as she finished saying the words, Master Nash appeared right next to her.

"Okay…" said Sara quietly.

"Samantha," said Nash, kneeling down next to her and Master Hua. "You were successful?"

"Yes," said Sam, tears rolling down her cheeks. "But Jaaku hit Hua with his lightning bolt. Nash…?"

"Osaka's on his way with Brock right now," said Nash. He placed two fingers on the side of Master Hua's neck. "This is not good," he said. "He's alive, but barely."

Katana felt her heart sink; tears welled up in her eyes.

Briefly, Sam told Nash what had happened. "We thought we were safe. I figured Jaaku would have moved the scroll immediately if he'd sensed our presence. We waited, and nothing happened. But then Jaaku showed up the moment Hua left the cave."

Nash thought about it for a moment. "His chi must have imprinted on the scroll. That's certainly plausible. We know he was obsessed with learning its secret since he acquired it last year. If so, he would have felt it when someone touched the scroll, the same way I can sense someone fading into the Hall."

Osaka walked in with Daniels right behind him. He stopped just inside the doorway, surveyed the room, and then turned to whisper something to Daniels. Daniels nodded. The two of them ran across the dojo.

"Osaka, give me a hand," said Nash. "Hua's almost dead. We need to get him up to the infirmary."

But as Osaka bent down to help, there was a deafening bang out in the atrium. It sounded like thunder.

Katana turned. Sato appeared in the doorway and stepped inside. Behind him stood another figure, clad in white samurai armor: Jaaku.

Katana, Chris and Sara looked on in terror. But just then someone grabbed Katana around the waist. The scene in front of her dissolved; an empty dojo filled her vision instead. She turned to see that it was Master Daniels who had faded her away.

She took a step toward the door, but Daniels blocked her path.

"Let me go!"

"Osaka said to keep you here until it's over."

Katana tried to duck around him, but Daniels grabbed her by the arm.

"Let go!" she screamed. She wrenched her arm free. Daniels tried to grab her again, but Katana shot twenty feet into the air. She landed with Daniels in hot pursuit. He was still between her and the exit.

Daniels chased her into the corner. Katana ran two steps up one wall, then kicked hard against the adjacent wall. She flipped right over Daniels, landing behind him.

She bolted for the door. Daniels faded directly in front of her. Katana bounced her chi against the floor, dove over his head and rolled out of the dojo. She vaulted over the edge of the balcony and floated down to the floor of the atrium. She ran, skidding to a stop at the door to Sam's dojo.

She froze on the spot.

Master Nash was walking toward Jaaku. "Leave this place," he said, but suddenly faded away. He appeared again behind Jaaku. A bolt of lightning struck the spot where Nash had been standing only a moment before, leaving a blackened hole in the mat.

Jaaku took a step toward Sam and Hua. "You will return that to me," he said. His voice was little more than a whisper. Sam got to her feet and backed away. Osaka reached to grab her arm. But at that moment, Sato hit Sam with an enormous fireball. Sam fell and the scroll flew out of her hand. It sailed through the air—directly toward Sato.

Osaka threw out his hand and shot a fireball at the scroll, incinerating it mid-flight.

Time seemed to stop. Everyone froze. Katana couldn't believe it: Osaka had just destroyed the Scroll of the Five Masters.

"FUSHI!" Jaaku screamed in a hoarse whisper, full of malice. He turned and disappeared behind a flash of light.

Sato faded as well, but reappeared behind Sam. He flung one arm around her neck, pushing his other hand against her sternum.

"Sato," said Nash, walking toward him. "What are you doing?"

"My master... I must kill Samantha."

"No!" Katana screamed. She ran across the dojo to them.

"Katana, no," said Osaka sternly.

Daniels came in behind Katana. She hadn't noticed him standing behind her. Sam struggled futilely against Sato's hold.

"Master Sato, *please*!" begged Katana. "Let her go!"

"I cannot. My master commands me..."

Sato cranked Sam's head farther back. Sam stopped struggling.

Katana couldn't believe this was happening. *Not Sam,* she thought. *Anyone but Sam...*

"She was my father's best friend," Katana pleaded, tears rolling down her cheeks. "She's the only connection I have to my parents. Don't do this!"

"Adrian..." said Sato. For a moment, he seemed to waver. But then he tightened his grip again. Sam whimpered.

"NO!" Katana screamed.

"Listen to her, Sato," Osaka said quietly. "Think of Adrian. Samantha has been like a mother to Adrian's daughter. If you kill her, you kill a part of Katana. Fight it, Sato! Focus on Adrian!"

"I CAN'T!"

It happened in an instant. Sato released his hold. Nash faded behind him, pulling him back in a chokehold. Sam fell to the ground.

"Brock! Help Osaka get Hua up to the infirmary," Nash commanded.

Daniels ran over to Master Hua.

"You've got him?" asked Nash.

Osaka nodded, looking grim. "Do what you need to do."

Master Nash wrangled Sato out of the room.

"We should carry him," said Osaka. "Fading again could further disrupt his energy."

Osaka and Daniels hoisted Hua up, and carried him away.

Katana dropped to her knees in front of Sam. Chris and Sara—who had been watching events unfold around them in sheer terror—ran over as well.

"Are you okay?" Katana asked between sobs.

"I think so," said Sam as she sat up. "But I've got a huge headache."

Chapter Seventeen: Loss

"So the mission was to steal back the Scroll of the Five Masters?" asked Sara quietly.

"Yes," said Sam, shaking her head. "That was the mission. Osaka blasted it, didn't he?" she asked. "When Sato hit me with the fireball and the scroll flew out of my hand." She looked down at her hands. "Osaka blasted it," she repeated.

Katana was worried. It seemed like Sam was in shock. She had never looked so unfocused.

"Yeah," said Chris quietly.

"Unbelievable," said Sam. "We went halfway around the world to steal back the scroll so Osaka could incinerate it. That makes sense, right?" Katana could see tears welling up in her eyes.

"No..." said Katana, "that doesn't make sense at all."

"Ah, well..." said Sam. She shook her head. "So Katana, I gather that you can levitate now?"

"Yeah," said Katana softly. "I got it in the middle of a sparring match two nights ago. But then I couldn't do it again... until Daniels grabbed me." She looked at Sara and giggled nervously.

"And I hear you two can both do *two* chen do now?" asked Sam, and sniffled.

"Yeah," said Sara. "We were down here goofing around a few weeks ago, and Kat was helping me do the tai chi form with the ball..."

"And then she threw it at me," said Chris, "and I deflected it."

"Wow," said Sam, getting to her feet. "I leave for a little while and you three turn into chen do masters."

"Sam, how did you hear about that?" asked Katana.

"One of the masters at the Shaolin Temple told us about it."

"Are you kidding me?" asked Sara.

Sam shook her head. "Let's go see how they're doing with Hua."

***

"He's beyond my ability to heal," Doctor Hubble said to Sam as they gathered around Master Hua's bed. "*Medically*, there's nothing wrong with him. This is going to be up to Osaka and Master Nash."

Master Hua was lying in the bed and someone had removed his shirt. Osaka had already inserted over a dozen acupuncture needles into various points in his chest and abdomen. He was currently inserting more needles in his neck.

"What do you think?" asked Sam. Osaka shook his head slightly. Sam stifled a sob.

Osaka worked for a few more minutes. "That is all I can do for him. Samantha, do you mind if we join you in your room for some dinner?"

"What?" said Sam with a sniffle. "Oh, no, that's fine..."

They followed Sam up to her apartment on the third floor. "Well, it's good to be home," she said as they walked into her suite. They sat down around the table in her sitting room, and Sam called in an order for a large amount of sushi, along with a sandwich for Chris.

When Sam was done ordering, Katana asked, "Osaka, why did Master Daniels take me away?"

"I instructed him that he should do so if Jaaku were to show up."

"Why?" Katana persisted.

"Katana, this is quite personal, it might be best if you and I discuss it in private," said Osaka.

"No," said Katana, "I tell these three everything anyway."

Osaka took a deep breath. "Katana, Jaaku murdered your parents."

"WHAT?!" Katana and Sam spoke at the same time.

"You told me they died in a *car accident*!" said Sam. "That's what I've believed all these years—now you're telling me Jaaku *killed* them?"

Katana looked from Osaka to Sam, and back to Osaka again to wait for his answer.

"They did die in a car accident," said Osaka. "But what I have never told either of you before now is that Jaaku caused that accident. Adrian and Kristine went to see me at my dojo the night that they died..."

"Yes," said Sam, "and you weren't there. I've heard this story a million times."

"I believe they went because Jesse Thompson called and told them to meet him there," said Osaka.

"Thompson... Thompson was still in China at that time," said Sam.

"Yes, but he came back briefly that night. He'd found Jaaku, and had begun training with him in dim mak. He betrayed Adrian to Jaaku, Samantha. He told him how powerful Adrian was, how he could do three chen do by the time he went to college. I believe Jaaku wanted Adrian to join his Arashi. They showed up in Hawaii that night. Jesse told Adrian to meet him at the dojo…"

"How do you know all of this? How can you be sure?" asked Sam.

"Because *I was there*, Samantha," said Osaka.

"No…" said Sam.

"I had been in China at the time, and I learned of Jaaku's intention to try to get to Adrian. I faded back to the dojo immediately, but I was too late. I tried to fend off Jaaku long enough for Adrian and Kristine to escape. But Jaaku faded out in front of the car and threw a fireball at them—I don't think he intended to kill them. I think he wanted to stop them from escaping so he could get to Adrian. But the car was in flames. I faded to Jaaku; I tried to stop him again. But the car swerved and went over the cliff."

"That explains why you didn't believe Lu was the new dim mak master last year," Katana observed. "You *knew* Jaaku was still alive."

"Yes," Osaka agreed, "although by that time, he had disappeared again for more than a decade. I told nobody what really happened the night your parents died. I waited to see what Jaaku would do next. Years went by and he did not reappear. But when we got word that there was a new dim mak master, I felt sure it had to be Jaaku. I waited until I could confirm it before notifying Shaolin."

"I still don't understand why you told Daniels to take me away when Jaaku showed up," said Katana.

Osaka's eyes filled with tears. "I lost your father, Katana. I couldn't risk losing you as well. When I walked in the dojo and saw you there... I had to make sure you were out of harm's way. So I instructed Master Daniels to fade away with you if Jaaku showed up."

"Why didn't you ever tell me? Or Sam, or anyone before now that Jaaku was responsible... for killing my parents?" asked Katana. She was no longer able to fight back the tears herself.

"I needed you to grow up happy and healthy," said Osaka. "Do you realize how different you could have turned out if you'd known your parents were murdered? Adrian and Kristine were gone, but you had Leanna and the Boyds there to raise you..."

"And you," said Katana quietly.

Osaka paused for a moment. A tear slipped down his cheek. "Thank you for that, Katana. Yes, and me. The point is that you have grown into someone who is caring and giving. You always contribute to the people around you," Osaka said, nodding to Chris and Sara.

"If you had known that a monster murdered your parents, would you have turned out the same? Or would you have grown up wanting to seek revenge one day? The knowledge of what happened to your parents could have consumed you and turned you into someone very different. I couldn't take that chance. I am sorry for keeping the truth from you for as long as I have. But I hope you can understand my reason for doing so."

There was a knock at the door. Gerty wheeled in a large cart that held their dinner, and Sam helped her set everything down on the table. The group sat in silence until Gerty left the room.

"Osaka," said Sam, "how did you know Jaaku would show up here?"

"I didn't know for certain," said Osaka. "It was only a hunch." He took a deep breath before continuing. "When Katana discovered that Sato was alive, we realized that he would still be able to enter the Hall of the Dragon. I was afraid Jaaku might use his connection to Sato to come here himself."

"Why did you destroy the scroll?" asked Katana.

"At that moment, I had no choice," Osaka said with a shrug. "We couldn't allow Sato to retake it. But with the scroll eliminated, Jaaku no longer has any reason to attack us, or the other temples."

"But now Chow's secret—the key to immortality—is gone, too," said Sam.

"Samantha..." Osaka took a deep breath. "The scroll was blank."

"*What*?" Sam exclaimed. Katana felt her jaw drop.

"The Scroll of the Five Masters was a blank piece of paper," Osaka repeated, grinning slightly at their reaction.

"Come on," said Chris. "How can an empty scroll hold the secret to immortality?"

"It can't, if you take the scroll literally like Jaaku did," Osaka replied. "Undoubtedly he was looking for some hidden message. But there was nothing special about the scroll itself. It was merely a koan."

"Ah..." Katana said pensively.

Sam suddenly seemed very upset.

"Wait," said Chris, his brow furrowed. "So... a blank piece of paper is supposed to be a riddle, to help you figure out..."

"How to become immortal?" Sara finished for him.

Osaka shrugged. "That's how Master Chow intended it."

There was another knock at the door. Sam got up to let Master Nash inside. "You're just in time for dinner," she said as they both sat down at the table.

"How is Master Hua?" Nash asked quietly.

Osaka met his eyes for a moment. He said nothing, but Nash clearly understood.

"Sam..." Sara said quietly. "Why didn't Sato..." She swallowed hard. "Why didn't he kill you?"

"Yeah," said Chris, "if Jaaku was commanding him to do it..."

"I'm guessing it must be the same for Sato as it was for Lu," Sam said tentatively, looking at Nash.

"Yes," Nash agreed. "Lu and Sato both became Arashi against their will. In that, they are unique. We found out from Lu that Jaaku has taken the prenatal chi of *all* the Arashi. For the others, there is no conflict in following Jaaku's orders—they joined willingly. Yet, for Lu and Sato, the desire to resist remains strong. Of course, Jaaku can still use his connection to compel them. And the more forcefully he bends them to his will, the harder it is for them to resist.

"But according to Sato, Samantha's death was not an obsessive desire for Jaaku, the way interpreting the scroll was. If it had been, Sato would not have been able to overcome Jaaku's directive. In Jaaku's mind, Sam is just a pawn. His command, in this case, was no more than an afterthought."

"Thank heaven for small miracles," Sam muttered.

They dug into their dinner. "So you guys have to tell me about the last two tournaments!" Sam said to Katana, Chris and Sara.

The three of them took turns filling her in on everything she'd missed while she was away. Everyone finished eating as they talked.

When they were done, Master Nash said, "I'm sorry kids, but I have to ask you to excuse us now. I need some time alone with Samantha and Osaka."

Once Katana, Sara and Chris had left, Sam said, "So basically, you sent Hua and me halfway around the world to risk life and limb to steal a blank piece of paper so you could destroy it. Do I have that right, or am I missing anything?"

"No, Samantha, you've got it exactly right," Nash said quietly.

Sam shook her head. Tears flowed down her cheeks. "Hua's lying on his deathbed!" she said, pointing up at the ceiling. "If the effing scroll was *blank*, why couldn't we let Jaaku keep it? What was the point..."

"We had to stop the attacks at the other temples," Nash reminded her gently.

Sam wanted to scream at him. How could he remain so calm and rational after what had happened? "You should have told us. If we knew it was blank..."

"That would have changed nothing," said Nash. "It wouldn't have mitigated the danger in any way. If we'd known that Jaaku could sense someone touching the scroll, perhaps we could have planned differently. I don't know... I'm sorry, Samantha."

She realized he was right. Although angry, she knew it wasn't Nash's fault. He'd spent months training them for the mission, giving them the greatest possible chance of success. Knowing the scroll was blank wouldn't have made a difference.

Sam took a minute to compose herself. "Tell me this: I tried to fade when Sato grabbed me. But I couldn't do it. He was stopping me somehow. And then it looked like you did the same thing to him. Am I losing my mind?"

"No," said Master Nash. "That's exactly what happened. But don't go trying that yourself yet—the technique is very advanced. You could obviously see from his shen that Sato was preparing to fade?" he asked. Sam nodded. "If you envelop someone in your shen as they are attempting to fade, *and* you anchor your own chi, you ground them to that spot. However, if you envelop them in your shen *without* simultaneously anchoring your chi, it will be as if *they* had enveloped *you* in their shen."

"So you would fade away with them," said Sam. "I get it. And when you say 'anchor your chi…'"

"Yes. Instead of projecting your chi somewhere else, you hold yourself in place," explained Master Nash.

"You're going to have to teach me how to do that sometime," said Sam.

"What did you learn from Sato?" asked Osaka.

"Not much that we didn't already know from Lu," said Nash. "He confirmed that Jaaku is able to share power with the Arashi. That is how he saved Sato last year, and that is why all of the Arashi can fade. It also explains why the Arashi have been so tough to take down during their raids on the temples. In the heat of battle, Jaaku lends them strength."

"Then why were Katana and Jason able to knock out those Arashi when they found Sato, after the Fall Ball?" asked Sam.

"I'm sure they were acting independently," said Nash. "That was just a routine meeting, not an attack on an enemy stronghold. There would have been no reason for Jaaku to lend them power at that point. And I'm sure they weren't *expecting* a fight, either."

"What about the lightning?" asked Sam. "Did Sato have any explanation for that?"

"No," said Master Nash. "I did ask. But he knows nothing more than we do. Somehow Jaaku is able to use his own shen to control the chi of everything around him.

"The only new information Sato provided was a confirmation of something we already suspected," said Nash. "Dim mak has two distinct chen do."

"Oh?" said Sam.

"Initially," said Osaka, "we assumed that taking someone's chi and taking someone's *prenatal* chi utilized the same skill. We thought it would work like deflecting intent. Whether you deflect a punch, or a chi hit, you are doing the same thing."

"Yes," Nash agreed. "The object you're acting upon may differ—a punch versus a fireball—but the skill itself is the same."

"That makes sense," said Sam. "But taking chi is different somehow?"

"Yes," Nash continued. "From everything Lu told us, it was starting to sound like draining someone's chi and taking only their *prenatal* chi were not the same skill at all. Sato has confirmed that indeed, they are two separate chen do.

"In any event, Jaaku's command to kill you, Samantha, pushed Sato over the edge. He does not want to be used like that again; he wants to fight back. He has agreed to turn spy for us. Between him and Lu, we should have a good idea what Jaaku is planning next."

"I can't imagine how difficult it must be for those two to work against Jaaku like this," said Sam, shaking her head.

Nash looked at Osaka. "We think we may have a way to ease that burden," he said. Osaka nodded in agreement.

"Nash," said Sam, "I had a very strange conversation with Master Liang while we were at Shaolin."

"Oh?" asked Master Nash.

"It was about Katana."

"I see."

"He says the headmaster there is concerned about her," said Sam.

"You mean paranoid," said Master Nash.

"Well, maybe," said Sam. "His greatest concern, apparently, is the way the kids around Katana are getting so many of the chen do. He fears that she may be able to share power with them the same way that Jaaku shares power with the Arashi. But obviously that's nonsense—there's no way Katana's going around stealing prenatal chi from people."

"No," said Master Nash. "But I, too, have become very curious about this. I doubt that it is mere coincidence that the people closest to Katana can do two of the chen do now. Having one student their age with that kind of power is rare enough. We now have *four*."

"Well, I was thinking," said Sam, "why don't we let Katana go to Shaolin so the headmaster can meet her. If he sees her in person, he'll know immediately that she isn't a secret student of Jaaku or anything. Right now, it seems like that's exactly what he's afraid of."

"Perhaps," said Master Nash. "I think, though, that the headmaster wants Katana for himself. He knows that one way or another—whatever the explanation for her friends learning the chen do—she is the most powerful student who has trained at any of the temples in a very long time. I believe the headmaster's paranoia is merely an act, an excuse to get Katana to go there. And if she does go there, mark my words, he will try to convince her to *stay*.

"I do not think we should send Katana to Shaolin unless there is a real reason to do so. And right now, I do not think such a reason exists," concluded Master Nash.

"I agree," said Osaka quietly.

"Well, it was a thought," said Sam.

***

Katana, Sara and Chris walked up to the girls' room in silence. Chris and Sara each sat down on one of the chairs, but Katana stayed on her feet, pacing back and forth across the floor.

"I'm going to have to face him someday," she said.

"Face Jaaku?" asked Chris.

Katana looked at him, then sat down on the couch, leaned her head back and looked up at the ceiling. "Yeah," she said. "Face Jaaku."

"Katana," Sara began with a worried look on her face, "you heard what Osaka said. You could be consumed by a desire for revenge..."

"That's not what she means," said Chris quietly. "She's going to *have* to face him; it's not going to be a *choice*."

"I don't get it..." said Sara.

Katana sat up. "Do you believe in destiny?"

"Destiny... Kat, sure," said Sara, "but you're saying you think it's your destiny to fight Jaaku? After what we saw him do today?"

"Especially after that," said Katana. "When I first found out about the Hall, before I'd ever seen the place, I got this weird feeling—like I'd always known I'd be coming here. Isn't that crazy? And now, after what we saw today, and after learning that Jaaku killed my parents... I feel like I am *meant* to face him someday."

Sara looked at her for a moment and sighed. "Well, you won't have to do it alone," she said. "We'll be right there with you."

***

On Monday morning, Master Nash addressed the whole school at their morning tai chi class. "As most of you have undoubtedly heard, Master Hua and Master Malloy returned to the Hall of the Dragon this weekend. Their mission was to retrieve the Scroll of the Five Masters that was taken exactly one year ago from this very dojo. They were successful. And we have since destroyed the scroll. Jaaku will not have any reason to attack this school again.

"Sadly, Master Hua sustained serious injuries near the end of their journey. He is currently staying in the infirmary and we are doing everything in our power to help him recover. In the meantime if you wish to visit Master Hua, please arrange a time with Master Osaka or myself. We do not wish to crowd everyone into the infirmary at once."

Katana attended Lincoln with everyone else that day, but schoolwork was the last thing on her mind. She couldn't stop thinking about Master Hua. She knew he might very well have sacrificed himself in the fight against Jaaku. She couldn't believe how important the tournament and the gainer flash had seemed to her a few short days ago. It all seemed so trivial now.

She went to the wushu dojo that afternoon. Master Nash was still teaching the class. Katana had half-hoped that she would find Master Hua there, resuming his post.

Master Nash sent everyone to practice their weapons after warm-ups and stretches. Katana grabbed a set of chains and worked with Dana and Donnie for a few minutes. But then Dana sat down on the floor and began to weep. Master Nash looked at Katana and nodded toward the door.

"Let's go, Dana," she said, helping her back to her feet.

They walked up to the infirmary and sat in the chairs next to Master Hua's bed. Dana sobbed uncontrollably. Katana took her hand and sat with her in silence.

Sam walked in a few minutes later and stood across the bed from them.

"Is he going to make it?" asked Dana, looking at Sam.

Tears streamed down Sam's face, and she closed her eyes for a moment.

"I don't think I can keep training if he dies," said Dana. "I don't want to work with anyone else. He's the only teacher I've ever had who really understands me."

"That's exactly why you *have* to keep training, Dana," said Sam. "Hua did this for you, you know."

"What do you mean?"

"We talked, Hua and I. A couple of nights before we got to Rebel's Cave. Do you know he could have been the deputy headmaster at the Shaolin Temple?"

Dana shook her head.

"He walked away from that because he loves to teach. He knew that if he took the post, he wouldn't work with the students much. So he turned it down. And he only went on this crazy mission because he knew that until we got the scroll back, Jaaku would keep raiding Shaolin, and might attack here.

"He accepted this assignment so the kids here could live without that fear. He went on this mission for you, Dana. I think you were his favorite. And if you stopped training after what he did, that would be a tragedy."

Katana and Sam walked out of the infirmary to give Dana a minute to be alone with Master Hua.

"Don't you have your classes now?" asked Katana.

"Bobby's going to keep doing them for me this week. I'm helping Master Nash with the arrangements..."

"He's not going to make it, is he?" asked Katana.

"No," said Sam. "He's not. Once that bolt of lightning hit him, he didn't have a chance. It's only a matter of time."

On Wednesday morning at their tai chi class, Master Nash made the fateful announcement. "I am profoundly saddened this morning... to have to inform you that Master Hua passed away earlier today. We will hold a memorial service for him on Friday afternoon when you return from Lincoln."

The whole school gathered in the atrium after school two days later. Master Nash and the other masters led them out the giant oak doors. They walked across the grounds, over the bridge that crossed Highway 101. Everyone gathered in the grass at the top of the cliff, looking out over the ocean.

Katana noticed a stone monument she'd never seen before, and that seemed to be the focal point of the crowd's attention. Master Nash walked to the front of the group and turned to address everyone.

"Master Hua hated long goodbyes," he said, "so we'll keep this simple."

Katana found it hard to hear Master Nash over the sound of the wind, so she stopped listening and looked out at the ocean. When Master Nash was done, she went up to get a closer look at the monument.

"The teaching of one virtuous person can influence many; that which has been learned well by one generation can be passed on to a hundred."
- Master Kano

In loving memory
Master Hua Xiang
A teacher, first and last

Katana noticed there was a picture embedded in the stone. It was Master Hua with his arm around Dana. She was holding up a big trophy, smiling ear to ear.

"That's me," said Dana. She'd walked up next to Katana to read the monument. "That was when I won grands the first time, at the end of seventh grade."

"You've got to keep going, Dana," said Katana.

"I know," said Dana, smiling in spite of the tears streaming down her face.

Chapter Eighteen: Sunset

Everyone tried to carry on with their lives for the next week. The teachers at Lincoln were gearing up for exams, but the classes at the Hall relaxed now that they were past nationals. Katana went down to Sam's dojo on Friday for the sparring team practice—Sam had resumed her teaching schedule.

"Well you guys had a great season," said Sam. "Bobby did an excellent job coaching everyone and keeping the team on track. We won both team divisions, and Bobby and Jason both won grands in their individual sparring events. Not bad for a team that was missing its coach for half the season."

"You were with us in spirit," said Jason. "Bobby kicked our butts so hard, it felt like you were still here."

"I just followed the instructions you left," said Bobby with a shrug. "We had it in the bag."

They goofed around for the rest of practice, then Sam invited them up to her apartment for a movie night. "Nash was able to collect footage of your sparring events from Golden Gate and nationals, and I haven't had a chance to watch it yet," she explained.

Katana went up to Sam's room with Sara and Chris after the wushu team practice. Sam had ordered pizza for everyone. They settled down to watch the video on the huge television screen mounted on the wall in her den.

Most of the kids were embarrassed to watch themselves. But Sam was thrilled to be seeing it for the first time. She coached them as they relived each match.

"You look mean when you spar, Kat," she said as they watched one of her bouts from Golden Gate.

"I don't do it on purpose!"

"You have the same look your dad always used to get," said Sam. "It's like you're staring straight into the person's soul—it's extremely intimidating."

"Yeah it is," said Jason knowingly.

They went to work out in Sam's dojo the next afternoon. Sara and Chris spent the whole time sparring with the chen do. Katana worked on tricks with Jelly and Scott, and she was relieved to find she could levitate at will. She'd been worried that she'd lose it again.

After a while, serious practice turned into horseplay. Chris and Jelly fought each other with their staves. When Chris failed to block one of Jelly's strikes, Jelly hit him on the top of the head.

"Ow!" said Chris. "That hurt, ya stupid midget!" He ran at Jelly, waving his staff. Jelly dropped his weapon and bolted, finally running up the wall, out of Chris's reach.

"I can do that too," said Katana. She got up to run after him. She followed him up the wall, chasing him around the room. But levitation or not, Jelly was too fast for her. She gave up and sat down next to Sara.

"Hey, are we going to Sam's for sushi tonight?" Sara asked.

"I don't know," said Katana. "I haven't talked to her about it."

They went with Chris up to Sam's room, but she was walking out her door when they arrived.

"Are we doing dinner tonight?" asked Sara.

"Yeah, but let's go eat at the sushi bar," suggested Sam.

They walked down to the cafeteria and sat on the stools across from Terry-san.

"Konichiwa," said Terry-san. "It's good to have you back, Master Samantha."

"It's good to *be* back," she said with a smile. She seemed to be taking in all the noise and chaos. "I missed this place."

Terry-san prepared their sushi, and Chris even gave it a try for once. "Hey... this isn't too bad," he said as he tried his first roll.

"Do we have another convert?" asked Sam.

"Maybe..." said Chris. He reached for another piece.

"Terry-san, do you know Katana can levitate now?" asked Sara.

"Yes, I have heard," said Terry-san. "*Three* chen do! That is truly remarkable."

"So can we assume Master Tanaka will hear about this?" asked Sam with an ironic smile.

"He already has," said Terry-san, winking at Katana. "Headmasters tell their sushi chefs everything, and we must return the favor."

Katana and Sara went with Chris up to his room after dinner. "Check this out you guys," said Jimmy when they walked in.

"What is it?" asked Chris.

"It's Beecher's interview in Black Belt magazine!" said Jimmy. "They talked a lot about you, Kat."

"What does it say?" asked Katana.

"Knox asked him what it was like having a girl on the team this year. Jason said you're just one of the guys," said Jimmy. "Oh, and he asked how Jason thought you woulda done if you hadn't been disqualified."

"What did he say?" asked Sara.

"He said Kat woulda won the whole thing," said Jimmy. "He said she's unstoppable when she sets her mind on something."

The last couple of weeks of the school year flew by, and before Katana knew it the final day of classes was upon them. The teachers had spent the last week feverishly reviewing the entire year's curriculum, and Katana actually paid attention. She wanted to make sure she still remembered everything so she could relax while everyone else stressed out about exams.

She went down to Sam's dojo that night for the last team practice of the term. When she walked in, Sam said, "Oh, Kat, I keep forgetting to tell you. You're testing for your second degree in tae kwon do tomorrow."

"WHAT?!" said Katana. "I'm supposed to take a black belt test with one day's notice?"

"You'll be fine. I talked to Bobby, and after watching the footage from the tournaments, I can say you're more than ready for this."

"No, Sam, I can't take a black belt test without any preparation."

"Sure you can," said Sam. "It's not the test that makes you a second degree—it's all the work you've done since your last test. This just makes it official. You have nothing to worry about. Be at the tai chi dojo tomorrow at three, and do what you do."

None of Katana's friends were testing this time, so Sara and Chris wished her luck, and Katana went up to the tai chi dojo by herself. The test wasn't as big as the one she'd taken the previous year. There were only ten students this time.

Master Nash started the test and took them through basics. Next he ran them through their forms as a group. After that, they came up individually to perform their newest kata.

Master Nash lined everyone up again and arranged them in two lines to do their self-defense combinations. After that, they split into two groups and came up individually to perform attack drills. Katana had to defend against an older girl she recognized from her wushu classes.

"Now, Katana, please use only the chen do," Osaka said after several exchanges.

The girl continued to attack and Katana deflected her intent, sending her sprawling on the mat every time.

Finally, Master Nash had them take a seat along the back wall. The candidates for second and third degree came up individually to perform the skills they needed for those higher ranks.

Sasha, who was from the demo team, did several wushu forms. She was testing for her third degree. Sasha would be graduating the following week, and Katana wondered if she might still make the team in her place.

An older boy was testing for second degree in aikido. Master Daniels had him do a series of advanced throws and locks on another boy, then defend himself freestyle.

After that, it was Katana's turn.

"You do not need to spar with a master of the Hall until you test for your third degree," said Master Nash. "But as you already know *three* of the chen do, you will have a chance to earn extra points on today's test. You will spar with Master Malloy, and for this first round, you must stick to external techniques only. I will not be calling points—instead, we will grade your overall performance. Are you ready?"

Katana nodded. She and Sam bowed to each other. "Fight!" yelled Master Nash.

Sam launched at Katana with a fierce sequence of kicks. Katana was a little taller than Sam now, but it made no difference. It was everything she could do to block the onslaught and avoid taking a kick to the face.

Finally Sam backed off. Katana launched at her with some of the kicking combinations she'd been working on all year. Sam dodged these with ease.

Back and forth they fought, neither of them able to land a single punch or kick. But finally as Sam threw a kick at Katana's head, Katana dropped and swept her other leg.

Sam fell flat on her back. She rocked back on her shoulders, kicked to her feet and came at Katana with another barrage of kicks.

A minute later, Master Nash called "UP!"

"You will proceed," he said, "but this time you may use the chen do.

"Fight!"

Sam faded away. An instant later, she choked Katana from behind. Katana grabbed Sam's arm and flipped her over onto the mat. But Sam disappeared again, this time reappearing directly in front of Katana. She dove at her, but Katana jumped in the air, levitating out of reach.

Sam threw a fireball at her instead; Katana deflected it as she floated to the floor. They went at each other for a minute with external techniques, and then Katana threw a fireball back at Sam.

Sam was ready; she caught Katana's fireball in her hands, spun around and threw it back at her. She hit Katana in the stomach and knocked her over.

Katana regained her feet as Sam ran in to engage her. After a fierce exchange of kicks, Sam backed off. Katana could see from her shen that she was gathering her energy for another chi hit. Katana formed a ball of energy in her arms, and used it to catch Sam's fireball. She hurled the combined energy back at her. Sam faded away just before it hit her.

"UP!" called Master Nash. "That's enough." Katana saw Daniels and Osaka scribbling away on their clipboards.

Master Nash lined everyone up again, and had them kneel down. He called them up one at a time to receive their new degrees.

"Congratulations," he said to Katana when it was her turn. "You are hereby promoted to second degree black belt in tae kwon do."

"Thank you," said Katana. She shook hands with the other masters before retaking her seat.

When the test was completed, Katana returned to her room.

"How'd it go?" asked Chris.

"Good," said Katana. "I passed."

"I still can't believe Sam 'forgot' to tell you that you were testing," said Sara. "You think she did that on purpose?"

"No doubt."

On Sunday night everyone went down to the lounge to study for their exams. Katana was bored. Even Paul was studying hard—the two of them had played a lot of video games during exam week the previous year. "Sorry, Kat," he said. "This year was way harder for me."

She decided to go for a walk. She went out the front doors, and strolled across the pedestrian bridge to the top of the cliff. She read Master Hua's memorial stone again, then sat down on one of the benches. She looked out at the ocean, listening to the waves crashing on the beach below, and watched the sun set in a brilliant display of color. As darkness grew, she walked along the beach for a while, gazing at the stars.

She missed Master Hua. It was hard, knowing she'd never train with him again. But she knew she'd always remember him. The image of him standing at the front of the wushu dojo, greeting his class with that infectious smile, was burned indelibly into her memory. His genuine love of teaching had always made her want to work hard for him. She'd never forget that either.

But she knew that Hua's death wouldn't be the last. As long as Jaaku survived, the nightmare would continue.

Katana returned to her room eventually and went right to sleep. She woke up a little before five the next morning. Master Nash always canceled their martial arts classes during exam weeks, and this policy included their morning tai chi lesson. Katana was awake, though, and had nothing to do until it was time to go to Lincoln. She got dressed as quietly as she could to avoid waking Sara, and went down to the atrium. She walked out the back doors, through the rock garden and across the field to the forest.

She followed the path that led to the old dojo in the woods. She found Osaka there, as expected. "I had a feeling I might see you here this morning," he said as she joined him on the foundation.

Katana smiled at him, and they began the long form together, master and pupil.

9 781737 683308